A COLUMBUS
OF SPACE

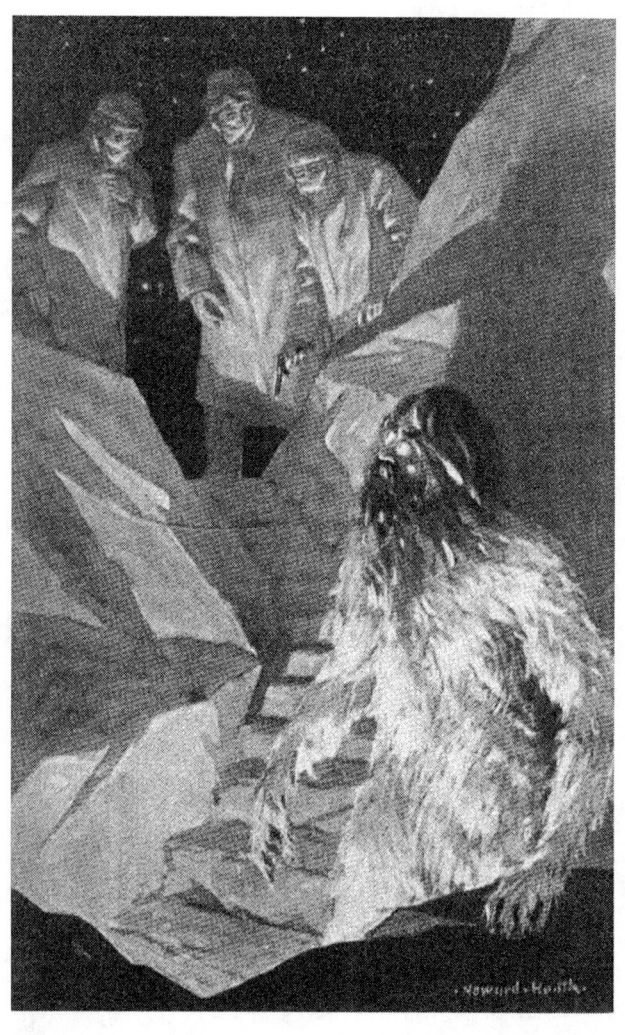

"Standing on the steps...was a creature shaped like a man, but more savage than a gorilla." Page 41.

A COLUMBUS OF SPACE

GARRETT P. SERVISS
Illustrations by Howard Heath

BLACK CAT PRESS/APOGEE BOOKS
2006

A Columbus of Space
Originally published 1909
Special contents copyright © 2006
Black Cat Press, King George, Virginia
Apogee Science Fiction, Box 62034, Burlington,
Ontario, Canada, L7R 4K2
www.apogeespacebooks.com
We acknowledge the financial support of the Government
of Canada through the Book Publishing Industry
Development Program for our
publishing activities. ISBN 09738203-7-3
Printed and bound in USA
Front Cover by Ron Miller

WorldCon 2006 First edition

TO THE READERS OF
JULES VERNE'S ROMANCES
THIS STORY IS DEDICATED

Not because the author flatters himself that he can walk in the Footsteps of that Immortal Dreamer, but because, like Jules Verne, he believes that the World of Imagination is as legitimate a Domain of the Human Mind as the World of Fact.

A COLUMBUS
OF SPACE

CHAPTER I
A MARVELOUS INVENTION

I am a hero worshiper; an insatiable devourer of biographies; and I say that no man in all the splendid list ever equaled Edmund Stonewall. You smile because you have never heard his name, for, until now, his biography has not been written. And this is not truly a biography; it is only the story of the crowning event in Stonewall's career.

Really it humbles one's pride of race to see how ignorant the world is of its true heroes. Many a man who cuts a great figure in history is, after all, a poor specimen of humanity, slavishly following old ruts, destitute of any real originality, and remarkable only for some exaggeration of the commonplace. But in the case of Edmund Stonewall the world cannot be blamed for its ignorance, because, as I have already said, his story remains to be written, and hitherto it has been guarded as a profound secret.

I do not wish to exaggerate; yet I cannot avoid seeming to do so in simply telling the facts. If Stonewall's proceedings had become Matter of common knowledge the world would have been—I must speak plainly—revolutionized. He held in his hands the means of realizing the wildest dreams of power, wealth, and human mastery over the forces of nature, that any enthusiast ever treasured in his prophetic soul. It was a part of his originality that he never entertained the thought of employing his advantage in any such way. His character was entirely free from the ordinary forms of avidity. He cared nothing for wealth in itself, and as little for fame. All his energies were concentrated upon the attainment of ends which nobody but himself would have regarded as of any practical importance. Thus it happened that, having made an invention which would have put every human industry upon a new footing, and multiplied beyond the limits of calculation the activities and achievements of mankind, this extraordinary person turned his back upon the colossal fortune which he had but to stretch forth his hand and grasp, refused to seize the unlimited power which his genius had laid at his feet, and used his unparalleled discovery for a purpose so eccentric, so wildly unpractical, so utterly beyond the pale of waking life, that to any ordinary man he must have seemed a lunatic lost in an endless dream of bedlam. And to this day I cannot, without a nervous thrill, think how the desire of all the ages, the ideal that has been the loadstar for thousands of philosophers, savants, inventors, prophets, and dreamers, was actually realized upon the earth; and yet of all its fifteen hundred million inhabitants but a single one knew it, possessed it, controlled it—and he would not reveal it, but hoarded and used his knowledge for the accomplishment of the craziest design that ever took shape in a human brain.

Now, to be more specific. Of Stonewall's antecedents I know very little. I only know that, in a moderate way, he was wealthy, and that he had no immediate family ties. He was somewhere near thirty years of age, and held the diploma of one of our oldest universities. But he was not, in a general way, sociable, and I never knew him to attend any of the reunions of his former classmates, or to show the slightest interest in any of the events or functions of society, although its doors were open to him through some distant relatives who were widely connected in New York, and who at times tried to draw him into their circle. He would certainly have adorned it, but it had no attraction for him. Nevertheless he was a member of the Olympus Club, where he frequently spent his evenings. But he

A COLUMBUS OF SPACE

made very few acquaintances even there, and I believe that except myself, Jack Ashton, Henry Darton, and Will Church, he had no intimates. And we knew him only at the club. There, when he was alone with us, he sometimes partly opened up his mind, and we were charmed by his variety of knowledge and the singularity of his conversation. I shall not disguise the fact that we thought him extremely eccentric, although the idea of anything in the nature of insanity never entered our heads. We knew that he was engaged in recondite researches of a scientific nature, and that he possessed a private laboratory, although none of us had ever entered it. Occasionally he would speak of some new advance of science, throwing a flood of light by his clear expositions upon things of which we should otherwise have remained profoundly ignorant. His imagination flashed like lightning over the subject of his talk, revealing it at the most unexpected angles, and often he roused us to real enthusiasm for things the very names of which we almost forgot amidst the next day's occupations.

There was one subject on which he was particularly eloquent—radioactivity; that most strange property of matter whose discovery had been the crowning glory of science in the closing decade of the nineteenth century. None of us really knew anything about it except what Stonewall taught us. If some new incomprehensible announcement appeared in the newspapers we skipped it, being sure that Edmund would make it all clear at the club in the evening. He made us understand, in a dim way, that some vast, tremendous secret lay behind it all. I recall his saying, on one occasion, not long before the blow fell:

"Listen to this! Here's Professor Thomson declaring that a single grain of radium contains in its padlocked atoms energy enough to lift a million tons three hundred yards high. Professor Thomson is too modest in his estimates, and he hasn't the ghost of an idea how to get at that energy. Neither has Professor Rutherford, nor Lord Kelvin; *but somebody will get at it, just the same.*"

GARRETT P. SERVISS

He positively thrilled us when he spoke thus, for there was a look in his eyes which seemed to penetrate depths unfathomable to our intelligence. Yet we had not the faintest conception of what was really passing in his mind. If we had understood it, if we had caught a single clear glimpse of the workings of his intellect, we should have been appalled. And if we had known how close we stood to the verge of an abyss of mystery about to be lighted by such a gleam as had never before been emitted from the human spirit, I believe that we would have started from our chairs and fled in dismay.

But we understood nothing, except that Edmund was indulging in one of his eccentric dreams, and Jack, in his large, careless, good-natured way broke in with:

"Well, Edmund, suppose *you* could 'get at it,' as you say; what would you do with it?"

Stonewall's eyes gleamed for a moment, and then he replied, with a curious emphasis:

"I might do what Archimedes dreamed of."

None of us happened to remember what it was that Archimedes had dreamed, and the subject was dropped.

For a considerable time afterwards we saw nothing of Stonewall. He did not come to the club, and we were beginning to think of looking him up, when one evening, quite unexpectedly, he dropped in, wearing an unusually cheerful expression. We had greatly missed him, and we now greeted him with effusion. His animation impressed us all, and he had no sooner shaken hands than he said, with suppressed excitement in his voice:

"Well, I've 'got at it.'"

"Got at what?" drawled Jack.

"The inter-atomic energy. I've got it under control."

"The deuce you have!" said Jack.

"Yes, I've arrived where a certain professor dreamed of being when he averred that 'when man knows that every breath of air he draws has contained within itself force enough to drive the workshops of the world he will find out some day, somehow, some way of tapping that energy.' The thing is done, for I've tapped it!"

We stared at one another, not knowing what to say, except Jack, who, inspired by the spirit of mischief, drawled out:

"Ah, yes, I remember. Well then, Edmund, as I asked you before, what are you going to do with it?"

There was not really any thought among us of poking fun at Edmund; we respected and admired him far too much for that; nevertheless, catching the infection of banter from Jack, we united in demanding, in a manner which I can now see must have appeared most provoking:

"Why, yes, Edmund, tell us what you are going to do with it."

And then Jack added fuel by mockingly, though with perfectly good-natured intention, taking Edmund by the hand and swinging him in front of us with:

"Gentlemen, Archimedes junior."

Stonewall's eyes flashed and his cheek darkened, but for a moment he said nothing. Presently, with a return of his former affability, he said:

"I wish you would come over to the laboratory and let me show you what I am going to do."

Of course we instantly assented. Nothing could have pleased us better than this invitation, for we had long been dying to see the inside of Edmund's laboratory. We all got our hats and started out with him. We knew where he lived, occupying a whole house though he was a bachelor, but none of us had ever seen the inside of it, and our curiosity was on the *qui vive*. He led us through a handsome hallway and a rear apartment directly into the back yard, half of which we were surprised to find inclosed and roofed over, forming a huge shanty, like a workshop. Edmund opened the door of the shanty and ushered us in.

• GARRETT P. SERVISS

A remarkable object at once concentrated our attention. In the center of the place was the queerest-looking thing that you can well imagine. I can hardly describe it. It was round and elongated like a boiler, with bulging ends, and seemed to be made of polished steel. Its total length was about eighteen feet, and its width ten feet. Edmund approached it and opened a door in the end, which was wide and high enough for us to enter without stooping or crowding.

"Step in, gentlemen," he said, and unhesitatingly we obeyed him, all except Church, who for some unknown reason remained outside, and when we looked for him had disappeared.

Edmund turned on a bright light, and we found ourselves in an oblong chamber, beautifully fitted up with polished woodwork, and leather-cushioned seats running round the sides. Many metallic knobs and handles shone on the walls.

"Sit down," said Edmund, "and I will tell you what I have got here."

He stepped to the door and called again for Church but there was no answer. We concluded that, thinking the thing would be too deep to be interesting, he had gone back to the club. That was not what he had done, as you will learn later, but he never regretted what he did do. Getting no response from Church, Edmund finally sat down with us on one of the leather-covered benches, and began his explanation.

"As I was telling you at the club," he said, "I've solved the mystery of the atoms. I'm sure you'll excuse me from explaining my method" (there was a little raillery in his manner), "but at least you can understand the plain statement that I've got unlimited power at my command. These knobs and handles that you see are my keys for turning it on and off, and controlling it as I wish. Mark you, this power comes right out of the heart of what we call matter; the world is chock full of it. We have known that it was there at least ever since radioactivity was discovered, but it looked as though human intelligence would never be able to set it free from its prison. Nevertheless I have not only set it free, but I am able to control it as perfectly as if it were steam from a boiler, or an electric current from a dynamo."

Jack, who was as unscientific a person as ever lived, yawned, and Edmund noticed it. But he showed no irritation, merely smiling, and saying, with a wink at me and Henry:

"Even this seems to be rather too deep, so perhaps I had better show you, instead of telling you, what I mean. Excuse me a moment."

He stepped out of the door, and we remained seated. We heard a noise outside like the opening of a barn door, and immediately Edmund reappeared and closed the door of the chamber in which we were. We watched him with growing curiosity. With a singular smile he pressed a knob on the wall, and instantly we felt that the chamber was rising in the air. It rocked a little like a boat in wavy water. We were startled, of course, but not alarmed.

"Hello!" exclaimed Jack. "What kind of a balloon is this?"

"It's something more than a balloon," was Edmund's reply, and as he spoke he touched another knob, and we felt the car, as I must now call it, come to rest. Then Edmund opened a shutter at one side, and we all sprang up to look out. Below us we saw roofs and the tops of two trees standing at the side of the street.

"We're about a hundred feet up," said Edmund quietly. "What do you think of it now?"

"Wonderful! wonderful!" we exclaimed in a breath. And I continued:

"And do you say that it is inter-atomic energy that does this?"

"Nothing else in the world," returned Edmund.

But bantering Jack must have his quip:

"By the way, Edmund," he demanded, "what was it that Archimedes dreamed? But no matter; you've knocked him silly.

• GARRETT P. SERVISS

Now, what are you going to do with your atomic balloon?"

Edmund's eyes flashed:

"You'll see in a minute."

The scene out of the window was beautiful, and for a moment we all remained watching it. The city lights were nearly all below our level, and away off over the New Jersey horizon I noticed the planet Venus, near to setting, but as brilliant as a diamond. I am fond of star-gazing, and I called Edmund's attention to the planet as he happened to be standing next to me.

"Lovely, isn't she?" he said with enthusiasm. "The finest world in the solar system, and what a strange thing that she should have one side always day and the other always night."

I was surprised by his exhibition of astronomic lore, for I had never known that he had given any attention to the subject, but a minute later the incident was forgotten as Edmund suddenly pushed us back from the window and closed the shutter.

"Going down again so soon?" asked Jack.

Edmund smiled. "Going," he said simply, and put his hand to one of the knobs. Immediately we felt ourselves moving very slowly.

"That's right, Edmund," put in Jack again, "let us down easy; I don't like bumps."

We expected at each instant to feel the car touch the cradle in which it had evidently rested, but never were three mortals so mistaken. What really did happen can better be described in the words of Will Church, who, you will remember, had disappeared at the beginning of our singular adventure. I got the account from him long afterwards. He had written it out carefully and put it away in a safe, as a sort of historic document. Here is Church's narrative, omitting the introduction, which read like a law paper:

"When we went over from the club to Stonewall's house, I dropped behind the others, because the four of them took up the whole width of the sidewalk. Stonewall was talking to them, and my attention was attracted by something uncommon in his manner. He had an indefinable carriage of the head which suggested to me the suspicion that everything was not just as it should be. I don't mean that I thought him crazy, or anything of that kind, but I felt that he had some scheme in his mind to fool us.

"I bitterly repented, after things turned out as they did, that I had not whispered a word to the others. But that would have been difficult, and, besides, I had no idea of the seriousness of the affair. Nevertheless, I determined to stay out of it, so that the laugh should not be on me at any rate. Accordingly when the others entered the car I stayed outside, and when Stonewall called me I did not answer.

"When he came out to open the roof of the shed, he did not see me in the shadow where I stood. The opening of the roof revealed the whole scheme in a flash. I had had no suspicion that the car was any kind of a balloon, and even after he had so significantly thrown the roof open, and then entered the car and closed the door, I was fairly amazed to see the thing began to rise without the slightest noise, and as if it were enchanted. It really looked diabolical as it floated silently upward and passed through the opening, and the sight gave me a shiver.

"But I was greatly relieved when it stopped at a height of a hundred feet or so, and then I said to myself that I should have been less of a fool if I had stayed with the others, for now they would have the laugh on me alone. Suddenly, while I watched, expecting every moment to see them drop down again, for I supposed that it was merely an experiment to show that the thing would float, the car started upward, very slowly at first, but increasing its speed until it had attained an elevation of perhaps five hundred feet. There it hung for a moment, like some mail-clad monster glinting in the quavering light of the street arcs, and then, without warning, made a dart skyward.

Garrett P. Serviss

For a minute it circled like a strange bird taking its bearings, and finally rushed off westward until I lost sight of it behind some tall buildings. I ran into the house to reach the street, but found the outer door locked, and not a person visible. I called but nobody came. Returning to the yard I discovered a place where I could get over the fence, and so I escaped into the street. Immediately I searched the sky for the mysterious car, but could see no sign of it. They were gone! I almost sank upon the pavement in a state of helpless excitement, which I could not have explained to myself if I had stopped to reason; for why, after all, should I take the thing so tragically. But something within me said that all was wrong. A policeman happened to pass.

"'Officer! officer!' I shouted, 'have you seen it?'

"'Seen what?' asked the blue-coat, twirling his club.

"'The car—the balloon,' I stammered.

"'Balloon in your head! You're drunk. Get long out o' here!'

"I realized the impossibility of explaining the matter to him, and running back to the place where I had got over the fence I climbed into the yard and entered the shed. Fortunately the policeman paid no further attention to my movements after I left him. I sat down on the empty cradle and stared up through the opening in the roof, hoping against hope to see them coming back. It must have been midnight before I gave up my vigil in despair, and went home, sorely puzzled, and blaming myself for having kept my suspicions unuttered. I finally got to sleep, but I had horrible dreams.

"The next day I was up early looking through all the papers in the hope of finding something about the car. But there was not a word. I watched the news columns for several days without result. Whenever the coast was clear I haunted Stonewall's yard, but the fatal shed yawned empty, and there was not a soul about the house. I cannot describe my feelings. My friends seemed to have been snatched away by some mysterious agency, and the horror of the thing almost drove me crazy. I felt that I was, in a manner, responsible for their disappearance.

"One day my heart sank at the sight of a cousin of Jack Ashton's motioning to me in the street. He approached, with a troubled look. 'Mr. Church,' he said, 'I think you know me; can you tell me what has become of Jack? I haven't seen him for several days.' What could I say? Still believing that they would soon come back, I invented, on the spur of the moment, a story that Jack, with a couple of intimate friends, had gone off on a hunting expedition. I took a little comfort in the reflection that my friends, like myself, were bachelors, and consequently at liberty to disappear if they chose.

"But when more than a week had passed with out any news of them I was thrown into despair. I had to give up all hope. Remembering how near we were to the coast, I concluded that they had drifted out over the sea and gone down. It was hard for me, after the lie I had told, to let out the truth to such of their friends as I knew, but I had to do it. Then the police took the matter in hand and ransacked Stonewall's laboratory and the shanty without finding anything to throw light on the mystery. It was a newspaper sensation for a few days, but as nothing came of it everybody soon forgot all about it—all except me. I was left to my loneliness and my regrets.

"A year has now passed with no news from them. I write this on the anniversary of their departure. My friends, I know, are dead—somewhere! Oh, what an experience it has been! When your friends die and are buried it is hard enough but when they disappear in a flash and leave no token—! It is almost beyond endurance!"

CHAPTER II
A TRIP OF TERROR

I take up the story at the point where I dropped it to introduce Church's narrative.

As minute after minute elapsed and we continued in motion we changed our minds about the descent, and concluded that the inventor was going to give us a much longer ride than we had anticipated. We were startled and puzzled but not really alarmed, for the car traveled so smoothly that it gave one a sense of confidence. On the other hand, we felt a little indignation that Edmund should treat us like a lot of boys, without wills of our own. No doubt we had provoked him, though unintentionally, but this was going too far on his part. I am sure we were all hot with this feeling and presently Jack flamed out:

"Look here, Edmund," he exclaimed, dropping his customary good-natured manner, "this is carrying things with a pretty high hand. It's a good deal like kidnapping, it seems to me. I didn't give you permission to carry me off in this way, and I want to know what you mean by it and what you are about. I've no objection to making a little trip in your car, which is certainly mighty comfortable, but first I'd like to be asked whether I want to go or no."

Edmund shrugged his shoulders and made no reply. He was very busy just then with the metallic knobs. Suddenly we were jerked off our feet as if we had been in a trolley driven by a green motorman. Edmund also would have fallen if he had

A Columbus of Space •

not clung to one of the handles. We felt that we were spinning through the air at a fearful speed. Still Edmund uttered not a word, but while we staggered upon our feet, and steadied ourselves with hands and knees on the leather-cushioned benches like so many drunken men, he continued pulling and pushing at his knobs. Finally the motion became more regular and it was evident that the car had slowed down from its wild rush.

"Excuse me," said Edmund, then, quite in his natural manner, "the thing is new yet and I've got to learn the stops by experience. But there's no occasion for alarm."

But our indignation had grown hotter with the shake-up that we had just had, and as usual Jack was spokesman for it:

"Maybe there is no occasion for alarm," he said excitedly, "but will you be kind enough to answer my question, and tell us what you're about and where we are going?"

And Henry, too, who was ordinarily as mute as a clam, broke out still more hotly:

"See here! I've had enough of this thing! Just go down and let me out. I won't be carried off so, against my will and knowledge."

By this time Edmund appeared to have got things in the shape he wanted, and he turned to face us. He always had a magnetism that was inexplicable, and now we felt it as never before. His features were perfectly calm, but there was a light in his eyes that seemed electric. As if disdaining to make a direct reply to the heated words of Jack and Henry he began in a quiet voice:

"It was my first intention to invite you to accompany me on a very interesting expedition. I knew that none of you had any ties of family or business to detain you, and I felt sure that you would readily consent. In case you should not, however, I had made up my mind to go alone. But you provoked me more than you knew, probably, at the club, and after we had entered the car, and, being myself hot-tempered, I determined to teach you a lesson. I have no intention, however, of abducting you. It is true that you are in my power at present, but if you now say that you do not wish to be concerned in what I assure you will prove the most wonderful enterprise ever undertaken by human beings, I will go back to the shed and let you out."

We looked at one another, in doubt what to reply until Jack, who, with all his impulsiveness had more of the milk of human kindness in his heart than anyone else I ever knew, seized Edmund's hand and exclaimed:

"All right, old boy, bygones are bygones; I'm with you. Now what do you fellows say?"

"I'm with you, too," I cried, yielding to the spur of Jack's enthusiasm and moved also by an intense curiosity. "I say go ahead."

Henry was more backward. But his curiosity, too, was aroused, and at length he gave in his voice with the others.

Jack swung his hat.

"Three cheers, then, for the modern Archimedes! You won't take that amiss now Edmund."

We gave the cheers, and I could see that Edmund was immensely pleased.

"And now," Jack continued, "tell us all about it. Where are we going?"

"Pardon me, Jack," was Edmund's reply, "but I'd rather keep that for a surprise. You shall know everything in good time; or at least everything that you can understand," he added, with a slightly malicious smile.

Feeling a little more interest than the others, perhaps, in the scientific aspects of the business, I asked Edmund to tell us something more about the nature of his wonderful invention. He responded with great good humor, but rather in the manner of a schoolmaster addressing pupils who, he knows, cannot entirely follow him.

"These knobs and handles on the walls," he said, "control

the driving power, which, as I have told you, comes from the atoms of matter which I have persuaded to unlock their hidden forces. I push or turn one way and we go ahead, or we rise; I push or turn another way and we stop, or go back. So I concentrate the atomic force just as I choose. It makes us go, or it carries us back to earth, or it holds us motionless, according to the way I apply it. The earth is what I kick against at present, and what I hold fast by; but any other sufficiently massive body would serve the same purpose. As to the machinery, you'd need a special education in order to understand it. You'd have to study the whole subject from the bottom up, and go through all the experiments that I have tried. I confess that there are some things the fundamental reason of which I don't understand myself. But I know how to apply and control the power, and if I had Professor Thomson and Professor Rutherford here, I'd make them open their eyes. I wish I had been able to kidnap them."

"That's a confession that, after all, you've kidnapped us," put in Jack, smiling.

"If you insist upon stating it in that way—yes," replied Edmund, smiling also. "But you know that now you've consented."

"Perhaps you'll treat us to a trip to Paris," Jack persisted.

"Better than that," was the reply. "Paris is only an ant-hill in comparison with what you are going to see."

And so, indeed, it turned out!

Finally all got out their pipes, and we began to make ourselves at home, for truly, as far as luxurious furniture was concerned, we were as comfortable as at the Olympus Club, and the motion of the strange craft was so smooth and regular that it soothed us like an anodyne. It was only those unnamed, subtle senses which man possesses almost without being aware of their existence that assured us that we were in motion at all.

After we had smoked for an hour or so, talking and telling

stories quite in the manner of the club, Edmund suddenly asked, with a peculiar smile:

"Aren't you a little surprised that this small room is not choking full of smoke? You know that the shutters are tightly closed."

"By Jo," exclaimed Jack, "that's so! Why here we've been pouring out clouds like old Vesuvius for an hour with no windows open, and yet the air is as clear as a bell."

"The smoke," said Edmund impressively, "has been turned into atomic energy to speed us on our way. I'm glad you're all good smokers, for that saves me fuel. Look," he continued, while we, amazed, stared at him, "those fellows there have been swallowing your smoke, and glad to get it."

He pointed at a row of what seemed to be grinning steel mouths, barred with innumerable black teeth, and half concealed by a projecting ledge at the bottom of the wall opposite the entrance, and as I looked I was thrilled by the sight of faint curls of smoke disappearing within their gaping jaws.

"They are omnivorous beasts," said Edmund. "They feed on the carbon from your breath, too. Rather remarkable, isn't it, that every time you expel the air from your lungs you help this car to go?"

None of us knew what to say; our astonishment was beyond speech. We began to look askance at Edmund, with creeping sensations about the spine. A formless, unacknowledged fear of him entered our souls. It never occurred to us to doubt the truth of what he had said. We knew him too well for that; and, then, were we not here, flying mysteriously through the air in a heavy metallic car that had no apparent motive power? For my part, instead of demanding any further explanations, I fell into a hazy reverie on the marvel of it all; and Jack and Henry must have been seized the same way, for not one of us spoke a word, or asked a question; while Edmund, satisfied, perhaps, with the impression he had made, kept equally quiet.

Thus another hour passed, and all of us, I think, had fallen into a doze, when Edmund aroused us by saying:

"I'll have to keep the first watch, and all the others, too, this night."

"So then we're not going to land to-night?"

"No, not to-night, and you may as well turn in. You see that I have prepared good, comfortable bunks, and I think you'll make out very well."

As Edmund spoke he lifted the tops from some of the benches along the walls, and revealed excellent beds, ready for occupancy.

"I believe that I have forgotten nothing that we shall really need," he added. "Beds, arms, instruments, books, clothing, furs, and good things to eat."

Again we looked at one another in surprise, but nobody spoke, although the same thought probably occurred to each—that this promised to be a pretty long trip, judging from the preparations. Arms! What in the world should we need of arms? Was he going to the Rocky Mountains for a bear hunt? And clothing, and furs!

But we were really sleepy, and none of us was very long in taking Edmund at his word and leaving him to watch alone. He considerately drew a shade over the light, and then noiselessly opened a shutter and looked out. When I saw that, I was strongly tempted to rise and take a look myself, but instead I fell asleep. My dreams were disturbed by visions of the grinning nondescripts at the foot of the wall, which transformed themselves into winged dragons, and remorselessly pursued me through the measureless abysses of space.

When I woke, windows were open on both sides of the car, and brilliant sunshine was streaming in through one of them. Henry was still asleep, Jack was yawning in his bunk, and Edmund stood at one of the windows staring out. I made a quick toilet, and hastened to Edmund's side.

"Good morning," he said heartily, taking my hand. "Look

out here, and tell me what you think of the prospect."

As I put my face close to the thick but very transparent glass covering the window, my heart jumped into my mouth!

"In Heaven's name, where are we?" I cried out.

Jack, hearing my agitated exclamation, jumped out of his bunk and ran to the window also. He gasped as he gazed out, and truly it was enough to take away one's breath!

We appeared to be at an infinite elevation, and the sky, as black as ink, was ablaze with stars, although the bright sunlight was streaming into the opposite window behind us. I could see nothing of the earth. Evidently we were too high for that.

"It must lie away down under our feet," I murmured half aloud, "so that even the horizon has sunk out of sight. Heavens, what a height!"

I had that queer uncontrollable qualm that comes to every one who finds himself suddenly on the edge of a soundless deep.

Presently I became aware that straight before us, but afar off, was a most singular appearance in the sky. At first glance I thought that it was a cloud, round and mottled, But it was strangely changeless in form, and it had an unvaporous look.

"Phew!" whistled Jack, suddenly catching sight of it and fixing his eyes in a stare, "what's *that?*"

"*That's the earth!*"

It was Edmund who spoke, looking at us with a quizzical smile. A shock ran through my nerves, and for an instant my brain whirled. I saw that it was the truth that he had uttered, for, as sure as I sit here, his words had hardly struck my ears when the great cloud rounded out and hardened, the deception vanished, and I recognized, as clearly as ever I saw them on a school globe, the outlines of Asia and the Pacific Ocean!

In a second I had become too weak to stand, and I sank trembling upon a bench. But Jack, whose eyes had not accommodated themselves as rapidly as mine to the gigantic perspective, remained at the window, exclaiming:

"Fiddlesticks! What are you trying to give us? The earth is down below, I reckon."

But in another minute he, too, saw it as it really was, and his astonishment equaled mine. In fact he made so much noise about it that he awoke Henry, who, jumping out of bed, came running to see, and when we had explained to him where we were, sank upon a seat with a despairing groan and covered his face. Our astonishment and dismay were too great to permit us quickly to recover our self-command, but after a while Jack seized Edmund's arm, and demanded:

"For God's sake, tell us what you've been doing."

"Nothing that ought to appear very extraordinary," answered Edmund, with uncommon warmth. "If men had not been fools for so many ages they might have done this, and more than this long ago. It's enough to make one ashamed of his race! For countless centuries, instead of grasping the power that nature had placed at the disposal of their intelligence, they have idled away their time gabbling about nothing. And even since, at last, they have begun to do something, look at the time that they have wasted upon such petty forces as steam and 'electricity,' burning whole mines of coal and whole lakes of oil, and childishly calling upon winds and tides and waterfalls to help them, when they had under their thumbs the limitless energy of the atoms, and no more understood it than a baby understands what makes its whistle scream! It's inter-atomic force that has brought us out here, and that is going to carry us a great deal farther."

We simply listened in silence; for what could we say? The facts were more eloquent than any words, and called for no commentary. Here we *were*, out in the middle of space; and *there* was the earth, hanging on nothing, like a summer cloud. At least we knew where we were if we didn't quite understand how we had got there.

Seeing us speechless, Edmund resumed in a different

tone:

"We made a fairly good run during the night. You must be hungry by this time, for you've slept late; suppose we have breakfast."

So saying, he opened a locker, took out a folding table, covered it with a white cloth, turned on something resembling a little electric range, and in a few minutes had ready as appetizing a breakfast of eggs and as good a cup of coffee as I ever tasted. It is one of the compensations of human nature that it is able to adjust itself to the most unheard-of conditions provided only that the inner man is not neglected. The smell of breakfast would almost reconcile a man to purgatory—anyhow it reconciled us for the time being to our unparalleled situation, and we ate and drank, and indulged in as cheerful good comradeship as that of a fishing party in the wilderness after a big morning's catch.

When the breakfast was finished we began to chat and smoke, which reminded me of those gulping mouths under the wainscot, and I leaned down to catch a glimpse of their rows of black fangs, thinking to ask Edmund for further explanation about them; but the sight gave me a shiver, and I felt the hopelessness of trying to understand their function.

Then we took a turn at looking out of the window to see the earth. Edmund furnished us with binoculars which enabled us to recognize many geographical features of our planet. The western shore of the Pacific was now in plain sight, and a few small spots, near the edge of the ocean, we knew to be Japan and the Philippines. The snowy Himalayas showed as a crinkling line, and a huge white smudge over the China Sea indicated where a storm was raging and where good ships, no doubt, were battling with the tossing waves.

After a time I noticed that Edmund was continually going from one window to the other and looking out with an air of anxiety. He seemed to be watching for something, and there was a look of mingled expectation and apprehension in his eyes. He had a peephole at the forward end of the car and another in the floor, and these he frequently visited. I now recalled that even while we were at breakfast he had seemed uneasy and occasionally left his seat to look out. At last I asked him:

"What are you looking for, Edmund?"

"Meteors."

"Meteors, out here!"

"Of course. You're something of an astronomer; don't you know that they hang about all the planets? They didn't give me any rest last night. I was on tender hooks all the time while you were sleeping. I was half inclined to call one of you to help me. We passed some pretty ugly fellows while you slept, I can tell you! You know that this is an unexplored sea that we are navigating, and I don't want to run on the rocks."

"But we seem to be a good way off from the earth now," I remarked, "and there ought not to be much danger."

"It's not as dangerous as it was, but there may be some of them yet around here. I'll feel safer when we have put a few more million miles behind us."

A few more million miles! We all stood aghast when we heard the words. We had, indeed, imagined that the earth looked as if it might be a million miles away, but, then, it was merely a passing impression, which had given us no sense of reality; but now when we heard Edmund say that we actually had traveled such a distance, the idea struck us with overwhelming force.

"In the name of all that's good, Edmund," cried Jack, "at what rate are we traveling, then?"

"Just at present," Edmund replied, glancing at an indicator, "we're making twenty miles a second."

Twenty miles a second! Our excited nerves had another shock.

"Why," I exclaimed, "that's faster than the earth moves in its orbit!"

"Yes, a trifle faster; but I'll probably have to work up to a little better speed in order to get where I want to go before our goal begins to run away from us."

"Ah, there you are," said Jack. "That's what I wanted to know. What is our goal? Where are we going?"

Before Edmund could reply we all sprang to our feet in affright. A loud grating noise had broken upon our ears. At the same instant the car gave a lurch, and a blaze of the most vicious lightning streamed through a window.

"Confound the things!" shouted Edmund, springing to the window, and then darting to one of his knobs and beginning to twist it with all his force.

In a second we were sprawling on the floor—all except Edmund, who kept his hold on the knob. Our course had been changed with amazing quickness, and our startled eyes beheld a huge misshapen object darting past the window.

"Here comes another!" cried Edmund, again seizing the knob.

I had managed to get my face to the window, and I certainly thought that we were done for. Apparently only a few rods away, and rushing straight at the car, was a vast black mass, shaped something like a dumb-bell, with ends as big as houses, tumbling over and over, and threatening us with annihilation. If it hit us, as it seemed sure that it would do, I knew that we should never return to the earth, unless in the form of pulverized ashes!

CHAPTER III
THE PLANETARY LIMITED

But Edmund had seen the meteor sooner than I, and as quick as thought he swerved the car, and threw us all off our feet once more. But we should have been thankful if he had broken our heads, since he had saved us from instant destruction.

The danger, however, was not yet passed. Scarcely had the immense dumb-bell (which Edmund declared must have been composed of solid iron, so great was its effect on his needles) disappeared, before there came from outside a blaze so fierce that it fairly slapped our lids shut.

"A collision!" Edmund exclaimed. "The thing has struck another big meteor, and they are exchanging fiery compliments."

He threw himself flat on the floor, and stared out of the peephole. Then he jumped to his feet and gave us another tumble.

"They're all about us," he faltered, breathless with exertion; then, having drawn a deep inspiration, he continued: "We're like a boat in a raging freshet, with rocks, tree trunks, and cakes of ice threatening it on all sides. But we'll get out of it. The car obeys its helm as if it appreciated the danger. Why, I got away from that last fellow by setting up atomic reaction against it, as a boatman pushes with his pole."

Even in the midst of our terror we could not but admire

our leader. His resources seemed boundless, and our confidence in him grew with every escape. While he kept guard at the peepholes we watched for meteors from the windows. We must have come almost within striking distance of a thousand in the course of an hour, but Edmund decided not to diminish our speed, for he said that he could control the car quicker when it was under full headway.

So on we rushed, dodging the things like a crow in a flock of pestering jays, and we really enjoyed the excitement. It was more fascinating sport than shooting rapids in a careening skiff, and at last we grew so confident in the powers of our car and its commander that we were rather sorry when the last meteor passed, and we found ourselves once more in open, unimpeded space.

After that the time passed quietly. We ate our meals and went to bed and rose as regularly as if we had been at home. In one respect, however, things were very different from what they were on the earth. We had no night! The sun shone continually, although the sky was black and always glittering with stars. None of us needed to be told by our conductor that this was due to the fact that we no longer had the shadow of the earth to make night for us when the sun was behind it. The sun was now never behind the earth, or any other great opaque body, and when we wished to sleep we made an artificial night, for our special use, by closing all the shutters. And there was no atmosphere about us to diffuse the sunlight, and so to hide the stars. We kept count of the days by the aid of a calendar clock; there seemed to be nothing that Edmund had forgotten. And it was a delightful experience, the wonder of which grew upon us hour by hour. It was too marvelous, too incredible, to be believed, and yet—*there we were!*

Once the idea suddenly came to me that it was astonishing that we had not long ago perished for lack of oxygen. I understood, of course, from what Edmund had said, that the mysterious machines along the wall absorbed the carbonic acid, but we must be constantly using up the oxygen. When I put my difficulty before Edmund he laughed.

"That's the easiest thing of all," he said. "Look here."

He threw open a little grating.

"In there," he continued, "there's an apparatus which manufactures just enough oxygen to keep the air in good condition. It is supplied with materials to last a month, which will be much longer than this expedition will take."

"There you are again," exclaimed Jack. "I was asking you about that when we ran into those pesky meteors. What *is* this expedition? Where are we going, anyway?"

"Well," Edmund replied, "since we have become pretty good shipmates, I don't see any objection to telling you. We are going to Venus."

"Going to Venus!" we all cried in a breath.

"To be sure. Why not? We've got the proper sort of conveyance, haven't we?"

There was no denying that. Our conveyance had already brought us some millions of miles out into space; why, indeed, should it not be able to carry us to Venus, or any other planet?

"How far is it to Venus?" asked Jack.

"When we quit the earth," Edmund answered, "Venus was rapidly approaching inferior conjunction. You know what that is," addressing me, "it's when the planet comes between the sun and the earth. The distance from the earth is not always the same at such a conjunction, but I figured out that on this occasion, after allowing for the circuit we should have to make, there would be just twenty-seven million miles to travel. At an average speed of twenty miles a second we could do that distance in fifteen days, fourteen and one half hours. But, of course, I had to lose some time going slow through the earth's atmosphere, for otherwise the car would have taken fire, like a meteor, on account of the friction. Then, too, I shall have to slow up on entering the atmosphere of Venus, which appears to be very deep and dense; so, upon the whole, I don't count on landing upon Venus in less than sixteen days from the time of our departure. We've already been out five days, and within eleven more I expect to introduce you to the inhabitants of another world."

The inhabitants of another world! Again Edmund had thrown out an idea which took us all aback.

"Do you believe there are any inhabitants on Venus?" I asked at length.

"Certainly. I know there are."

"For sure," put in Jack, stretching out his legs and pulling at his pipe. "Who'd go twenty-seven million miles to pay a visit if he didn't know there was somebody at home?"

"Then that's what you put the arms aboard for," I remarked.

"Yes, but I hope we shall not have to use them."

"Strikes me that this is a sort of pirate ship," said Jack. "But what kind of arms have you got, Edmund?"

For answer Edmund threw open a locker and showed us a gleaming array of automatic guns and pistols and even some cutlasses.

"Decidedly piratical!" exclaimed the incorrigible Jack. "You'd better hoist the black flag. But, see here, Edmund, with all this inter-atomic energy that you talk about, why in the world didn't you invent something new—something that would just knock the Venustians silly, and blow their old planet up if necessary? Automatic arms are pretty good at home, on that unprogressive earth that you have spurned with your heels, but they'll likely be rather small pumpkins on Venus."

"I didn't prepare anything else," Edmund replied, "because, in the first place, I was too busy with more important things, and in the second place because I don't really anticipate that we shall have any use for arms. I only took these as a precaution."

"You mean to try moral suasion, I suppose," drawled Jack. "Well, anyhow, I hope they'll be glad to see us, and since it is Venus that we are going to visit, I don't look for much fighting. I'm glad you made it Venus instead of Mars, Edmund, for, from all I've heard of Mars with its fourteen-foot giants, I don't think I should like to try the pirate business in that direction."

We all laughed at Jack's fancies; but there was something tremendously thrilling in the idea. Think of landing on another world! Think of meeting inhabitants there! Really, it made one's head spin.

"Confound it, this is all a dream," I said to myself. "I'm on my back in bed with a nightmare. I'll kick myself awake."

But do what I would I could make no dream of it. On the contrary, I felt that I had never been quite so much awake in all my life before.

After a while we all settled down to take the thing in earnest. And then the charm of it began to master our imaginations. We talked over the prospects in all their aspects. Edmund said little, and Henry nothing, but Jack and I were stirred to the bottom of our romantic souls. Henry was different. He had no romance in his make-up. He always looked at the money in a thing. To his mind, going to Venus was playing the fool, when we had at our command the means of owning the earth.

"Edmund," he said, after mumbling for a while under his breath, "this is the most utter tomfoolery that ever I heard of. Here you've got an invention that would revolutionize mechanics, and instead of utilizing it you rush off into space on a hairbrained adventure. You might have been twenty times a billionaire inside of a year if you had stayed at home and developed the thing. Why, it's folly; pure, beastly folly! Going to Venus! What can you make on Venus?"

Edmund only smiled. After a little he said:

"Well, I'm sorry for you, Henry. But then you're cut out on the ordinary pattern. But cheer up. When we go back, perhaps I'll let you take out a patent, and you can make the billions. For my part, Venus is more interesting to me than all the money you could pile up between the Atlantic Ocean and the Rocky Mountains. Why," he continued, warming up, and straightening with a certain pride which he had, "am I not the Columbus of Space?—And you my lieutenants," he added, with a smile.

"Right you are," cried Jack enthusiastically. "The Columbus of Space, that's the ticket! Where's old Archimedes now? Buried, by Jo! *He* couldn't go to Venus! And what need we care for your billionaires?"

Edmund patted Jack on the back, and I rather sympathized with his enthusiasm myself.

The time ran on, and we watched anxiously the day-hand of the calendar clock. Soon it had marked a week; then ten days; then a fortnight. We knew we must be getting very close to our goal, yet up to this time neither Jack, nor Henry, nor I had caught a glimpse of Venus. Edmund, however, had seen it, but he told us that in order to do so he had been obliged to alter our course because the planet was directly in the eye of the sun. In consequence of the change of course we were now approaching Venus from the east—flanking her, so to speak—and Edmund described her appearance as that of an enormous crescent. Finally he invited us to take a look for ourselves.

I shall never forget that first view! It was only a glimpse, for Edmund was nervous about meteors again, and would allow us only a moment at the peephole because he wished to be continually on the watch himself. But, brief as was the view, that vast gleaming sickle hanging in the black sky was the most tremendous thing I ever looked upon!

Soon afterwards Edmund changed the course again, and then we saw her no more. We had not come upon the swarms of meteors that Edmund had expected to find lurking about the planet, and he said that he now felt safe in running into her shadow, and making a landing on her night hemisphere. You will allow me to remind you that Schiaparelli had long before found out that Venus doesn't turn on her axis once every twenty-four hours, like the earth, but keeps always the same face to the sun; the consequence being that she has perpetual day on one side and perpetual night on the other. I asked Edmund why he should not rather land on the daylight side; but he replied that his plan was safer, and that we could easily go from one side to the other whenever we chose. It didn't turn out to be so easy after all, but that is another part of the story.

"I hardly expect to find any inhabitants on the night side," Edmund remarked, "for it must be fearfully cold there—too cold for life to exist, perhaps; but I have provided against that as far as we are concerned. Still, one can never tell. There *may* be inhabitants there, and at any rate I am going to find out. If there are none, we'll just stop long enough to take a look at things, and then the car will quickly transport us to the daylight hemisphere, where life certainly exists. By landing on the uninhabited side, you see, we shall have a chance to reconnoiter a little, and can approach the inhabitants on the other side so much the more safely."

"That sounds all right enough," said Jack, "but if Venus is correctly named, I'm for getting where the inhabitants are as quick as possible."

When we swung round into the shadow of the planet we got her between the sun and ourselves, and as she completely hid the sun, we now had perpetual night about the car. Out of the peephole she looked like a stupendous black circle, blacker than the sky itself, but round the rim was a beautiful ring of light.

"That's her atmosphere," Edmund explained, "lighted up by the sun from behind. But, for the life of me, I cannot tell what those immense flames mean."

He referred to a vast circle of many-colored spires that blazed and flickered like a burning rainbow at the inner edge of the ring of light. It was one of the most awful, and yet beautiful, sights that I had ever gazed upon.

"That's something altogether outside my calculations," Edmund added. "I can't account for it at all."

"Perhaps they are already celebrating our arrival with fireworks," suggested Jack, always ready to take the humorous view of everything.

"That's not fire," Edmund responded earnestly. "But what it is I confess I can't imagine. We'll find out, however, for I haven't come all this distance to be scared off."

And here I must try to explain a very curious thing which had puzzled our senses, though not our understanding (because Edmund had promptly explained it), throughout the voyage, and that was—levitation. On our first day out from the earth, we began to notice the remarkable ease with which we handled things, and the strange tendency we had to bump into one another because we seemed to be all the time employing more strength than was necessary and almost to be able to walk on air. Jack declared that he felt as if his head had become a toy balloon.

"It's the lack of weight," said Edmund. "Every time we double our distance from the earth we lose another three quarters of our weight. If I had thought to bring along a spring dynamometer, I could have shown you, Jack, that when we were 4,000 miles above the earth's surface the 200 good pounds with which you depress the scales at home had diminished to 50, and that when we had passed about 150,000 miles into space you weighed no more than a couple of ounces. From that point on, it has been the attraction of the sun to which we have owed whatever weight we had, and the floor of the car has been toward the sun, because, at that distance from the earth, the latter ceases to exercise the master force, and the pull of the sun becomes greater than the earth's. But as we approach Venus the latter begins to restore our weight, and when we arrive on her surface we shall weigh about four fifths as much as when we started from the earth."

"But I don't look as if I had lost any avoirdupois," said

Jack, glancing at his round limbs. "And when you give us a fling I seem to strike pretty hard, though in other respects I confess I do feel a good deal like an angel."

"Ah," said Edmund, laughing, "that's the *inertia of mass*. Your mass is the same, although your weight has almost disappeared. Weight depends upon the distance from the attracting body, but mass is independent of everything."

"Do you mean to say that angels are massive?"

"They may be as massive as they like provided they keep well away from great centers of gravitation."

"But Venus is such a center—then there can't be any angels there."

"I hope to find something better than angels," was Edmund's smiling reply.

Now, as we drew near to Venus, the truth of Edmund's statements became apparent. We felt that our weight was returning, and our muscular activity sinking back to the normal again. We imagined that every minute we could feel our feet pressing more heavily upon the floor.

Our approach was so rapid that the immense black circle grew visibly minute by minute. Soon it was so large that we could no longer see its boundaries through the peephole in the floor.

"We're now within a thousand miles," said Edmund, "and must be close to the upper limits of the atmosphere. I'll have to slow down, or else we'll be burnt up by the heat of friction."

He proceeded to slow down a little more rapidly than was comfortable. It was jerk after jerk, as he dropped off the power, and put on the brakes, but at last we got down to the speed of a fast express train. Soon we were so close that the surface of the planet became dimly visible, simply from the starlight. We were now settling down very cautiously, and presently we began to notice curious shafts of light which appeared to issue from the ground, as if the surface beneath us had been sprinkled with iron founderies.

"Aha!" cried Edmund, "I believe there *are* inhabitants on this side after all. Those lights don't come from volcanoes. I'm going to make for the nearest one, and we'll soon know what they are."

Accordingly we steered for one of the gleaming shafts. It was a thrilling moment, I can tell you—that when we first saw another world than ours under our feet! As we approached the light it threw a pale illumination on the ground around. Everything appeared to be perfectly flat and level. It was like dropping down at night upon a vast prairie. But the features of the landscape were indistinguishable in the gloom. Edmund boldly continued to approach until we were within a hundred feet of the shaft of light, which we could now perceive issued directly from the ground. Suddenly, with the slightest perceptible bump, we touched the soil, and the car came to rest. We had landed on Venus!

"It's unquestionably frightfully cold outside," said Edmund, "and we'll now put on these things."

He dragged out of one of his many lockers four suits of thick fur garments, and as many pairs of fur gloves, together with caps and shields for the face, leaving only narrow openings for the eyes. When we had got them on we looked like so many Esquimaux. Finally Edmund handed each of us a pair of small automatic pistols, telling us to put them where they would be handy in our side pockets.

"Boarders all!" cried the irrepressible Jack. "Pirates, do your duty!"

Our preparations being made, we opened the door. The air that rushed in almost hardened us into icicles!

"It won't hurt you," said Edmund in a whisper. "It can't be down to absolute zero on account of the dense atmosphere. You'll get used to it in a few minutes. Come on."

His whispering gave us a sense of imminent danger, but nevertheless we followed as he led the way straight toward the shaft of light. On nearing it we saw that it came out of an irregularly round hole in the ground. When we got yet nearer we were astonished to see rough steps which led down into the pit. The next instant we were frozen in our tracks! For a moment my heart stopped beating.

Standing on the steps, just below the level of the ground, and intently watching us, with eyes as big and luminous as moons, was a creature shaped like a man, but more savage than a gorilla!

CHAPTER IV
THE CAVERNS OF VENUS

For two or three minutes the creature continued to stare at us, motionless; and we stared at him. It was so dramatic that it makes my nerves tingle now when I think of it. His eyes alone were enough to harrow up your soul. Huge beyond belief, round and luminous as full moons, they were filled with the phosphorescent greenish-yellow glare that sometimes appears in the expanded pupils of a cat or a wild beast. The great hairy head was black, but the stocky body was as white as a polar bear. The arms were apelike and very long and muscular, and the entire aspect of the creature betokened immense strength and activity.

Edmund was the first to recover from the stupor of surprise, and instantly he did a thing so apparently absurd but so marvelous in its calculated effect that no brain but his could have conceived it. It shakes me at once with laughter and recollected terror when I recall it.

"WELL, HELLO YOU!" he called out in a voice of such stentorian power that we jumped as at a thunderclap. The effect on the strange brute was electric. A film shot across the big eyes, he leaped into the air, uttering a squeak that was ridiculous, coming from an animal of such size and strength, and instantly disappeared, tumbling down the steps.

But we were as much frightened as the ugly monster himself. We stared at Edmund, speechless in our amazement.

Never could I have believed it possible for such a voice to issue from the human throat. It was not the voice of our friend, nor the voice of a man at all, but an indescribable clangor; and the words I have quoted had been scarcely distinguishable, so shattered were they by the crash of sound that whirled them into our astonished ears. Edmund, seeing us gaping in speechless wonder, laughed with such an appearance of hearty enjoyment as I had never known him to exhibit—and his merriment produced another thunderous explosion that shook the air.

Then the truth burst upon me, and I exclaimed:

"It's the atmosphere!"

I had not spoken very loudly, but the words seemed to reverberate in my mouth, as if to testify to the correctness of my explanation.

"Yes," said Edmund, taking pains to moderate his voice, "you've hit it, it's the atmosphere. I had calculated on an effect of the kind, but the reality exceeds all that I had anticipated. Spectroscopic analysis as well as telescopic appearances demonstrated long ago that the atmosphere of Venus was extraordinarily extensive and dense, from which fact I inferred that we should encounter some wonderful acoustic phenomena here, and this was in my mind when, on stepping out of the car, I addressed you in a whisper. The reaction even of the whisper on my organs of speech told me that I was right, and showed me what to expect if the full power of the voice were used. When we caught sight of the creature at the top of the pit I had no desire to shoot him, and I saw that he was too powerful to be captured alive. In a second I had decided what to do. It ran through my mind that, in a world where the density, and probably something also in the peculiar constitution of the air, had the effect of vastly magnifying sound, the phonetic and acoustic organs of the inhabitants would be modified, and that the sounds uttered by them would be much fainter than those that we are accustomed to hear from living creatures on the earth. That being so, I argued that a very great and heavy sound coming from a strange animal would produce in the creature before us a paralyzing terror. You have seen that it did so. I expect that this will give us an immense advantage to begin with. We have already inspired so great a fear that I believe that we can now safely follow the creature into its habitation, and encounter without danger any of its congeners that may be there. Nevertheless, I shall not ask you to run any risks, and I will alone descend into the pit."

"If you do, may I be hanged for sheep stealing!"

You will guess at once that it was Jack who had spoken thus.

"No, sir," he continued, "if you go, we all go. Isn't that so, boys?"

In answer to an appeal thus put, neither Henry nor myself could have hung back even if we had had the disposition to do so. But I believe that we all instinctively felt that our place was by Edmund's side, wherever he might choose to go.

"Go ahead, then, Edmund," Jack added, seeing that we consented, "we're with you." And then his enthusiasm taking fire, as usual, he exclaimed: "Hurrah! Columbus forever! We've conquered a hemisphere with a blank shot."

And so we began our descent into the mysterious pit. The strange light that came from it, and formed a shaft in the dense atmosphere above like sunlight in a haymow, was accompanied by a considerable degree of heat, which was very grateful to our lungs after the frigid plunge that we had taken from the comfortable car. As we descended, the temperature continually rose until we were glad to throw off our Arctic togs, and leave them on a shelf of rock to await our return. But, fortunately, we did not forget to take the pistols from the pockets before leaving the garments. I am very uncertain what would have been the future course of our history if we had neglected this precaution.

It was an awful hole for depth. The steps, rudely cut,

wound round and round the sides like those in a cathedral tower, but the pit was not perfectly circular. It looked like a natural formation, such as the vertical entrance to a limestone cavern, or the throat of a sleeping volcano. But whatever the nature of the pit might be, I was convinced that the steps were of artificial origin. They were reasonably regular in height and broad enough for two, or even three, persons to go abreast.

When we had descended perhaps as much as two hundred feet, we suddenly found ourselves in a broad cavern with a surprisingly level floor. The temperature had been steadily rising all the time, and here it was as warm as in an ordinary living room. The cavern appeared to be about twenty yards broad and eight or ten feet in height, with a flat roof of rock. It was dimly illuminated by a small heap of what seemed to be hard coal, burning in a very roughly constructed brazier, which, as far as looks went, one would have said was constructed of iron.

You will imagine our surprise upon seeing these things. The appearance of the gorilla-like beast with the awful eyes had certainly not led us to anticipate the finding in his lair of any such evidences of human intelligence, and we stood fast in our tracks for a minute or two, nobody speaking a word. Then Edmund said:

"This is far better than I hoped. I had not thought about caverns, though I ought to have foreseen the probability of something of the kind. It is hard to drive out life as long as a world has solid foundations, and air for breathing. I shall be greatly surprised now if these creatures do not turn out to be at least as intelligent as our African or Australian savages."

"But," said I, "the fellow that we saw surely cannot have more intelligence than a beast. There must be some more highly developed creatures living here."

"I'm not so sure of that," Edmund responded. "Looks go for nothing in such a case. He had arms and hands, and his brain may be well organized."

"If his brain is as big as his eyes," Jack put in, "he ought to be able to give odds to old Solomon and beat him easy. My, but I'd like to see their spectacles—if they ever wear any!"

Jack's humor recalled us from our meditation, and we began to look about more carefully. There was not a living creature in sight, but over in a corner I detected a broad hole, down which the steps continued to descend.

"Here's the way," said Edmund, discovering the steps at the same moment. "Down we go."

He again led the way, and we resumed the descent. As we stumbled along downward we began to talk of a strange but agreeable odor which we had noticed in the cavern. Edmund said that it was due, perhaps, to some peculiar quality of the atmosphere.

"I think," he continued, "that it is heavily charged with oxygen. You have noticed that none of us feels the slightest fatigue, notwithstanding the precipitancy of our long descent."

I reflected that this might also be the cause of our rising courage, for I was sure that not one of us felt the slightest fear in thus pushing on toward dangers of whose nature we could form no idea. The steps, precisely like those above, wound round and round and led us down I should say as much as three hundred feet before we entered another cavern, larger and loftier than the first.

And there we found them!

There was never another such sight! It made our blood run cold once more, rather with surprise than fear, though the latter quickly followed.

Ranged along the farther side of the cavern, and visible in the light of another glowing heap in the center, were as many as thirty of those huge hairy creatures, standing shoulder to shoulder, their great eyes glaring like bull's-eye lanterns. But the thing that filled us with terror was their motions.

You have read, with thrilling nerves, how a huge cobra, reared on his coils, sways his terrible head from side to side before striking. Well, all those black heads before us were swaying in unison, but with a sickening circular movement, which was regularly reversed in direction. Three times by the right and then three times by the left those heads circled, in rhythmic cadence, while the luminous eyes seemed to leave phosphorescent rings in the air, intersecting one another in consequence of the rapidity of the motion.

It was such a spectacle as I had never beheld in the wildest dream. It was baleful. It was the charm of the serpent fascinating his terrified prey. In an instant I felt my brain turning, and I staggered in spite of my utmost efforts. A kind of paralysis stiffened my limbs.

Presently, all moving together, and uttering a hissing, whistling sound, they began slowly to approach us, keeping in line, each shaggy leg lifted at the same moment, like so many soldiers on parade, while the heads continued to swing, and the glowing eyes to cut linked circles in the air. But for Edmund we should certainly have been lost. Standing a little to the fore, he spoke to us over his shoulder, in a low voice:

"Take out your pistols, but don't shoot unless they make a rush. Then kill as many as you can. I'll knock over the leader in the center, and I think that will be enough."

We could as easily have stirred our arms if we had been marble statues, but he promptly raised his pistol, and the explosion followed on the instant. The report was like an earthquake. It shocked us into our senses and almost out of them again. The weight of the air and the confinement of the cavern magnified and concentrated the sound so that it was awful beyond belief. The fellow in the center was hurled back as if shot from a catapult, and the others fell at flat as he, and lay there groveling, their big eyes filming and swaying, but no longer in unison.

The charm was broken, and as we saw our fearful enemies prostrate, our courage returned at a bound.

"I thought as much," said Edmund coolly. "But I'm sorry

now that I aimed at that fellow; the sound alone would have sufficed. It was not necessary to take life. However, we should probably have had to come to it eventually, and now we have them thoroughly cowed. Our safety consists in keeping them terrified."

Thus speaking, Edmund boldly approached the groveling row, and pushed with his foot the furry body of the one he had shot. The bullet had gone through his head. At Edmund's approach the creatures sank lower on the rocky floor, and those nearest him turned up their moon eyes with an expression of submission and supplication that was grotesque. He motioned us to join him and, imitating him, we began to pat and smooth the shrinking bodies until, understanding that we would not hurt them, they gradually acquired confidence.

In the meantime the crowd in the cavern increased, others coming in through side passages, and exhibiting the utmost astonishment at the spectacle which greeted them. It was clear that those who had taken part in the opening scene imparted to the newcomers a knowledge of the situation of affairs, and we could see that our prestige was thoroughly established. It remained to utilize our advantage, and we looked to Edmund to show how it should be done. He was equal to the undertaking, but I shall not trouble you with the details of his diplomacy. Let it suffice to say that by a combination of gentleness and firmness he quickly reduced almost the entire population of the caverns (for, as we afterwards discovered, there were a dozen or more of these underground dwellings connected by horizontal passages through the rocks) into subjection to his will. I say "almost," because, as you will see in a little while, there were certain members of this extraordinary community who possessed a spirit of independence too strong to be so easily subdued.

As we became better acquainted with the cave dwellers we found that they were by no means as savage as they looked. Their appearance was certainly grotesque, and even unaccountable. Why, for instance, should their heads have been covered with coarse black disordered hair while their bodies, from the neck down, were almost beautiful with a natural raiment of golden white, as soft as silk and as brilliant as floss? I never could explain it, and Edmund was no less puzzled by this peculiarity. The immense size of their eyes did not seem astonishing after we began to reflect upon the consequences of the relative lack of light in their world. It was but a natural adjustment to their environment; with such eyes they could see in the dark better than cats. Their feet were bare and covered on the soles with thick soft skin, while the insides of their long hands were almost as white and delicate as those of a human being.

Their intelligence was sufficiently demonstrated by the construction of the hundreds of rocky steps leading from the caverns to the surface of the ground, and by their employment of fire, and manufacture of the metallic braziers which contained it. But this was not all. We found that in some of the winding passages connecting the caverns they cultivated food. It consisted entirely of vegetables of various kinds, and all unlike any that I ever saw on the earth. Water dripped from the roofs of these particular passages, and the almost colorless vegetation thrived there with astonishing luxuriance. They had many simple ways of cooking their food, and it was evident that they possessed some form of salt, though we did not discover the deposit from which they must have drawn it. They collected water in cisterns hollowed in the rock.

Although we still had abundance of food in the car, Edmund insisted on trying theirs, and it proved to be very palatable.

"This is fortunate, though hardly surprising," said Edmund. "If we had found the food on Venus uneatable, we should indeed have been in a fine fix. While we remain here we will eat as the natives eat, and save our own supplies for future need."

The only brute animals that we saw in the caverns were some doglike creatures, about as large as terriers, but very furry, which showed the utmost terror whenever we appeared.

One of the first things that we discovered outside the main cavern where we had made our debut was the burial ground of the community. This happened when they came to dispose of the fellow that Edmund had shot. They formed a regular procession, which greatly impressed us, and we followed them as they bore the body through several winding ways into a large cavern, at a considerable distance from any of the others. Here they had dug a grave, and, to our astonishment, there appeared to be something resembling a religious ceremony connected with the interment. And then, for the first time, we distinguished the females from the others. But a still greater surprise awaited us. It was no less than plain evidence of regular family relationship.

As the body was lowered into the grave one of the females approached with every sign of distress and sorrow. Jack declared that he saw tears running down her hairy cheeks. She held two little ones by the hand, and this spectacle produced an astonishing effect upon Edmund, revealing an entirely new side of his character. I have told you that he expressed regret for having killed the fellow in the cavern, but now, at the sight before him, he seemed filled with remorse.

"I wish I had never come here!" he said bitterly. "The first thing I have done is to kill an inoffensive and intelligent creature."

"Intelligent, perhaps," said Jack, "but inoffensive—not by a long shot! Where'd we have been if you hadn't killed him? They'd have made mincemeat of us."

"No," replied Edmund, sorrowfully shaking his head, "it wasn't necessary. The noise would have sufficed; and I ought to have known it."

"Why didn't you shout, then? That scared the first one," put in Henry, whose soul, it must be said, was not overflowing with sympathy.

"I did what I thought was best at the moment," Edmund replied, with a broken voice. "They were so many and so threatening that I imagined my voice alone might not be effective. But I'm sorry, sorry!"

"Henry, you're a fool!" cried the sympathetic Jack. "Come now, Edmund," he continued, kindly laying a hand on his shoulder, "what you did was the only thing under heaven that could have been done. You're wrong to blame yourself. By Jo, if you hadn't done it I would!"

But Edmund only shook his head, as if refusing to be comforted. It was the first sign of weakness that we had seen in our incomparable leader, but I am sure it only increased our respect for him—at least that's true of Jack and me. After that I noticed that Edmund was far more gentle than before in his relations with the people of the caverns.

Not long after this painful incident we made a discovery of extreme interest. It was nothing less than a big smithy! Edmund had foretold that we should find something of the kind.

"Those braziers and cooking pots," he had said, "and the tools that must have been needed to build the steps and to dig their graves, prove that they know how to work in iron. If it is not done in these caverns, then they get it from some other similar community. But I think it likely that we shall come upon some signs of the work hereabouts."

"Maybe they import it from Pittsburg," was the remark that fun-loving Jack could not refrain from making.

"Well, you'll see," said Edmund.

And, as I have already told you, he was right. We did find the smithy, with several stout fellows pounding out rude tools with equally rude hammers of iron. Of course we could ask them no questions, for their language was only a kind of squeak, and they seemed to converse mostly by means of expressive signs. But Edmund was not long in drawing his conclusions.

"This," he said, after closely examining the metal, "is native iron. There's nothing remarkable in the fact that it should be here. All the solid planets, as you know" (turning to me), "are very largely composed of iron, and Venus, being nearer the center of the system, may have proportionally more of it than the earth. And these fellows have found out its usefulness, and how to work it. There's nothing surprising in that, either, for some of our savages have done as much on the earth. Now I'll make another prediction—we are going to find coal here. That is inevitable, since we know that they burn it in the caverns. I shouldn't wonder if it were close at hand, from the look of these rocks."

He approached the wall of the cavern containing the smithy, and immediately exclaimed:

"Look here! Here it is!"

And sure enough, on joining him we saw a seam of as fine anthracite as Pennsylvania ever produced.

"A Carboniferous Age on Venus!" Edmund continued. "What do you think of that? But, of course, it was sure to be so; all the planets that are old enough have been through practically the same stages. Think of it! The plants that gave origin to this coal must have flourished here when Venus still rotated on her axis rapidly enough to have day and night succeeding one another on all sides of her, for now no vegetation except the insignificant plants that grow in these caverns can live on this hemisphere. And think, too, of the countless ages that must have been consumed in slowing down her rotation by the friction of her ocean tides."

"Has Venus got any oceans?" asked Jack.

"I haven't a doubt of it; but we shall find none on this side, although they must once have been here."

We all mused for a time on the subject that Edmund had started, when suddenly his face lighted up with the greatest animation, and he exclaimed, but as if speaking to himself rather than to us:

"Capital! It couldn't have happened better!"

"What's capital?" drawled Jack.

"Why, this smithy, and these Tubal Cains here. Unconsciously they have solved for me a problem that has given me considerable trouble. Almost as soon as we got acquainted with the people of the caverns the idea occurred to me that I should like to take some of them with us when we visit the other hemisphere. There are many interesting observations that their presence on that side of Venus would give rise to, and, besides, they might be of great use to us. Of course I meant to bring them back to their home. But the puzzling question has been how to transport them. The car has a full load already."

"They've got good legs; make 'em walk," said Jack.

Edmund burst into a laugh.

"Why, Jack," he asked, "how far do you think it is to the other side of Venus?"

"I don't know," said Jack, "but I suppose it's not very far round her. How far is it?"

"Five thousand miles, at least, to the edge of the sunlit hemisphere."

Jack whistled.

"By Jo! I wouldn't have believed it."

"Well, it's a fact," said Edmund, "and of course I don't propose to take several months to make the journey. Now the sight of these fellows at work has shown me just how it can be done in short order. It's this way: I'll have iron sleds made, put the natives that I propose to take along upon them, hitch them by wire cables, which luckily I've got, to the car, and away we'll spin. The power of the car is practically unlimited, and, as you have observed, the ground is as flat and smooth as a prairie, and, moreover, is coated with an icy covering."

Jack glowed with enthusiasm over this project, and was about to indulge in one of his characteristic outbreaks, when there came an interruption which ended in a drama that put silver streaks among my coal-black locks! Some one came in where we were and called off the workmen, who went out with the others in great haste. Of course we followed at their heels. On reaching the principal cavern, we found a singular scene. Two natives, whom we had never seen before, were evidently in charge of some kind of a ceremony. They wore tall, conical hats made of polished metal and covered with hieroglyphics, and carried staves of iron in their hands.

"Priests," Edmund immediately whispered. "Now we'll see something interesting."

The "priests" marshaled all the others, numbering several hundreds, into a long column, and then began a slow, solemn march up the steps. The leaders produced a squeaking music by blowing into the ends of their staves. Women were mingled with men, and even the children were there, too. We followed at the tail of the procession, our curiosity at the highest pitch. At the rate we went it must have taken nearly an hour to mount the steps, but at last all emerged in the open air, where the cold struck to our marrow. The natives didn't seem to mind it, but we ran back and donned our furs. Then we re-ascended and stepped out into the Arctic night, finding the crowd assembled not far from the entrance to the cavern. The frosty sky was ablaze with stars, and directly overhead shone a planet of amazing size and splendor with a little one beside it.

"The earth and the moon!" exclaimed Edmund.

I cannot describe the flood of feeling that went over me at that sight! But in a moment Edmund interrupted my meditation by saying, in a quick, nervous way:

"Look at that!"

The natives had formed themselves in a circle with the two priests standing alone in the center. All but these two had dropped on their knees, while the leaders, elevating their long arms toward the zenith, gazed upward, uttering a kind of chant in their queer, squeaking voices.

"Don't you see what they're about?" demanded Edmund, twitching me irritably by the sleeve. "They're worshipping the earth!"

It was the truth—the amazing truth! They were worshipping our planet in the sky! And, indeed, she looked worth worshipping. Never have I seen so splendid a star. She was twenty times as bright as the most brilliant planet that any terrestrial astronomer ever beheld; and the moon, glowing beside her like an attendant, redoubled the beauty of the sight.

"It's just the moment of the conjunction," said Edmund. "This is their religion; the earth is their goddess, and when she is nearest and brightest they perform this ceremony in her honor. I wouldn't have missed this for a world."

Suddenly the two priests began to pirouette, and as they whirled more and more rapidly, their huge glowing eyes made phosphorescent circles in the gloom like those that had so alarmed and fascinated us in the cavern. They gyrated round the ring of worshipers with accelerated speed, and all those poor creatures fell under the fascination and drooped with heads to the ground. Now for the first time I caught sight of an oblong object rising a couple of feet above the ground in the center of the circle. I was wondering what it might be when the spinning priests, who had gradually drawn closer to the ring of worshipers, dived into the circle, and, catching each a native in his arms, ran with their captives to the curious object that I have just described.

"It's a sacrificial stone!" exclaimed Edmund. "They're going to kill them as an offering to the earth and her child the moon."

I was frozen with horror at the sight, but just as the second priest reached the altar, where the first victim had already been pinned with the sharp point of the sacrificial staff, his captive, suddenly recovering his senses, and terrified by the awful fate confronting him, uttered a cry, wrenched himself loose, and, running like the wind, leaped over the circle and disappeared in the darkness. The fugitive passed close by us, and Jack shouted as he darted past:

"Good boy!"

The enraged priest was after him like lightning, and as he came near us his awful eyes seemed to emit actual flames. But the runner had vanished. Without an instant's hesitation the priest shot out his great arm and caught *me* by the throat! In another second I felt myself carried in a bound, as if a tiger had seized me, over the drooping heads of the worshipers and toward the horrible altar.

CHAPTER V
OFF FOR THE SUN LANDS

Dreadful as the moment was, I did not lose my senses. On the contrary, my mind was fearfully clear and active. There was not a horror that I missed. The strength and agility of my captor were astounding. I could no more have struggled with him than with a lion. Only one thing flashed upon me to do; I yelled with all the strength of my lungs. But they had become accustomed to our voices now, and the maddened creature was so intent upon his fell purpose that a cannon-shot would not have diverted him from it.

He got me to the altar, where the preceding victim already lay with his heart torn out, and, pressing me against it with all his bestial force, raised the pointed staff to transfix me. With dying eyes I saw the earth gleaming, magnificent, directly over my head, and my heart bounded with unreasoning hope at the sight. It was my mother planet, powerful to save!

All this passed in a second, while the dreadful spear was poised for its work. Even in that fraction of time I noticed the bunching muscles of the murderer's hairy arm, and then I pressed my eyes shut.

Bang!

Something touched me, and I felt the warm blood gushing. Then I knew no more.

* * * *

• GARRETT P. SERVISS

In the midst of a dream of boyhood scenes a murmur of familiar voices awoke me. I opened my eyes, but as I could not make out where I was, closed them again.

Then I heard Edmund saying:

"He's coming out all right."

Thereupon, I reopened my eyes, but still the scene puzzled me. I saw Edmund's face, and behind those of Jack and Henry, wearing anxious looks. But this was not my room! It seemed to be a cave, with faint firelight reflections on the walls.

"Where am I?" I asked.

"Back in the cavern, and coming along all right," said Edmund.

Back in the cavern! What did he mean? Then, suddenly, memory returned.

"So he didn't sacrifice me!" I cried.

"Not on your life!" Jack's hearty voice responded. "Edmund was too quick for that."

"But only by a fraction of a second!" said Edmund, smiling.

"What happened, then?" I asked, my recollections coming back stronger and stronger.

"A mighty good shot happened," said Jack. "The best I ever saw."

I looked inquiringly at Edmund. He saw that I could bear it, and he began:

"When that fellow snatched you up and leaped inside the circle I had my furs wrapped so closely around me, not anticipating any danger, that for quite ten seconds I was unable to get out my pistol. I tore the garment open just in time, for already he was pressing you against the accursed altar with his spear poised. I didn't waste any time finding my aim, but even as it was the iron point had touched you when the bullet crashed through his brain. The shock swerved the weapon a little and you were only wounded in the shoulder. You got a scratch which might have been serious but for your Arctic coat.

The fellow fell dead beside you, and under the circumstances I felt compelled to shoot the other one also, for he was insane with the delirium of their bloody rite, and I knew that our lives would never be safe if he remained ready for mischief.

"I'm sorry to have had to begin killing right and left again, but I guess that's the lot of all invaders, wherever they may go. It's the second lesson for these savages, and I believe it will prove final. When their priests were dead and the others had no fight in them, even if they had intended any harm to us. Nobody knows to what those chaps might have led them, and my conscience is easy this time."

"How long have I been here?" I asked.

"Two days by the calendar clock?" replied Jack.

"Yes, two days," Edmund assented. "I never saw a man so knocked out by a shock, for the wound wasn't much; I fixed that up in five minutes. But I don't blame you. In your place I should have been scared to the bottom of my soul also. But look at yourself."

He held a pocket mirror before me, and then I saw that my hair was streaked with gray!

"But we haven't been idle in the meanwhile," Edmund went on. "I've got two sleds nearly completed, and to-morrow at midnight—earth time—I mean to set out for the sunny lands of Venus."

"How in the world could you have worked so fast?" I asked in surprise.

"Because I had certain tools in the car which vastly facilitated the operation; but I must admit that the savage blacksmiths worked well, too, and showed surprising intelligence in comprehending my directions. Perhaps that was because I had learned their language."

"Learned their language!" I exclaimed, staring in amazement.

"Well, perhaps that's putting it a little too strong; but I have learned enough to establish a pretty good understanding with them. There's nothing like working together to make intelligent creatures comprehend one another."

"But what kind of a language is it, then?" I asked.

"A language to make your hair stand on end," put in Jack. "The language that ghosts speak, I reckon! Not that I understand the least little bit of it, but I judge from what Edmund says."

With increasing bewilderment I looked at our leader. He smiled, and then looked thoughtful for a moment before again speaking. At last he said:

"It's a subject that I may be better able to discuss after I have learned more about it. All I can say at present is that it appears to be a kind of telepathy. You know that their voices seem hardly more cultivated, or capable of regular articulation, than those of mere brutes; and, besides, they have a certain horror of sound. These smiths wear coverings over their ears to minify the noise of their hammering. Yet they are able to converse, partly by physical signs, but more, I am sure, by some means which they possess of transferring thought without the mediation of any senses familiar to us. Sometimes I imagine that their extraordinary eyes play a large part in the phenomenon. But, however that may be, they certainly are able to read some of my thoughts, when we are in close relations and working together. One of them is especially gifted in this way, and what do you think? I have discovered his name!"

"Now, Edmund—" I began incredulously.

"Yes," he persisted, "it's a fact. You are to remember that they do interchange some of their ideas by means of sounds, and they have certain words, among which I am disposed to think are their individual designations. One of these words particularly attracted my attention because I observed that it was always addressed to the person I have just spoken of, and I finally concluded that it was his name. As near as I can imitate it, it sounds something like 'Juba.' So that's what I call him, and he's going to be the chief of the party that I propose to take with us. His services may be invaluable to us."

A great deal more was said on this curious subject, but since we did not arrive at a complete understanding of it until after we had reached the other side of the planet, I shall postpone any further explanation to the chapters which will be devoted to our astonishing adventures on that part of Venus.

My wound, as Edmund had said, was very slight, and the effects of the shock having passed off during the period of my unconsciousness, I was soon busy with the others in making the final preparations for our departure. The sleds were, of course, very rude affairs, but they were also very strong. Among the innumerable stores which Edmund's foresight had led him to put into the car were a number of exceedingly strong but light metallic cables. With these the two sleds were hitched, one behind the other, and a line about a hundred feet long connected them with the car. The latter could thus rise to a considerable height without lifting the sleds from the ground.

The sleds were provisioned from the stores of the natives, and we also took some of their food in the car, not only to eke out our own but because we had come to like it.

Edmund had already chosen the fellows who were to accompany us, and among them were two of the smiths besides Juba. In all they were eight. How he succeeded in persuading them I do not know, but not the slightest objection was apparent on their part, or on the part of their compatriots in the caverns. We were all ready at the predetermined time, and the scene at our departure was a strange one.

At least five hundred natives had assembled in a furry crowd around the entrance to the caverns to see us off. When we started, the fellows on the sleds, being unused to the motion, clung together like so many awkward white bears taking a ride in the circus. Their friends stood about the ill-omened sacrificial altar, waving their long arms, while their huge eyes goggled in the starlight.

Jack, in a burst of enthusiasm, fired four or five parting shots from his pistol. As the reports crashed through the heavy air, you should have seen the crowd vanish down the hole! The sight made me wince, for they must have gone down like a cataract, all heaped together. But they were tough, and I trust no heads were broken. The effect on the eight fellows on the sleds came near being disastrous. I expected to see them leap off and run, which no doubt they would have done if Edmund had not taken, for other reasons, the precaution to tie them fast. But they strained at their bonds, and squealed in terror.

"Give me your pistol!" commanded Edmund, in a voice of thunder, and with blazing eyes.

Jack was almost twice his size, but he handed over the pistol with the air of a rebuked schoolboy.

"When you learn how to use it, I'll give it back to you," said Edmund sternly, and that closed the incident.

Then we began gradually to put on speed, and as the ground was icy smooth and entirely unobstructed, we were soon traveling at the rate of sixty miles an hour. The plan of the sleds worked like magic, and after their first terror had passed away it was plain to be seen that the natives enjoyed the new sensation immensely. And, indeed, it was a glorious spin!

But in a little while a danger developed which we had not thought of. It arose from the existence of other caverns whose mouths opened upon the plain. To have precipitated the sleds into these would have been fatal. Luckily, shafts of light issued from all of them, and warned by these, we managed to avoid the danger. But it was not entirely passed before we had traveled at least a hundred miles. It was like an immense city of prairie dogs without mounds. The cavern that we had discovered on our arrival was evidently situated on the outskirts of the group, and now we were passing through the center of it. Occasionally we saw a huge white form disappear in one of the holes as we swiftly approached, but that was all we beheld of the inhabitants. But the spectacle of the shafts of light rising all around us was amazing. When we were in the midst of it Edmund hesitated for a moment, muttering that we had been too hasty and should have remained longer to study the peculiarities of this wonderful world of night; but finally he decided to keep on, and soon afterwards we saw the last of the caverns. Then, as there appeared to be no obstructions of any kind, the speed was worked up to a hundred miles an hour. Going straight ahead as we did, there was no danger of the sleds being overturned.

Having, as Edmund had calculated, about five thousand miles to go before reaching the edge of the sun-illuminated hemisphere, it was evident that, at our present rate of progress, we should arrive there in a little over two days by the calendar clock. We guided our course by the stars, and for me one of the most interesting things was to see the earth sinking toward the horizon, accompanied by the stars, as if the heavens were revolving in a direction opposed to our line of travel. We smoked and talked and ate and slept in the old way, while the marvelous mouths in the wall resumed their strange deglutition. Thus the time passed, without ennui, until, unexpectedly, a new phenomenon captured our attention.

Ahead, through the peephole, Edmund had descried again the flaming spires which had so astonished us on our approach to Venus. But now their appearance was splendid and imposing beyond words. Above them rose an arc of pearly light which grew higher every hour. And with the arc of light rose the flames also. At the same time they seemed to spread to the right and the left, until they were simultaneously visible from both of the side windows of the car. Their colors were wonderful—red, green, purple, orange—all the hues of the prism.

"There is the old mystery again," exclaimed Edmund, "and I can no more explain it now than I could when we first saw it on nearing the planet. The arc of light above is natural enough; it's simply the dawn. The sun never rises on this side of Venus, but it will rise for us because we are approaching it, and the light is the first indication that we are getting near enough to the border between day and night for some of the sun's rays to be bent over the horizon by refraction. But those flames! See how steady they are as a whole, and yet how they change color like a slowly turning prism."

"Don't, for God's sake, run us into a conflagration," said Jack. "I'm ready to believe anything of this topsy-turvy old planet, and I shouldn't be surprised if the other side is all fire as this one is all frost. I can stand these hairy beasts, but I'll be hanged if I want to be introduced among salamanders."

"That's not real fire," said Edmund. "When we get a little nearer we can see what it is. In the meantime I'll try to think it out."

The result of Edmund's meditations, when he announced it to us, an hour later, awoke as much amazement in our minds as anything that had yet occurred. He had been sitting silent in his corner, occasionally taking a glimpse through the peephole, or one of the windows, when suddenly he slapped his thigh, and springing to his feet, exclaimed:

"They're mountains of crystal!"

"Mountains of crystal!" we echoed.

"Nothing else in the world, and I am ashamed not to have foreseen the thing. It's plain enough when you come to think about it. Remember that Venus being a world lying half in the daylight and half in the night, is necessarily as hot on one side as it is cold on the other. All of the clouds and floating vapors are on the day side, where the sunbeams act. The heated air charged with moisture rises over the sunward hemisphere, and flows off above, on all sides, toward the night side, while from the latter cold air flows in beneath to take its place. Along the junction of the two hemispheres the clouds and moisture are condensed by the intense cold, and fall in ceaseless snowstorms. This snow descending for ages has piled up in mountainous masses whose height may be increased in some places by real mountain ranges buried beneath. The atmospheric moisture cannot pass very far into the night hemisphere without being condensed, and so it is all arrested within a ring, or band, extending completely around the planet, and marking the division between perpetual day and perpetual night. The appearance of gigantic flames is produced by the sunbeams striking these mountains of ice and snow from behind and breaking into prismatic fire."

We listened to this explanation, so simple and yet so wonderful, with mingled feelings of astonishment and admiration. And then we turned again to regard the phenomenon, which now, with our nearer approach, had become splendid and awful beyond description.

In a few minutes Edmund addressed us again. "I foresee now," he said, "considerable trouble for us. There has been a warning of that, too, if I had but heeded it. I've noticed for some time that a wind, getting gradually stronger, has been following us, sometimes dying out and then coming on again stronger than before. It is likely that this wind gets to be a perfect hurricane in the neighborhood of those strange mountains. It is the back suction, caused, as I have already told you, by the rising of the heated air on the sunny side of the planet. It may play the deuce with us when we get into the midst of it. I shall have to be cautious."

He immediately reduced the speed to not more than ten miles an hour, and at once we noticed the wind of which he had spoken. It came now in great gusts from behind, rapidly increasing in frequency and fury. Soon it was strong enough to drive the sleds without any pull upon the cable, and sometimes they were forced directly under the car, and even ahead of it, the natives clinging to one another in the utmost terror. Edmund managed to govern the motions of the car for a time, holding it back against the storm, but as he confessed, this was a contingency he had made no provision for, and eventually we became almost as helpless as a ship in a typhoon.

"Of course I could cut loose from the sleds and run right

GARRETT P. SERVISS

"We were in the heart of the Crystal Mountains!"
Page 71.

out of this," said Edmund, "but that would never do. I've taken them into my service and I'm bound to look out for them. If there was room for them in the car it would be all right. Let's see. Yes! I've got it. I'll fetch up the sleds and fasten them underneath the car, like baskets to a balloon, and so carry the whole thing. There's plenty of power; it's only room that's wanting."

No sooner said than done with Edmund. By this time we were getting into the ice, huge hills of which surrounded us. Edmund dropped the car in the lee of one of these strange hummocks. Here the force of the wind was broken, and the sky directly over us was free from clouds, but a short distance ahead we could see them whirling and tumbling in mighty masses of tumultuous vapor. Lashing the two sleds together we attached them about ten feet below the bottom of the car. Then the natives, who had been unbound, and had stood looking on in utter bewilderment, were securely fastened on the sleds. We entered the car and the power was turned on.

"We'll rise straight up," said Edmund, "and as soon as we are out of the wind current we will sail over the mountains and come down on the other side as nice as you please. Strange that I didn't think of carrying the sleds in this way to begin with."

It was a beautiful program that Edmund had outlined, and we had complete confidence in our leader's ability to carry it through; but it didn't work as expected. Even his genius had met its match this time.

No sooner had we risen out of the protection of the hill of ice than the hurricane caught us. It was a blast of such power and ferocity that in an instant it had the car spinning like a teetotum, and then it shot us ahead, banging the sleds against the car as if they had been tassels. It is a wonder of wonders that the poor creatures on them were not flung off, but fortunately we had taken particular pains with their lashings, and as for knocks, they could stand them like so many bears.

In the course of twenty minutes we must have traveled

twice as many miles, perfectly helpless to arrest our mad rush because, Edmund said, the atomic reaction partly refused to work, and he could not rise as he had expected to do. We were pitched hither and thither, and were sprawling on the floor more than half the time. The noise was awful, and nobody tried to speak after Edmund had shouted his single communication about the power, which would have filled us with dismay if we had had leisure to think.

The shutters were open, and suddenly I saw through one of the windows a sight which I thought must surely be my last. The car had been sweeping through a dense cloud of boiling vapors, and these had without warning split open before my eyes—and there, almost in contact with the car, was a glittering precipice of solid ice, gleaming with wicked blue flashes, and we were rushing upon it as if shot out of a cannon!

The next instant came a terrific shock, which I thought must have crushed the car like an eggshell, and down we fell—down and down!

CHAPTER VI
LOST IN THE CRYSTAL MOUNTAINS

If we had seen the danger earlier, and had not been so tumbled about by the pitching of the car, it is possible that Edmund would have prevented the collision, in spite of the partial disablement of his apparatus. The blow against the precipice of ice was not as severe as it had seemed to me, and the car was not smashed; but the fall was terrible! There was only one thing which saved us from destruction. At the base of the mighty cliff against which the wind had hurled the car an immense deposit of snow had collected, and into this we plunged. We were all thrown together in a heap, the car and the sleds being entangled with the wire ropes.

Fortunately the stout glass windows were not broken, and after we had struggled to our feet Edmund managed to open the door. Before emerging he bade us put on our furs, but even with them we found the cold outside all but unendurable. Yet the natives paid no attention to it. Not one of them was seriously hurt, although they were firmly attached to the sleds, and unable to undo their fastenings. We set them loose, and then began seriously to examine the situation.

Above us towered the vertical precipice disappearing in the whirling clouds, and the wind drove square against it with the roar of Niagara. The air was filled with snow and ice dust, and at intervals we could not see objects three feet away from our noses. Our poor furry companions huddled together, and being of no use to themselves or us, suffered more from the noise, and from the terror inspired by the snow than from any injuries that they had received.

"We've got to get out of this mighty quick," shouted Edward. "Hustle now and repair ship."

We got to work at once, Juba aiding us a little under Edmund's direction, and soon we had the sleds out of the tangle and properly attached. Then we replaced the natives on their seats, and entered the car. Edmund began to fumble with his apparatus. After some ten minutes' work he said, in an evasive way, that the damage was not serious enough to prevent the working of the car, but I thought I caught an expression of extreme anxiety in his face. Still, his manner indicated that he considered himself master of the situation.

"You notice," he said, "that this wind is variable, and there lies our chance. When the blasts weaken, the air springs back from the face of the cliff and then whirls round to the right. I've no doubt that there is a passage in that direction through which the wind finds its way behind this icy mountain, and if we can get there, too, we shall undoubtedly find at least partial shelter. I'm going to take advantage of the first lull."

It worked out just as he had predicted. As the wind surged back after a particularly vicious rush against the great blue cliff, we cut loose and went sailing up into it, rushing past the glittering wall so swiftly that it made our heads swim. In two or three minutes we rounded a corner, and then found ourselves in a kind of atmospheric eddy, where the car simply spun round and round, with the sleds whirling below it.

"Now for it!" shouted Edmund. "Hang on!"

He touched a knob, and instantly we rose with immense speed. We must have shot up a couple of thousand feet, when the wind, coming over the top of the icy barrier we had just flanked, caught us again, and swept us off on a horizontal course. Then, suddenly, the air cleared all round about, as if a magic broom had swept away the clouds. The spectacle that was

A Columbus of Space •

revealed—but why try to describe it! No language could do it. Yet I must tell you what we saw.

We were in the heart of the *Crystal Mountains!* They towered round us on every side, and stretched away in interminable ranges of shining pinnacles. Such shapes! Such colors! Such flashing and blazing of gigantic rainbows and prisms! There were mountains that looked to my amazed eyes as lofty as Mont Blanc, and as massive, every solid mile of which was composed of crystalline ice, refracting and reflecting the sunbeams with iridescent splendor. For now we could begin to see a part of the orb of the sun itself, prodigious in size, and poised on the edge of the gem-glittering horizon, where the jeweled summits split its beams into a thousand haloes.

There was one mighty peak, still ahead of us, but toward which we were rushed sidewise by the wind, which surpassed all the others in marvelousness. It towered majestically above our level—a superb, stupendous, coruscating *Alp of Light!* On every side it darted blinding rays of a hundred splendid hues, as if a worldful of emeralds, rubies, sapphires, and diamonds had been heaped together in one gigantic pile and transfused with a sunburst. Even Edmund was for a moment speechless with astonishment at this wildly magnificent sight. But presently he spoke, very calmly, though what he said changed our amazement to terror.

"The trouble with the apparatus is very serious. I am unable to make the car rise higher. It will no longer react against an obstacle. We are entirely at the mercy of the wind. If it carries us against that glittering devil no power under heaven can save us."

If my hair had not whitened before it surely would have whitened now!

When we were swept against the first icy precipice the danger had come unexpectedly, out of a concealing cloud, and anticipation was swallowed up in the event. But now we had to bear the fearful strain of expectation, with the paralyzing knowledge that nothing that we could do could aid us in the least. I thought that even Edmund's face paled with fear.

On we rushed, still borne sidewise, so that the spectacle was burned into our eyes, as, with the fascination of impending death, we gazed helpless out of the window. Now we were upon it! Instinctively I threw myself backward; but the blow did not come. Instead there was a wild rush of ice crystals sweeping the thick glass.

"Look!" shouted Edmund. "We are safe! See how the particles of ice are swept from the face of the peak by the tempest. They leap toward us, and are then whirled round the mountain. The compacted air forms a buffer. We may yet touch the precipice, but the wind, having free vent on both sides, will carry us one way or the other without a serious shock."

He had hardly finished speaking, in a voice that had risen to a shriek with the effort to make himself heard, when the crisis came. We did just touch a projecting ridge, but the wind, howling past it, carried us in an instant round the obstruction.

"Scared ourselves for nothing," said Edmund, in a quieter voice, as the roar died down. "We were really as safe all the time as a boat in a deep rapid. The velocity of the current sheered us off."

Our hearts beat more steadily again, but there was a greater danger, of which he had warned us, but which we had not had time to contemplate. I, at least, began to think of it with dismay when the scintillant peak was left behind, and I saw Edmund again working away at his machinery. Presently it was manifest that we were rapidly sinking.

"What's the matter?" I cried. "We seem to be going down."

"So we are," he replied quietly, "and I fear that we shall not go up again very soon. The power is failing all the time. It will be pretty hard to have to stop indefinitely in this frightful place, but I am afraid that that is our destiny."

Lost and helpless in these mountains of ice and this world

of gloom and storm! The thought was too terrible to be entertained. Yet it was forced into our minds even more by our leader's manner than by his words. Not one of us failed to comprehend its meaning, and it was characteristic that, while talkative Jack now said not a word, uncommunicative Henry burst into a brief fury of denunciation. I was startled by the energy of his words:

"Edmund Stonewall," he cried, agitating his arms, "you have brought me to my death with your infernal invention! May you be—"

But he never finished the sentence. His face turned as white as a sheet, and he sank in a heap upon the floor.

"Poor fellow," said Edmund, pityingly. "Would to God that he instead of Church had remained at home. But I'll get him and all of us out of this trouble; only give me a little time."

In a few minutes Jack and I had restored Henry to his senses, but he was as weak as a child, and remained lying on one of the cushioned benches. In the meantime the car descended until at last it rested upon the snow in a deep valley, where we were protected from the wind. In this profound depression a kind of twilight prevailed, for the sun, which we had glimpsed when we were on the level of the peaks, was at least thirty degrees below our present horizon. Henry having recovered his nerve, we all got out of the car, unloosed the natives, and began to look about us.

The scene was more disheartening than ever. All about towered the crystal mountains, their bases leaden-hued and formless in the ghostly gloom, while their middle parts showed deep gleams of ultramarine, brightening to purple higher up, and a few aspiring peaks behind us sparkled brilliantly where the sunlight touched them. It was such a spectacle as the imagination could not have conceived, and I have often tried in vain to reproduce it satisfactorily in my own mind.

Was there ever such a situation as ours? Cast away in a place wild and wonderful beyond description, millions of miles from all human aid and sympathy, millions of miles from the world that had given us birth! I could, in bitterness of spirit, have laughed at the suggestion that there was any hope for us. And yet, at that very moment, not only was there hope, but there was even the certainty of deliverance. But, unknown to us, it lay in the brain of the incomparable man who had brought us hither.

I have told you that it was twilight in the valley where we lay. But when, as frequently happened, tempests of snow burst over the mountains, and choked the air about us, the twilight turned to deepest night, and we had to illumine the lamps in the car. By great good fortune, Edmund said, enough power remained to furnish us with light and heat, and now I looked upon those mysterious black-tusked muzzles in the car with a new sentiment, praying that they would not turn to mouths of death.

The natives, being used to darkness, needed no artificial illumination. In fact, we had observed that whenever the sunlight had streamed over them their great eyes were almost blinded, and they suffered cruelly from an affliction so completely outside of all their experience. Edmund now began to speak to us of this, saying that he ought to have foreseen and provided against it.

"I shall try to find some means of affording protection to their eyes when we arrive in the sunlit hemisphere," he said. "It must be my first duty."

We heard these words with a thrill of hope.

"Then you think that we shall escape?" I asked.

"Of course we shall escape," he replied cheerfully. "I give you my word for it, but do not ask me for any particulars yet. The exact means I have not yet found, but find them I will. We may have to stay where we are for a considerable time, and our companions must be made comfortable. Even under their furry skins they'll suffer from this kind of weather."

Following his directions we took a lot of extra furs from the car, and constructed a kind of tent, under which the natives could huddle on the sleds. There being but little wind in the valley, this was not so difficult an undertaking as it may seem. And the poor fellows were very glad of the shelter, for some of them were shivering, since, not knowing what to do, they were less active than ourselves. No sooner were they housed than they fell to eating ravenously. Both the car and the sleds had been abundantly provisioned, so that there was no immediate fear of a famine among us.

Inside the car we soon had things organized very much as they were during our voyage from the earth. We read, talked, and smoked to our hearts' content, almost forgetting the icy mountains that tottered over us, and the howling tempest which, with hardly an intermission, tore through the cloud-choked air a thousand or two thousand feet above our heads. We talked of our adventure with the meteors, which seemed an event of long ago, and then we talked of home—home twenty-six million miles away! In fact, it may have been thirty millions by this time, for Edmund had told us that Venus, having passed conjunction while we were at the caverns, was now receding from the earth.

But while we thus strove to kill the time and banish thoughts of our actual situation, Edmund sat apart much of the time absorbed in thought, and we respected his privacy, knowing that our only chance of escape lay in him. One day (I speak always of "days," because we religiously counted the passage of time by our clock) he issued alone from the car and was absent a long time, so that we began to be concerned, and, going outside looked everywhere for signs of him. At length, to our infinite relief, he appeared stumbling and crawling along the foot of an icy mountain. As he drew nearer we saw that he was smiling, and as soon as he was within easy earshot he called out:

"It's all right. I've found the solution."

Then upon joining us he continued:

"We'll get out all right, but we shall have to be patient for a while longer."

"What is it?" we asked eagerly. "What have you found out?"

"Peter," he said, turning to me, "you know what libration means; well, it's libration that is going to save us. As Venus travels round the sun she turns just once on her axis in making a complete circuit, the consequence being, as you already know, that she has one side on which the sun never rises while the other half is in perpetual daylight. But, since her orbit is not a perfect circle, she travels a little faster than the average during about half of her year and a little slower during the other half, but, at the same time, her steady rotation on her axis never varies. This produces the phenomenon that is called libration, the result of which is that, along the border between the day and night hemispheres there is a narrow strip where the sun rises and sets once in each of her years, which are about two hundred and twenty-five of our days in length. Within this strip the sun shines continuously for about sixteen weeks, gradually rising during eight weeks and sinking during the following eight. Then, during the next sixteen weeks, the strip lies in unceasing night.

"Now the kind fates have willed that we should fall just within this lucky strip. By the utmost good fortune after we passed the blazing peak which so nearly wrecked us, we were carried on by the wind so far, before the ascensional power of the car gave out, that we descended on the sunward side of the crest of the range. The sun is now just beginning to rise on the part of the strip where we are, and it will get higher for several weeks to come. The result will be that a great melting of ice and snow will occur here, and in this deep valley a river will form, flowing off toward the sunward hemisphere, exactly where we want to go. I shall take advantage of the torrent that will flow here and float down with it until we are out of the labyrinth. It's our only chance, for we couldn't possibly clamber over the hummocky ice and drag the car with us."

"Why not leave the car here?" asked Henry.

Edmund looked at him and smiled.

"Do you want to stay on Venus all your life?" he asked. "I thought you didn't like it well enough for that. How could we ever get back to the earth without the car? I can repair the mechanism as soon as I can find certain substances, which I am sure exist on this planet as well as on the earth. But it is no use looking for them in this icy wilderness. No, we can never abandon the car. We must take it with us, and the only possible way to transport it is with the aid of the coming river."

"But how will you manage to float?" I asked.

"The car, being air-tight, will float like a buoy."

"But the natives, will you abandon them?"

"God forbid. I'll contrive a way for them."

The effects of libration on Venus were not new to me, but they were to Jack and Henry, who had never studied such things, and they expressed much doubt about Edmund's plan, but I had confidence in it from the beginning, and it turned out just as he had predicted, as things always did. Every twenty-four hours we saw, with thankful hearts, that the sun had perceptibly risen, and as it rose, the sky gradually cleared, while the sunbeams, falling uninterruptedly, grew hotter and hotter. Soon we no longer had any use for furs, or for artificial heat. At the same time the melting of the ice began. It formed, in fact, a new danger, by bringing down avalanches into the valley, yet we watched the process joyously, since it fell so entirely within Edmund's program. While we were awaiting the flood, Edmund had prepared screens to protect the eyes of the natives.

We were just at the bottom of the trough of the valley, near its head. It wound away before us, turning out of sight beyond an icy bulwark. Streams were soon pouring down from the heights all around, and uniting, they formed a little torrent, which flowed swiftly over the smooth, hard ice. Edmund now completed his plan.

"I'll take Juba in the car with us," he said. "There's just room for him. As for the others, we'll fasten the sleds on each side of the car, which will be buoyant enough to float them, and they'll have to take their chances outside."

We made the final arrangements while the little torrent was swelling to a river. Before it became too broad and deep we managed to place the car across the center of its course, the sleds forming outriders. Then all took their places and waited. Higher and higher rose the waters, while avalanches, continually increasing in size and number, thundered down the heights, and vast cataracts leaped and poured from the precipices. It was a mercy that we were so situated that the avalanches could not reach the car. But we received some pretty hard knocks before the stream became deep and steady enough to float us off. Shall I ever forget that moment?

There came a sudden wave, forced onward by a great slide of ice, which lifted car and sleds on its crest, and away we went! The car proved more buoyant than I had believed possible. The sleds, fastened on each side, tended to give it extra stability, and it did not sink deeper than the middle of the windows. The latter, though formed of very thick glass, might have been broken by the tossing ice if they had not been divided into small panes separated by bars of steel, which projected a few inches outside.

"I made that arrangement for meteors," said Edmund, "but I never thought that they would have to be defended against ice."

The increasing force of the current sent us spinning down the valley with accelerated speed. We swept round the nearest ice peak on the left, and as we passed under its projecting buttresses a fearful roar above informed us that an avalanche of unexampled magnitude had been unchained. We could not withdraw our eyes from the window on that side of the car, and almost instantly immense masses of ice appeared crashing into the water, throwing it over us in floods and half drowning the unfortunate wretches on the sleds. Still, they clung on, fastened together, and we could do nothing to aid them. The uproar grew worse, and the ice came plunging down faster and faster, accompanied with a deluge of water from the heights above. The car pitched and rolled until we were all flung off our feet. Poor Juba was a picture of abject terror. He hung moaning to a bench, his huge eyes aglow with fright.

Suddenly the car seemed to be lifted clear from the water, and then it fell back again and was submerged, so that we were buried in night. Slowly we rose to the surface, and Edmund, springing to a window, shouted:

"They're gone! Heaven have pity on them—and on me!"

In spite of their fastenings the water had swept every living soul from the sled on the left. We rushed to the other window. It was the same story there—the sled on that side was also empty. I saw a furry body tossed in the torrent alongside, but in a second it disappeared beneath the raging water. At the same time Edmund exclaimed:

"God forgive us for bringing those poor creatures here only to meet their death!"

CHAPTER VII
THE CHILDREN OF THE SUN

But the situation was too critical to permit us to think of the unfortunates whose death we had undoubtedly caused. There seemed less than an even chance of our getting through with our own lives. As we tossed and whirled onward the water rose yet higher, and blocks of ice assailed us on all sides. First the sled on the left was torn loose; then the other followed it, leaving the car to fight its battle alone. But the loss of the sleds was a good thing now that their occupants were gone, for it eased off the weight and the car rose much higher in the water. Moreover, it gave way more readily when pressed by the ice. To be sure, it rolled more than before, but still, being well ballasted, it did not turn turtle, and most of the time we were able to keep on our feet by holding fast to the inside window bars.

Once we took a terrible plunge, over a vertical fall of not less than twenty or thirty feet. But the water below the fall was very deep, a profound hole having been quickly scooped out in the unfathomable ice beneath, so that we did not strike bottom, as I had feared, but came bobbing to the top again like a cork. Below this fall there was a very long series of rapids, extending, it seemed, for miles upon miles, and we shot down them with the speed of an express train, lurching from side to side, and colliding with hundreds of ice floes. It must not be supposed that we went through this experience without suffering any injuries. On the contrary, our hands were all bleeding, our faces cut, Henry had one eye closed by a blow, and our clothing, for we were not wearing our Arctic outfit, was badly used up. Yet none of our injuries was really serious, although we looked as if we had just come out of the toughest kind of a street brawl.

But there is no use in prolonging the story of this awful ride. It seemed to us to last for days upon days, though, in fact, the worst of it was over within twelve hours after we were lifted from our moorings in the valley. The tumbling stream gradually broadened out as it left the region of the high mountains, and then we found ourselves in a district covered with icy hills of no great elevation. But we could still see, by glances, as the stream curved this way and that, the glittering peaks behind. It was an appalling thing to watch many of the nearer hills as they suddenly sank, collapsed, and disappeared, like pinnacles of loaf sugar melting and falling to pieces in a basin of water.

Edmund said that all of the ice-hills and mounds through which we were passing no doubt owed their existence to pressure from behind, in the belt where the sun never rose, and where the ice was piled up in actual mountains. These foothills were, in fact, enormous glaciers thrust out toward the sunward hemisphere.

After a long time the now broad river widened yet more until it became a great lake, or bay. The surface of the planet around appeared nearly level, and, as far as we could see, was mostly covered by the water. Here vast fields of ice floated, and the water was not muddy, as it would have been if it had passed over soil, but of crystal purity and wonderfully blue in places where shafts of sunlight penetrated to great depths—for now the sun was high above the horizon ahead, and shining in an almost clear sky. Presently we began to notice the wind again. It came fitfully, first from one quarter and then another, rapidly increasing until, at times, it rose into a tempest. It lifted the water in huge combing waves, but the car rode them like a lifeboat.

"There is peril for us in this," said Edmund, at last. "We are being carried by the current into a region where the contending winds may play havoc. It is the place where the hot air from the sunward side begins to be chilled and to descend, meeting the colder air from the night side. It must form a veritable belt of storms, which may be as difficult to pass, circumstanced as we are, as the crystal mountains themselves."

"Suppose it should turn out that there is nothing but an ocean on this side of the planet," I suggested.

"That I believe to be impossible," Edmund responded. "This hemisphere must be, as a whole, broken up into highlands and depressions. The geological formation of the other side, as far as I could make it out from the appearance of the rocks in the caverns, indicates that Venus has undergone the same experience of upheavals and fracturings of the crust that the earth has been through. If that is true of one side it must be true of the other also, for during a large part of these geological changes she undoubtedly rotated rapidly on her axis like the earth."

"But we traveled five thousand miles on the other side without encountering anything but a frozen prairie," I objected.

"True enough, and yet I would lay a wager that all of that side of the planet is not equally level. Remember the vast plains of Russia and Siberia."

"Well," put in Jack, whose spirits were beginning to revive, "if there's a shore somewheres, let's find it. I want to see the other kind of inhabitants. These that we've met don't accord with my ideas of Venus."

"We shall find them," responded Edmund, "and I think I can promise you that they will not disappoint your expectations."

Yet there seemed to be nothing in our present situation to

warrant the confidence expressed by our leader's words and manner. The current that had carried us out of the crystal mountains gradually disappeared in a vast waste of waters, and we were driven hither and thither by the tempestuous wind. Its force increased hour by hour, and at last the sky, which at brief intervals had been clear and exquisitely blue, became choked with black clouds, sweeping down upon the face of the waters, and often whirled into great *trombes* by the tornadic blasts. Several times the car was deluged by waterspouts, and once it was actually lifted up into the air by the mighty suction. An ordinary vessel would not have lived five minutes in that hell of winds and waters. But the car, if it had been built for this kind of navigation, could not have behaved better.

I do not know how long all this lasted. It grew worse and worse. Sometimes a flood of rain fell, and then would come a storm of lightning, and a downpour of gigantic hailstones that rattled upon the steel shell of the car like a rain of bullets from a battery of machine guns. Half the time one window or the other was submerged by the waves, and when we got an opportunity to glance out, we saw nothing but torn streamers of cloud whipping the face of the waters. But when the change came at last, it was as sudden as the dropping of a curtain. The clouds broke away, a soft light filled the atmosphere, the waves ceased to break and rolled in long undulations, and a marvelous dome appeared overhead.

That dome, at its first dramatic appearance, was one of the most astonishing things that we saw in the whole course of our adventures. It was not a cerulean vault like that which covers the earth in halcyon weather, but an indescribably soft, pinkish-gray concavity that seemed nearer than the sky and yet farther than the clouds. Here and there, far beneath it, but still at a vast elevation, floated delicate gauzy curtains, tinted like sheets of mother-of-pearl. The sun was no longer visible, but the air was filled with a delicious luminousness, which bathed the eyes as if it had been an ethereal liquid.

Below each window was a steel ledge, broad enough to stand on, with convenient hold-fasts for the hands. These had evidently been prepared for some such contingency, and Edmund, throwing open the windows, invited us to go outside. We gladly accepted the invitation, and all, except Juba, issued into the open air. The temperature was that of an early spring day, and the air was splendidly fresh and stimulating. The rolling of the car had now nearly ceased, and we had no difficulty in maintaining our positions. For a long while we admired, and talked of, the great dome overhead, which drew our attention, for the time, from the sea that had so strangely brought us hither.

"There," said Edmund, pointing to the dome, "is the inside of the shell of cloud whose exterior, gleaming in the sunshine, baffles our astronomers in their efforts to see the surface of Venus. I believe that we shall find the whole of this hemisphere covered by it. It is a shield for the inhabitants against the fervors of an unsetting sun. Its presence prevents their real world from being seen from outside."

"Well," said Jack, laughing, "I never heard before that Venus was fond of a veil."

"Not only can they not be seen," continued Edmund, "but they cannot themselves see beyond the screen that covers them."

"Worse and worse!" exclaimed Jack. "The astronomers have certainly made a mistake in naming this bashful planet Venus."

We continued for a long time to gaze at the great dome, admiring the magnificent play of iridescent colors over its vast surface, until suddenly Jack, who had gone to the other side of the car, called out to us:

"Come here and tell me what this is."

We hurried to his side and were astonished to see a number of glittering objects which appeared to be floating in the atmosphere. They were arranged in an almost straight row, at an elevation of perhaps two thousand feet, and were apparently about three miles away. After a few moments of silence, Edmund said, in his quiet way:

"Those are air ships."

"Air ships!"

"Yes, surely. An exploring expedition, I shouldn't wonder. I anticipated something of that kind. You know already how dense the atmosphere of Venus is. It follows that balloons, and all sorts of machines for aerial navigation, can float much more easily here than over the earth. I was prepared to find the inhabitants of Venus skilled in such things, and I'm not surprised by what we see."

"Venus with wings!" cried Jack. "Now, Edmund, that sounds more like it. I guess we've struck the right planet after all."

"But," I said, "you spoke of an exploring expedition. How in the world do you make that out?"

"It seems perfectly natural to me," replied Edmund. "Remember the two sides of the planet, so wonderfully different from one another. If we on the earth are so curious about the poles of our planet, simply because they are unlike other parts of the world, don't you think that the inhabitants of Venus should be at least equally curious concerning a whole hemisphere of their world, which differs *in toto* from the half on which they live?"

"That does seem reasonable," I assented.

"Of course it's reasonable, and I imagine that we, ourselves, are about to be submitted to investigation."

"By Jo!" exclaimed Jack, running his hands through his hair, and smoothing his torn and rumpled garments, "then we must make ready for inspection. But I'm afraid we won't do much honor to old New York. Can I get a shave aboard your craft, Edmund?"

"Oh, yes," Edmund replied, laughing. "I didn't forget soap and razors."

But Jack would have had no time to make his toilet even if he had seriously thought of it. The strange objects in the air approached with great rapidity, and we soon saw that Edmund had correctly divined their nature. They were certainly air ships, and I was greatly interested in the observation that they seemed to be constructed somewhat upon the principles upon which our inventors were then working on the earth. But they were neither aeroplanes nor balloons. They bore a resemblance to mechanical birds, and seemed to be sustained and forced ahead by a wing-like action.

This, of course, did not escape Edmund's notice.

"Look," he said admiringly, "how easily and gracefully they fly. Perhaps with our relatively light atmosphere we shall never be able to do that on the earth; but no matter," he added, with a flush, "for with the inter-atomic energy at our command, we shall have no need to imitate the birds."

"Perhaps they have made that discovery here, too," I suggested.

"No, it is evident that they have not, else they would not be employing mechanical means of flight. Once let me get the car fixed up and we'll give them a surprise."

"Yes, and if you had used common sense," growled Henry, nursing his injured eye, "you would not be here fooling away your time and ours, and risking our lives every minute, but you'd be making millions and revolutionizing life at home."

"And where'd the Columbus of Space be then?" demanded Jack. "Hanged if Edmund is not right! I'd rather be here meeting these doves of Venus than grinding out dollars on the earth. And can't we go back and scoop in the money when we get ready?"

The discussion went no further, for, by this time, two of the air ships were close at hand. And now we perceived, for the first time, the beings that they carried. Our surprise at the sight was even greater than that which we had experienced upon meeting the inhabitants of the dark hemisphere. The latter were extraordinary—but we were looking for extraordinary things. Indeed they were, except for certain peculiarities, much more like some members of our own race than we should have deemed possible. How great, then, was our astonishment upon seeing the two air ships apparently in charge of *real human beings!*

At least that was our first impression. In the midst of the strange apparatus, which evidently fulfilled the function of wings for the air ships, we saw decks, spacious enough to contain twenty persons, and surmounted with deck houses, and along the railings inclosing the decks were gathered the crews, among whom we believed that we could recognize their officers. The two vessels had approached within a hundred yards before being suddenly arrested. Then they settled gracefully down upon the water, where they floated like swans.

At first, as I have said, the resemblance of their crews to inhabitants of the earth seemed complete. One would have said that we had met a yachting party, composed of tall, well-formed, light-complexioned, yellow-haired Englishmen, the pick of their race. At a distance their dress alone appeared strange, though it, too, might easily be imitated on the earth. As well as I can describe it, it bore some resemblance, in general effect, to the draperies of a Greek statue, and it was specially remarkable for the harmonious blending of soft hues in its texture.

During a space of at least five minutes we gazed at them, and they at us. Probably their surprise was greater than ours, because we had been on the lookout for strange sights, being, of our own volition, in a foreign world, while they could have had no expectation of such an encounter, even if, as Edmund had conjectured, they were engaged in exploration. We could read their astonishment in their gesticulations. Slowly the car and the nearer of the two air ships drifted closer together. When we were within less than fifty yards of one another, Jack suddenly called out:

"A woman! By Jo, it's Venus herself!"

His excited voice rang like a rattle of musketry in the heavy air, and the beings on the air ship started back in alarm. But although, like the inhabitants of the dark hemisphere, they were, evidently, unaccustomed to hearing sounds of such forcefulness issue from a living creature no larger than themselves, they were not faint-hearted, and the air ship did not, as we half expected it would, take flight. The momentary commotion was quickly quieted, and our visitors continued their inspection. All of us immediately recognized the personage whom Jack had singled out as the subject of his startling exclamation. It was clear that he had rightly guessed her sex, and she appeared worthy of his admiring designation. Even at the distance of a hundred feet we could see that she was very beautiful. Her complexion was light, with a flame upon the cheeks; her hair a chestnut blond; and her large, round eyes were sapphire blue, and seemed to radiate a light of their own. This last statement (about the eyes) must not be taken for a conventional exaggeration, such as writers of fiction employ in describing heroines who never existed. On the contrary, it expresses a literal fact; and moreover, as the reader will see further on, this peculiarity of the eyes was shared, in varying degrees, by all these people of Venus, and was connected with the most amazing of all our discoveries on that planet. I should say here that, while the eyes of the inhabitants of the day side were larger than ours, they did not, in respect of size, resemble the extraordinary organs of vision possessed by the compatriots of Juba.

In a few minutes we became aware that the beautiful creature we had been admiring was not the only representative of the female sex on the air ship. Several others surrounded her, and the fact quickly became manifest that they recognized her as a superior. Still more surprising was the discovery, which we were not long in making, that she was actually the commander of the craft. We could see that the orders which determined its movements emanated from her.

"Amazons!" exclaimed Jack, taking pains this time to moderate his voice. "And what a queen they've got!"

During all this time the car and the air ship were slowly drifting nearer to one another, drawn by that strange attraction which seems to affect inanimate things when in close neighborhood, and when they were not more than fifteen yards apart the personage we had been watching slowly lifted her arm, revealing a glittering bracelet, and, with an ineffably winning smile, made a gesture which said plainer than any words could have done:

"Welcome, strangers."

CHAPTER VIII
LANGUAGE WITHOUT SPEECH

"That breaks the ice," said the irrepressible Jack. "We're introduced! Now for the conquest of Venus."

We had all instinctively returned the smile of our beautiful interlocutor, with bows and gestures of amity, and it looked as though we might soon be within touch of her hand, for the vessels continued to drift nearer, when suddenly Juba clambered out of the window and stood beside us, his moon eyes blinking in the unaccustomed light. The greatest agitation was immediately manifest among the crowd on the deck of the air ship. They seemed to be even more startled than they had been by the sound of Jack's voice. They interchanged looks, and, apparently, a few words, spoken in very low voices, and glanced from Juba to us in a way which plainly showed that they were astonished at our being together.

Edmund, whose perspicacity never deserted him, immediately penetrated their thoughts.

"It is clear," he said, "that these people recognize Juba as an inhabitant of the dark hemisphere, while, as to us, they are puzzled, and all the more so now that Juba has made his appearance. I think it certain that they have never actually met any representative of Juba's race before, but no doubt he bears, to their eyes, ethnological characteristics which escape our discernment, and it is likely that tradition has handed down to them facts about the inhabitants of the other side of their planet which accord with his appearance."

"Then, they must conclude that we have come from the other side, and brought Juba along as a captive," I said.

"Undoubtedly."

"And what must they think of us—that we are inhabitants of the dark hemisphere also?"

"What else can they think?"

I do not know into what train of speculation this might have led us if a new incident had not suddenly changed the current of our thoughts. Unnoticed by us the second air ship had drawn near. Signals were interchanged between it and the first, and we observed that she who seemed to be the commander in chief gave orders that the second air ship should lay us aboard. The order was no sooner given than executed, and we found ourselves face to face with a dozen of the blond-haired natives, led by one who was clearly their captain. The deck of the air ship touched the side of the car, and, as if instinctively recognizing our leader, the captain laid his hand on Edmund's arm, but with a smile which gave assurance that no violence was intended.

"Come," said Edmund, in a low voice, "it is best that we should go aboard their craft. We are in their hands, and luckily so, for they will take us where we want to go."

Accordingly, all, including Juba, passed upon the deck of the air ship. You will readily imagine the intensity of interest with which we studied the faces and forms of those whom I will call our captors. Now that we were in contact with them we could better observe their resemblances to, and differences from, ourselves. In all the main features of body they were human beings, but of a somewhat superior stature. Noses and mouths were small and delicate; hair long, silken, and either light gold or rich chestnut in color; skin white and smooth; ears small and peculiarly formed, with a curious mobility; and eyes large, round, invariably light blue, and possessing that strange luminousness of which I have already spoken. One could not look directly into these eyes without a certain shrinking, for some wonderful power seemed to radiate from them, and one had the feeling that the intelligence behind them could dip to the bottom of his mind. We were gently treated and could perceive no indication of peril to ourselves. Nevertheless, we were glad to feel our pistols in our pockets. There were seats on the deck to which we were civilly conducted, but Edmund refused to sit.

"I must see the commander herself," he whispered. "These are only subordinates, and I cannot deal with them. It will not do to leave the car here at the mercy of the waves. I must find the means of making them understand that it is to go with us."

Accordingly, he approached the captain, and we watched him with beating hearts, not being able to divine what an attempt to dictate terms on our part might lead to. Jack shook his head, and put his hand on his pistol, which Edmund had restored to him while we were in the ice mountains.

"I'll drop the jackanapes in his tracks if he shows up ugly," he said.

"You'd better keep quiet," I whispered, "and don't let them see your weapon. They appear to have no arms, and you should trust to Edmund to manage the affair. When he gives the word it will be time enough to begin shooting."

Jack grumbled, but kept the pistol in his pocket, although he did not withdraw his hand from it.

I have already told you how, at the caverns, Edmund had discovered that the inhabitants there possessed a means of converse which he likened to telepathy, and from what I had seen of the people here I was convinced that they had the same mysterious power, and probably in a higher degree. To be sure, they used words occasionally, but for the most part they communed together in some other way. I felt sure that Edmund was now about to apply what he had learned, and his actions quickly demonstrated that my conjecture was well

A Columbus of Space •

founded. Just what he did, I do not know, but the result of his conference was promptly apparent.

The first air ship had withdrawn a short distance when the other boarded the car, but now the two mutually approached until it was possible to step from one deck to the other. As soon as they touched, Edmund was conducted by the captain, at whose side he had remained standing, to the presence of the important personage whom Jack had begun to designate as the queen. We remained where we were, watching with all eyes, while Jack persisted in keeping his hand on the pistol in his pocket. A crowd immediately surrounded Edmund and we were unable to see exactly what went on, a fact that rendered Jack so much the more impatient. But it turned out that there was no cause for alarm. In about ten minutes the crowd opened and Edmund appeared. Uninterfered with, he came to the edge of the deck, close by us, and said:

"It is all arranged. The car will be towed by one of the air ships. I am to stay here and you will remain where you are until we reach our destination."

"Have you had a talk with her?" asked Jack.

"Not in any language that you understand," Edmund responded, smiling. "But I have made good use of what I learned in the caverns. These people are intellectually vastly superior to the others, and, as I guessed, they possess a more perfect command of the sort of telepathy that I told you about. I have not found much difficulty in making my wish understood, and your amazon is a very obliging person. It is only necessary to be discreet and we shall have no trouble."

"But why are you to be separated from us?" asked Jack anxiously. "That looks bad, for it is exactly what they would do if they meant to kill us one at a time."

"Why should they kill us?" retorted Edmund.

"And why should we be separated?" persisted Jack. "I tell you, Edmund, I don't like it."

"Very well, then," Edmund said, after a moment's

thought; "if that's the way you feel about it, I'll see what I can do. It will be another exercise for me in this new kind of language. But, mark this, if I succeed in persuading the chieftainess to keep us together, you will have to acknowledge that your fears were groundless. Perhaps it's worth trying on that very account."

He disappeared from our eyes again—for as soon as he approached their leader the people of the air ship crowded close around as if to afford her protection—and, after another ten minutes' conference, came back smiling to the edge of the deck.

"Dismiss your fears, friend Jack," he said cheerfully. "You are all to come aboard here with me. So you see there could have been no thought of treachery; but I'm glad that we are not to be separated, and I thank you for your solicitude on my account. I'm sure that the original arrangement was made only because of lack of room aboard this craft, and you'll see that that was the reason."

He was right, for immediately half a dozen of the crew of the principal air ship were sent aboard ours while we were transferred to take their place.

We now had an opportunity to study the countenance of the "amazon" commander, and we found her to be an even more remarkable personage than she had appeared at a distance. Of the beauty of her features and form I shall say no more, but about her eyes I could write a chapter. The pupils, widely expanded amidst their circles of sky-blue iris, seemed to speak. I can describe the impression that they made in no other way. I no longer wondered at Edmund's ability to converse with her, for I felt that, with a little instruction, and more of our leader's mental penetration, I could do it myself. At times I shrank from encountering her gaze, for I verily believed that she read my inmost thoughts. And I could see that *thought came out of her eyes*, but it escaped all my efforts to grasp it; it was too evanescent, or I was too dull. Sometimes I imagined that the meaning was at the threshold of comprehension, but yet it evaded me, like forgotten words whose general sense dimly irradiates the mind, while they refuse to take a definite shape, and keep flitting just beyond the reach of memory. Still, charity and good will shone out so plainly that anybody could read them, and I do not know how to express the feeling that came over me at this evidence of friendliness exhibited by an inhabitant of a world so far from our own. It was as if a dim sense of ultimate fraternity bound her to us. Jack's enthusiasm, as you may guess, was without bounds, and strangely enough it rendered him almost speechless.

"By Jo!" he kept repeating to himself in an undertone, without venturing upon any further expression of his feelings.

Henry, as usual, was silent, but I know that he felt the influence no less than the rest of us. Edmund, too, said nothing, but it was plain that he was continually studying the phenomenon, and I felt sure that his analytic mind would find a more complete explanation than we yet possessed. Of course you are not to suppose that the power that I have been trying to describe was peculiar to this woman. On the contrary, as I have already intimated, it was common to all of them; but with her it seemed to have reached a higher development, and, what was of special interest, she alone exhibited a marked benevolence toward us.

The car was attached by a cable to the air ship that we had just quitted, and our voyage into a new unknown began. The other air ships, which had been hovering about, moved up into line, and, with the exception of the one which towed the car, all rose to an elevation of perhaps a thousand feet, and moved rapidly away from a row of dark clouds which we could now see low on the horizon behind. We found the air ship splendidly fitted up, with everything that could contribute to the comfort of its inmates. And what a voyage it was! "Yachting on Venus," as Jack called it. We sat on the deck, with a pleasant breeze, produced by the swift, steady motion, fanning our faces; the temperature was delightful; the air was wonderfully stimulating; the light, softly and evenly diffused from the great shell-like dome of the sky, seemed to bewitch the eyesight; and the sea beneath us, reflecting the dome, was a marvel of refluent colors.

We had left the calendar clock in the car, but, with our watches, which we had never ceased to wind up regularly, we were able to measure the time. The voyage lasted about seventy-two hours, but could, perhaps, have been performed in less time if we had not been somewhat delayed by the towing of the car. They had on the air ship ingenious clocks, driven by weights, and governed by pendulums, but the divisions of time were unlike ours, and there was nothing corresponding to our days. This, of course, arose from the fact that there was never any night, and, being unable to see either sun or stars, they had no measure of the year. With them time was simply endless duration, with no return in cycles.

"What interests me most," said Edmund, "is the fact that they should have established any chronological measure at all. It would puzzle some of our metaphysicians on the earth to account for the origin of their sense of time. To me it seems evident that the consciousness of duration is fundamental in all intelligent life, and does not necessarily demand natural recurrences, like the succession of day and night, and the passage of sun and stars across the meridian, to give it birth. Did you ever read St. Augustine's reply to the question, 'What is time'— 'I know if you don't ask me'?"

"If they haven't any years," said Jack, "how do they know when they are old enough to die?"

"They have the years, but no measure for them," replied Edmund, and then added quizzically, "Perhaps they *don't* die."

"Well, I shouldn't wonder," Jack returned, "for this seems to me to be Paradise for sure."

When we felt sleepy, we imitated the natives themselves, and, just as we had done during the voyage from the earth, created an artificial night by shutting ourselves up in the cabins that had been assigned to us. Rest was taken by all of them in this manner as regularly as it is taken at night on the earth.

One subject which we frequently discussed during the voyage was the astonishing resemblance of our hosts to the *genus homo*. Influenced by speculations which I had read at home about the probable unlikeness to one another of the inhabitants of different planets, I was particularly insistent upon this point, and declared that the facts as we found them were utterly inexplicable.

"Not at all," Edmund averred. "It is perfectly natural, and quite as I expected. Venus resembles the earth in composition, in form, in physical constitution, and in subordination to the sun, the great ruler of the entire system. Here are the same chemical elements, and the same laws of matter. The human type is manifestly the highest possible that could be developed with such materials to work upon. Why, then, should you be surprised to find that it prevails here as well as upon our planet? Intelligent life could find no more suitable abode than in a human body. The details are simply varied in accordance with the environment—a principle that works on the earth also."

I was not altogether satisfied with the reasoning—but as to the facts, we had to believe our eyes.

Palatable food was served to us, and during the waking time Edmund was frequently engaged in his mysterious conversation with the "queen." Within forty-eight hours after we had set out in the air ship, he came to us, wearing one of his enigmatic smiles, and said:

"I've got another aphroditic word for you to remember. It is the name of our hostess—Ala."

We were not so much surprised by this news as we should have been but for what had occurred at the caverns, where he had discovered the patronymic of Juba.

"Good!" cried Jack, "it's a fine name. I was going to call her Aphrodite, myself, but this is better as well as shorter."

"But, Edmund," I said, "how does it happen that these

people, if they converse by 'telepathy' as you say, and as I fully believe, nevertheless occasionally use sounds and words? I should think it would be all one thing or all the other."

"Think a moment," he replied. "Is it so with us? Do we not use signs and gestures as well as words? And what do we mean by 'silent converse,' when mind speaks to mind and soul to soul without the intervention of spoken language? We have the potentiality of telepathic intercommunication, but we have not yet developed it into a kinetic form as these people have done. Ah, when will men begin to appreciate *what mind means?*"

I made no reply, and after a moment's musing, he continued:

"I suspect that here, too, speech preceded the higher form of converse, and that the spoken language remains only as a survival, presenting certain advantages for particular cases. But we shall learn more as time goes on."

There was no disputing Edmund's conclusions. He was the greatest accepter and defender of facts as he found them that I have ever known.

It was written that before this voyage ended we should have another phase of language without speech presented for our wonderment. It came about near the end of the trip. We were standing apart in a group, greatly interested and excited by the discovery, which had just been made, of land ahead. Far in advance we could see a curving, yellow shore line, and, dim in the distance behind it, a range of mountains. Edmund had just called our attention to these, with the remark that now I must admit that he had reasoned correctly about the existence of elevated regions on this side of Venus, when Jack, always the first to note a new phenomenon, exclaimed:

"Hurrah! Here they come! We're going to have a royal reception."

He pointed toward the land in a different direction from that in which we had been gazing, and immediately we beheld an extraordinary assemblage of air ships, perhaps ten miles off, but rapidly making toward us. More were coming up from behind, as if rising out of the land, and soon they resembled flocks of large birds all converging to a common center. In a little while they became almost innumerable, but their number soon ceased to be as great a cause of surprise to us as their peculiar appearance. Viewed with our binoculars they showed an infinite variety of shapes and sizes. Chinese kites could not, for a moment, be compared in grotesqueness with the forms which many of them presented. Some soared in vast circles at a great height, with the steady flight of eagles; others spread out to right and left, as if to flank us on either hand; and in the center, directly ahead, about a hundred advanced in column deployed in a semicircle, each keeping its place with the precision of a soldier in line of battle.

As we continued to gaze, fascinated by the splendor and strangeness of the spectacle, suddenly the air was filled with fluttering colors. I do not mean flags and streamers, but *colors in the air itself!* Colors the most exquisite that ever the eye looked upon! They changed, flickered, melted, brightened, flowed over one another in iridescent waves, mingled, separated, turned the whole atmosphere into a spectral kaleidoscope. And it was evident that, in some inexplicable way, the approaching squadrons were the sources of this marvelous display. Presently from the craft that carried us, answering colors flashed out, as if the air around us had suddenly been changed to crystal with a thousand quivering rainbows shot through it, their beautiful arches shifting and interchanging so rapidly that the eye could not follow them.

Then I began to notice that all this incessant play of colors was based upon an unmistakable rhythm. I can think of no better way to describe it than to say that it was as if a great organ should send forth from its keys harmonic vibrations consisting not of concordant sounds but of even more perfectly related undulations of color. The permutations and combinations of this truly chromatic scale were marvelous and magical in their infinite variety. It thrilled us with awe and wonder. But none was so rapt as Edmund himself. He gazed as if his soul were in his eyes, and finally he turned to us, with a strange look, and said, almost under his breath:

"This, too, is language, and more than that—it is music!"

"Impossible!" I exclaimed.

"No, not impossible, since it *is*. They are not only exchanging intelligence in this way, but we are being greeted with a great anthem played in the heaven itself!"

There was the force of enthusiastic conviction in Edmund's words, and we could only look at him, and at one another, in silent astonishment.

"Oh, what a people! What a people!" he muttered. "And yet I am not surprised. I dimly fore-read this in Ala's eyes."

Even Jack's levity was subdued for the time, but after a while he said to me with a shrug, half in earnest, half in derision:

"Well, this Yankee-doodling in the air gets me! I'd prefer a little plain English and the Old Folks at Home."

After about ten minutes the display ceased as suddenly as it had begun, and the nearer of the approaching air craft began to circle around us. Finally one of them ran so close alongside that an officer of high rank, for such he seemed to be, leaped aboard us, and was quickly at Ala's side. There was a rapid interchange of communications between them, and then the newcomer was, I may say, presented. Ala led him to where we were standing, and I could read in his eyes the astonishment that the sight of such strangers produced in him.

CHAPTER IX
AN AMAZING METROPOLIS

If I should undertake to describe in detail all the events that now followed in rapid succession, this history would take a lifetime to write. I must choose only the more significant facts.

The newcomer, whose remarkable face had immediately impressed me, and not altogether favorably, proved to be a personage of very great importance, second only, as we could see, to Ala herself. And, what was particularly important for us, he showed none of her friendly disposition. I do not mean to suggest that he seemed inclined to any active hostility, but evidently we were, in his eyes, no better than savages, and consequently entitled to no special consideration, and especially to no favors. Jack, who, with all his careless ways, had a penetrating mind for the perception of character, whispered to me, within five minutes after the fellow came aboard:

"If that galoot had his way, we'd make our entry in irons. Mark my words, there's mischief in him. Hang him! I'm going to keep my pistol handy when he's around."

Edmund, who happened to overhear Jack's remark, interposed:

"See here, Master Jack, this is no time to be talking of pistols. I trust that we are done with shooting."

We were not done with it; but that comes later.

It was not long before Edmund had discovered a name

for the newcomer also; he called him Ingra. It was singular, he said, that all the names seemed to be characterized by the prevalence of vowels sounds, but he thought it likely that this arose from the greater ease with which they could be enunciated. They were like Spanish words, which are the easiest of all for foreigners, and probably also for natives, to pronounce.

After we reached the coast we descended to the ground, at Edmund's request, I believe, because he wished to superintend the loading of the car upon one of the largest air ships, and it was an unforgettable sight to watch him managing the work as coolly and effectively as if he had been in charge of a gang of workmen at home! And, while I looked, I found myself again doubting if, after all, this was not a dream. The workers hurrying about, Edmund following them, pointing, objecting, urging and directing, with his derby hat, which had come through all our adventures (though somewhat damaged), stuck on the back of his head—and all this on the planet Venus! No! I could not be awake. But yet I was.

When we started again, we were escorted by a hundred air ships, forming a complete circle about us. Now I noticed, what had escaped attention during the extraordinary atmospheric display, viz., that these craft were painted in colors that I should call gorgeous if they had not been so perfectly harmonious and pleasing. Every one looked like the careful creation of an artist, and the variety of tints exhibited was incredible. Our own air ship, and its consorts, on the other hand, were very plain in their decorations. I called Edmund's attention to this and immediately he said:

"Remember what I told you—this has been an exploring expedition, and the craft taking part in it have been fitted up for rough work. That reminds me that I have not yet made the inquiries that I intended on that subject. I shall go to Ala now and see what I can learn."

She was standing on the deck near the other end, with Ingra beside her. As Edmund approached them, Jack nudged me:

"Look at that fellow," he said. "Wasn't I right?"

There was no doubt about it; Ingra scowled and showed every sign of displeasure at Edmund's presence. But Ala greeted him graciously, and, apparently, Ingra did not dare to interfere. I could see that Jack was grasping his pistol again, but I did not anticipate that there would be any occasion to use it. Nevertheless, I watched them closely for a time, hoping to discover Edmund's method of reading her meaning; as to her comprehension of his I had no question about that. But I got no light on the subject, and, as it soon became evident, even to Jack, that there was no danger this time, we fell to examining the land over which we were passing.

We flew at a height of about two thousand feet, so that the range of vision was very wide. The sea behind us curved into the land in three great scallops, separated by acuminate promontories, whose terminal bluffs of sand were as yellow as gold. Away ahead the line of mountains, that we had noticed before, appeared as a dark sierra, and between it and the sea the country seemed to be very little broken by hills. Large forests were visible, but from our elevation it was impossible to tell whether the trees composing them bore any resemblance to terrestrial forms. The open land was about equally divided in area between bare yellowish soil (or what we took to be soil) and bright green expanses whose color suggested vegetation. Scattered here and there we saw what appeared to be habitations, but we could not be sure of their nature; and, upon the whole, the land seemed to us to be very thinly populated.

Many birds accompanied us in our flight, frequently alighting on the deck and other parts of the air ship. They were remarkably tame, allowing us to approach them closely, and we were delighted by their beautiful plumage and their singular forms. This reminds me to say that the motion of the craft was extremely curious—a kind of gentle rising and falling, which was very agreeable when once we were accustomed to it, and which resembled what one would suppose to be the movement of a bird in flight. This, of course, arose from the structure of the air ship, which, as I have before said, seemed to be modeled, as far as its motive parts were concerned, upon the principle of wings rather than of simple aeroplanes. But the mechanism was very complicated, and I never arrived at a full comprehension of it.

Edmund remained a long time in conference with Ala, Ingra staying constantly with them, and when he had apparently finished his "conversation" we were surprised to see them begin a tour of inspection of the air ship, finally descending into the interior. This greatly excited Jack, who was for following them at once.

"I can't be easy," he declared. "Nobody can tell what may happen to him if they get him alone."

But I succeeded in persuading him that there could be no danger, and that we ought to trust to Edmund's discretion. They were gone so long, however, that at last I became anxious myself, and was on the point of suggesting to Jack that we try to find them, when they reappeared, and Edmund at once came to us, his face irradiated with smiles.

"I have plenty of news for you," he said, as soon as he had joined us. "Never in my life have I spent two hours more delightfully. In the first place, I have found out practically all that I wished to know about this expedition, and, second, I have thoroughly examined the mechanism of the ship. Its complication is only apparent, and the management of it is so simple that a single man can pilot it easily. I could do it myself."

We did not appreciate at the time what the knowledge that Edmund had thus acquired meant for us.

"Well, what about the expedition?" asked Jack. "And where are we going?"

"From what I can make out," replied Edmund musingly, "Ala is really what you called her, Jack, a queen. But such a queen! If we had some like her on the earth, monarchy might not be such a bad thing after all. She is a *savant*."

"Bluestocking," put in Jack. "This is a new kind of amazon."

Edmund did not smile.

"I am in earnest," he continued. "Of course you understand that most of my conclusions are really based upon inference. I cannot grasp all that she tries to tell me, but her gestures are so speaking, and her eyes so full of a kind of meaning which seems to force its way into my mind, I cannot tell how, that I am virtually sure of the correctness of my interpretation. The expedition, which I am certain was planned by her, was intended to explore the outskirts of the dark hemisphere. Perhaps they meant to penetrate within it, but, if so, the stormy belt that we crossed was too serious an obstacle for them to overcome. Our encountering them was the greatest stroke of good fortune that we have yet had. It places us right at the center of affairs."

"Where are they going now?"

"Evidently back to their starting point; which is likely to be a great city—the capital and metropolis, most probably. The more I think of it the stronger becomes my conviction that Ala is really, at least in power and influence, a queen. And you can see for yourselves that it must be a great and rich empire that she rules, for remember the extraordinary reception with which she was greeted, the innumerable air ships, the splendor of everything."

"But are we to be well treated? Is there no danger for us in accompanying them?"

"If there were danger, it would be hard for us to escape from it now; but why should there be danger? We did not kill the Esquimaux that our polar explorers brought from the Arctic regions, and for these people, we are a greater curiosity than ever the Esquimaux, or the Pygmies of Africa, were for us. Instead of encountering any danger, I anticipate that we shall be very well treated."

"Perhaps they'll put us in a cage," said Jack, with a

ludicrous grimace, "and tote us about as a great moral show for children. If there's a Barnum on Venus, our fate is sealed."

Jack's humorous suggestion struck home, for there seemed to be probability behind it, and Henry groaned, while, for my part, I confess that I felt rather uncomfortable over the prospect. But Edmund did not pursue the conversation, and soon we fell to regarding again the landscape beneath and far around us. We were gradually nearing the mountains, although they were still distant, and presently we caught sight of what resembled, as much as anything, gigantic cobwebs glittering with dew, and rising out of the plain between us and the mountains.

"There, Edmund," said Jack, "there's another chance to exercise your genius for explaining mysteries. What are those things?"

Edmund watched the objects for several minutes before replying. At length he said, with the decision characteristic of him:

"Palaces."

Jack burst out laughing.

"Castles in Spain, I reckon," he said. "But, really, Edmund, what do you think they can be?"

"I have already told you, palaces, or castles, if you prefer."

"You are serious?" I asked.

"Perfectly so. They cannot be anything else."

Seeing our astonishment and incredulity, Edmund added:

"Since they retain their places, it is evident that they are edifices of some kind, attached to the ground. But their great height and aerial structure indicate that they are erected in the air—floating, I should say, but firmly anchored at the bottom. Really, I cannot see anything astonishing about it; it accords with everything else that we have seen. Your minds are too hidebound to terrestrial analogies, and you do not give your imaginations sufficient play with the new materials that are here offered.

"This atmosphere," he continued, after a pause, "is exactly suited for such things. It is a region of atmospheric calm. If we were not moving, you would hardly feel a breeze, and I doubt if there is ever a high wind here. To build their habitations in the air and make them float like gossamers—could any idea be more beautiful than that, or more in harmony with the nature of this planet, which is the favorite of the sun, for first he inundates it with a splendor unknown to the earth, and then generously covers it with a gorgeous screen of cloud which cuts off his scorching beams but suffers the light to pass, filtered to opalescent ether?"

When Edmund spoke like that, as he sometimes did, suffusing his words with the fervor of his imagination, even Henry, I believe, felt his soul lifted to unaccustomed heights. We hung upon his lips, and, without a word, waited for him to continue. Presently he murmured, in an undertone:

"Yes, all this I foresaw in my dream. A world of crystal, houses that seemed not made with hands, reaching toward heaven, and a people, beautiful beyond compare, dwelling in the aerial home of birds"; and then, addressing us, in his ordinary tones: "You will see that the capital, which we are unquestionably approaching, is to a large extent composed of this airy architecture."

And it turned out to be as he had said—when, indeed, was it ever otherwise? As we drew nearer, the aerial structures which we had first seen began to tower up to an amazing height, just perceptibly swaying and undulating with the gentle currents of air that flowed through their traceried lattices, while behind them began to loom an immense number of floating towers, rising stage above stage, like the steel monsters of New York before they have received their outer coverings, but incomparably lighter in appearance, and more delicate and graceful; truly fairy constructions, bespangled with countless brilliant points. Yet nearer, and we could see cables attached to the higher structures, and running downward as if anchored to the ground beneath, but the ground itself we could not see, because now we had dropped lower in the air, and a long hill rose between us and the fairy towers, whose slight sinuous motion, affecting so many together, produced a trifling sense of dizziness as we gazed. Still nearer, and we believed that we could see people in the buoyant towers. A minute later there was no doubt about their presence, for the *colors* broke forth, and that marvelous interchange of chromatic signals, which had so astonished us as we drew near the coast, was resumed.

"It is my belief," said Edmund, "that, notwithstanding the buoyancy of the heavy atmosphere, those structures cannot be maintained at such elevations without mechanical aid. You will see when we get nearer that every stage is furnished with some means of support, probably vertical screws reacting upon the air."

Again he had guessed right, for in a little while we were near enough to see the screws, working in a maze of motion, like the wings of a multitude of insects. The resemblance was increased by their gauzy structure, and, as they turned, they flashed and glittered as if enameled. (The supernatant structures that they maintained were, as we afterwards ascertained, framed of hollow beams and trusses—a kind of bamboo, of great strength and lightness.)

Now we rose over the intervening hill, and as we did so a cry burst from our lips. A vast city made its appearance as by magic, a magnified counterpart of the aerial city above it. Put all the glories of Constantinople, Damascus, Cairo, and Bombay, with all their spires, towers, minarets, and domes together, and multiply their splendor a thousand times, and yet your imagination will be unable to picture the scene of enchantment on which our eyes rested.

"It is the capital of Venus," exclaimed Edmund. "There can be nothing greater than this!"

It must, indeed, be the capital, for in the midst of it rose an edifice of unparalleled splendor, which could only be the palace of a mighty monarch. Above this magnificent building, which gleamed with metallic reflections, although it was as light and airy in construction as frostwork, rose the loftiest of the aerial towers, a hundred, two hundred—I cannot tell you how many stories in height, for I never succeeded in counting them.

The other air ships now dropped back, and ours alone approached this stupendous tower, making apparently for its principal landing stage. Along the sides of the tower a multitude of small air ships ran up and down, stopping at various stages to discharge their living cargoes.

"Elevators," said Edmund.

Glancing round we saw that similar scenes were occurring at all the towers. They were filling up with people, and the continual rising and descending of the little craft that bore them, the holiday aspect of the gay colors everywhere displayed, and the brilliancy of the whole spectacle moved us beyond words. But the most astonishing scene still awaited us.

Just before our vessel reached the landing stage, the enormous tower, from foot to apex, broke out with all the hues of the rainbow, like an enchanted rose tree covered with millions of brilliant flowers at the touch of a wand. The effect was overwhelming. The air became tremulous with rippling colors, whose vibrant waves, with quick succession of concordant tints afforded to the eye an exquisite pleasure akin to that which the ear receives from a carillon of bells. Our companions, and the people crowded on the towers, seemed to be transported with ecstatic delight.

"Again the music of the spectrum!" cried Edmund. "The diapason of color! It is their national hymn, or the hymn of their race, written on a prismatic, instead of a sonometric, staff. And, mark me, this has a significance beyond your conjectures!"

I believe that our enjoyment of this astonishing spectacle was hardly less than that of the natives themselves, but the pleasure was suddenly broken off by a tragedy that struck cold to our hearts.

GARRETT P. SERVISS

We had nearly touched the landing, when we observed that a discussion was going on between Ala and Ingra, and it quickly became evident that we were the subject of it. Before we could exchange a word, they approached us, and Ingra, in a threatening manner, laid his hand on Edmund's shoulder. In a second Jack had his pistol covering Ingra. Edmund saw the motion, and struck Jack's arm aside, but the weapon exploded, and, clutching her breast, Ala fell at our feet!

CHAPTER X
IMPRISONMENT AND A WONDERFUL ESCAPE

The shock of this terrible accident, the full import of which must have flashed simultaneously through the mind of every one of us, drove the blood from Edmund's face, while Jack staggered, uttering a pitiful moan, Henry collapsed, and I stood trembling in every limb. The report of the pistol produced upon the natives the effect that was to have been expected. Ingra sprang backward with a cry like that of a startled beast, and many upon the deck fell prostrate, either through terror or the effect of collision with one another in their wild flight. What occurred among the waiting crowd on the tower I do not precisely know, but a wind of fear seemed to pass through the air—a weird, heart-quaking *shadow of sound*.

For a few moments, I believe, no one but ourselves understood what had happened to Ala. Ingra may have thought, if he thought at all in his terror and surprise, that she had fallen as the result of nervous shock. This moment of paralysis on the part of those whom we had now to regard as our enemies, whatever they may have been before, afforded the opportunity for escape—if there had been any way to escape. But we were completely trapped; there was no direction in which we could flee. Yet I doubt if the thought of flight occurred to any of us. Certainly it did not to Edmund, who was the first to recover his self-command.

• GARRETT P. SERVISS

"We have shot down our only friend!" he said with terrible emphasis, and, as he spoke, he lifted Ala in his arms and laid her on a seat. Her breast was stained with blood.

At the sight of this, a flash of comprehension passed over the features of Ingra; then, instantly, his face changed to a look of fury, and he sprang upon Edmund. With trembling hand, I tried to draw my pistol, but before I could get it from my pocket there was a rush, a hairy form darted past me, and Ingra lay sprawling on his back. Over him, with foot planted on his breast, stood the burly form of Juba, with his muscular arms uplifted, and his enormous eyes blazing fire!

God only knows what would have happened next, but at this instant Ala—to my amazement, for I had thought that the bullet had gone through her heart—rose to an upright posture, and made a commanding gesture, which arrested those who were now hurrying to take a part in the scene. All, natives as well as ourselves, stood as motionless as stone. Her face was pale and her eyes were wonderful to look upon. With a gasp of thankfulness, I noticed that the blood on her breast was but a narrow streak Juba, staring at her, slowly withdrew his foot from his prostrate opponent, and Ingra first sat up, and then got upon his feet. Ala, who had been seated, rose at the same moment, and looked Ingra straight in the face. I saw Edmund glancing from one to the other, and I knew he was trying to follow the communication that was taking place between them.

The general sense of it I could follow, myself. Ingra, metaphorically, stormed and Ala commanded. That she was defending us was plain, and it was but natural that my admiration for this wonderful woman should rise to the highest pitch. I thanked God, in my heart, that her wound could be no more than a scratch—and yet it was a wound, inflicted upon the person of her who, there could be no doubt, was the ruler of a powerful empire. It was less majesty, or worse, and she, herself, might not be able to protect us against its consequences.

At last, it became evident that a decision had been made. Ala turned to us with a smile, which we took for an assurance of encouragement, at least, and started to leave the deck. Edmund instantly stepped in front of her, and pointed to the stain of blood, with a gesture and a look which meant, at the same time, an inquiry as to the nature of the wound and an expression of the wish to do something to repair the injury. She shook her head and smiled again, in a manner which clearly said that the hurt was not serious and that she understood that it was an accident. Then, surrounded by her female attendants, she passed out of our sight in the crowd on the landing. Edmund turned to us:

"We shall probably get out of it all right," he said, "but not without some difficulty. They will surely imprison us. Make no resistance. Leave all to me. Jack's pistol will, no doubt, be seized, but if the rest of you keep yours concealed, they may not search for them, as they know nothing about the weapons."

Edmund had spoken hurriedly, and had hardly finished when a dozen stout fellows, under Ingra's directions, took us in charge, Juba included, and we were led from the deck, through the vast throng on the platform, who made room for our passage, while devouring us with curious, though frightened eyes. In a minute we embarked on one of the "elevators," and made a thrillingly rapid descent. Arrived at the bottom, we were conducted, through long, stone-walled passages, into a veritable dungeon. And there they left us. I wondered if this had been done at Ala's order, or in defiance of her wishes. After all, I reflected, what claim have we upon her?

In the absolute darkness where we now found ourselves, we remained silent for a minute or two, feeling about for one another, until the quiet voice of Edmund said:

"Fortune still favors us."

As he spoke, a light dazzled our eyes. He had turned on a pocket electric lamp. We looked about and found that we were in a square chamber, about fifteen feet on a side, with walls of heavy stone.

"They make things solid enough down here," said Jack, with some return of his usual spirits, "however airy and fairy they may be above."

"All the better for us," returned Edmund enigmatically.

Henry sank upon the floor, the picture of dejection and despair. I expected another outbreak from him, but he spoke not a word. His heart was too full for utterance, and I pitied him so much that I tried to reanimate his spirits.

"Come, now," I said, "don't take it this way, man. Have confidence in Edmund. He has never yet been beaten."

"I reckon he's got his hands full this time," put in Jack. "What do you think, Edmund, can your atomic energy bore a hole through these walls?"

"If I had it here, you'd see," Edmund replied. "But there's no occasion to worry, we'll come out all right."

It was his unfailing remark when in difficulties, and somehow it always enheartened us. Juba, more accustomed to such situations, seemed the least disturbed member of the party. He rolled his huge eyes around the apartment once or twice, and then lay down on the floor, and seemed at once to fall asleep.

"That's a good idea of Juba's," said Edmund, smiling; "it's a long time since we have had a nap. Let's all try a little sleep. I may dream of some way out of this."

It was a fact that we were all exhausted for want of sleep, and, in spite of our situation, I soon fell into deep slumber, as peaceful as if I had been in my bed at home. Edmund had turned out the lamp, and the silence and darkness were equally profound.

I dreamt that I was at the Olympus Club on the point of trumping an ace, when a flash of light in the eyes awoke me. I started up and found Edmund standing over me. The others were all on their feet. Edmund immediately whispered:

"Come quietly; I've found a way out."

"What have you found?"

"Something extremely simple. This is no prison cell, but a part of what appears to be the engine rooms—probably it is an unused storeroom. They have put us here for convenience, trusting more to the darkness than to the lock, for the corridors outside are as black as Erebus and as crooked as a labyrinth."

"How do you know?"

"Because, while you were all asleep, I made an exploration. The lock was nothing; the merest tyro could pick it. Fortunately they never guessed that I had a lamp. In this world of daylight, it is not likely that pocket lamps have ever been thought of. Just around the corner, there is another door opening into a passage that leads by a power house. That passage gives access to a sort of garage of air craft, and when I stole into it five minutes ago, there was not a soul in sight. We'll simply slip in there, and if I can't run away with one of those fliers, then I'm no engineer. To tell the truth, I'm not altogether sure that it is wise for us to escape, for I have a feeling that Ala will help us; still, when Providence throws one a rope, it's best, perhaps, to test its strength. Come on, now, and make no noise."

Accompanied by Juba, we stepped noiselessly outside, extinguishing the light, and, led by Edmund, passed what he had called the power house, where we saw several fellows absorbed in their work, lighted somehow from above. Then we slipped into the "garage." Here light entered from without, through a large opening at the side. There may have been twenty small air ships resting on cradles. Edmund selected one, which he appeared to have examined in advance, and motioning us to step upon its little deck, he began to manipulate the mechanism as confidently as if it had been his own invention.

"You see that I did not waste my time in examining the air ship that brought us," he whispered, and never before had I admired and trusted him as I did now. In less than a minute after we had stepped aboard, we were circling in the air outside.

We rose with stunning rapidity, swooping away in a curve like an eagle.

At this instant we were seen!

There was a quick flashing of signals, and two air craft shot into sight above us.

"Now for a chase!" cried Edmund, actually laughing with exultation.

We darted upward, curving aside to avoid the pursuers. And then they swooped after us. We rose so rapidly that within a couple of seconds we were skirting the upper part of the great tower. Then others saw us, and joined in the chase. Jack's spirits soared with the excitement:

"Sorry to take rogue's leave of these Venuses," he exclaimed. "But no dungeons for us, if you please."

"We're not away, yet," said Edmund over his shoulder; and, indeed, we were not!

The air ships swarmed out on every side like hornets; the atmosphere seemed full of them. I gave up all hope of escape, but Edmund was like a racer who hears the thud of hoofs behind him. He put on more and more speed until we were compelled to hang on to anything within reach in order to save ourselves from being blown off by the wind which we made, or whirled overboard on sharp turns.

Crash! We had run straight into a huge craft that persisted in getting in our way. She dipped and rolled like a floating log. I saw the fellows on her tumble over one another, as we shot by, and I glanced anxiously to see if any had gone overboard. We could afford to do no killing if we could avoid it; for, in case of recapture, that would be another indictment against us. I saw no one falling from the discomfited air ship, and I felt reassured. Occupied as he was, dodging and turning, Edmund did not cease to address a few words to us occasionally.

"There's just one chance to beat them," he said, "and only one. I'm going to try it as soon as I can get out of this press."

I had no notion of what he meant, but a few minutes later

A Columbus of Space •

"Who and what are you, and whence do you come?" Page 129

I divined his intention. I had observed that all the while he was working higher and higher, and this, as you will presently see, was the key to his plan.

Up and up we shot, Edmund making the necessary circles as short as possible, and so recklessly did he turn on the speed that it really began to look as if we might get away after all. Two thirds of our pursuers were now far below our level, but none showed a disposition to give up the chase, and those which were yet above tried to cross our bow. While I saw that Edmund's idea was to hold a skyward course, I was far from guessing the particular reason he had for doing so, and, finally, Jack, who comprehended it still less, exclaimed:

"See here, Edmund, if you keep on going up instead of running off in one direction or another, they'll corner you in the middle of the sky. Don't you see how they have circled out on all sides so as to surround us? Then when we get as high as we can go, they'll simply close in, and we'll be trapped."

"Oh, no, we won't," Edmund replied.

"I don't see why."

"Because they can't go as high as we can."

"The deuce they can't! I guess they understand these ships as well as you do."

"Can a fish live out of water?" asked Edmund, laughing.

"What's that got to do with it?"

"Why, it's plain enough. These people are used to breathing an atmosphere surcharged with oxygen and twice as dense as that of the earth. It doesn't trouble our breathing, simply giving us more energy; but we can live where they would gasp for breath. Air impossibly rare for them is all right for us, and that's what I am in search of, and we shall find it if we can get high enough."

The beauty and simplicity of this unexpected plan struck us all with admiration, and Jack, his doubts instantly turning to enthusiasm, cried:

"By Jo, Edmund, you're a trump! I'd like to get a gaff into

the gills of that catfish, Ingra, when he begins to blow. By Jo, I'd pickle him and make a present of him to the Museum of Natural History. '*Catfishia Venusensis*, presented by Jack Ashton, Esq.'—how'd that look on a label, hey?"

And Jack hugged himself with delight over his conceit.

In a short time the accuracy of Edmund's conjecture became apparent. Our pursuers, one by one, dropped off. Their own strategy, to which Jack had called attention, was simply a playing into our hands. They had really thought to catch us in the center of a contracting circle, when, to their amazement, we rose straight up into air so rare that they could not live in it. Edmund roared with laughter when he saw the assured success of his maneuver.

But there was one thing which even he had overlooked, and it struck to our hearts when we became aware of it. Poor, faithful Juba, who had so recently proved his devotion to us, could endure this rare air no better than our pursuers. Already, unnoticed in the excitement, he had fallen upon the deck, where he lay gasping.

"Good God, he's dying!" exclaimed Jack.

"He shall not die!" responded Edmund, setting his lips, and turning to his machinery.

"But, you're not going back down there!"

"I'll run beyond the edge of the circle, and drop down far enough to revive him. Then we can keep dodging up and down just out of their reach, and so be out of danger both ways."

No sooner said than done. We ran rapidly on a horizontal course until we had cleared the air ships below, and then dropped like a shot. Juba came to his senses in a few moments after we entered the denser air. But now our pursuers, thinking, no doubt, that we had found it impracticable to remain where they knew they could not go, began to close in upon us. I reflected that here was the only mistake that Edmund had made—I mean the bringing along with us of the natives of the dark hemisphere. It was only their presence that had prevented us from sailing triumphantly over the crystal mountains; it was because of them that we had wrecked the car; and now it was Juba who baffled our best chance of escape. And yet—and I am glad to be able to say it—I could not regret his presence, for had he not made himself one of us; had he not proved himself entitled to all the privileges of comradeship?

But Henry (I am sorry to write it) did not share these feelings.

"Edmund," he said, "why do you insist upon endangering our lives for the sake of this—this—animal here?"

Never have I beheld such a blaze of anger as that which burst from Edmund's eyes as he turned upon Henry:

"You cowardly brute!" he shouted. "I ought to throw you overboard!"

He seemed about to execute his threat, dropping the controller from his hand as he spoke, and Henry, with ashen face, ran from him like a madman. I caught him in my arms, fearing that he would tumble overboard in his fright, and Edmund, instantly recovering his composure, turned back to his work.

Finding Juba sufficiently recovered, although yet weak and almost helpless, he rose again, but more cautiously than before. And now our pursuers, plainly believing that these maneuvers could have but one ending, began to set their net, and I could not help admiring their plan, which would surely have succeeded if they had not made a fundamental error in their calculations, but one for which they were not to blame. There was such a multitude of their craft, fresh ones coming up all the while, that they were able to form themselves into the shape of a huge bag net, the edge of which was carried as high as they dared to go, while the sides and receding bottom were composed of air ships so numerous that they were packed almost as closely as meshes. Edmund laughed again as he looked down into this immense net.

"No, no," he shouted. "We're no gudgeons! You'll have

to do better than that!"

"See here, Edmund," Jack suddenly exclaimed, "why don't you make off and leave them? By keeping just above their reach we could easily escape."

"And leave the car?" was the reply.

"By Jo," returned Jack, "I never thought of that. But, then, what did you run away for at all?"

"Because," said Edmund quietly, "I thought it better to parley than to lie in prison."

"Parley! How are you going to parley?"

"That remains to be seen; but I guess we'll manage it."

We were now, as far as I could estimate, five or six miles high. When we were highest, the great cloud dome seemed to be but a little way above our heads, and I thought, at first, that Edmund intended to run up into it and thus conceal our movements. The highest of our pursuers were about half a mile below us. They circled about, and were evidently parleying on their own account, for waves of color flowed all about them, making a spectacle so brilliant and beautiful that sometimes I almost forgot our critical situation in watching it.

"I suppose you'll play them a prismatic symphony," said Henry mockingly.

I looked at him in surprise. Evidently his fear of Edmund had vanished; no doubt because he knew in his heart the magnanimity of our great leader.

"Who knows?" Edmund replied. "I've no doubt the materials are aboard, and if I had been here a month, I'd probably try it. As things stand, we shall have to resort to other methods."

While we were talking, Edmund did not relax his vigilance, and two or three times, when he had dropped to a lesser elevation for Juba's sake, he baffled a dash of the enemy. At last we noticed a movement in the crowd which betokened something of importance, and in a moment we saw what it was. A splendid air ship, by far the most beautiful that we had yet seen, was swiftly approaching from below.

"It's the queen," said Edmund. "I thought she'd come."

The approaching ship made its way straight toward us, and, without the slightest hesitation, Edmund dropped down to meet it. Those who had been our pursuers now made no attempt to interfere with us; they recognized the presence of a superior authority. Soon we were so near that we could recognize Ala, who looked like Cleopatra in her barge on the charmed waves of Cydnus. Beside her, to the intense disappointment of Jack and myself, stood Ingra.

"Confound him!" growled Jack. "He's always got to have his oar in the puddle. Blamed if I'm not sorry Edmund spoiled my aim. I'd have had his scalp to hang up at the Olympus to be smoked at!"

Of what now occurred, I can give no detailed account, because it was all beyond my comprehension. We approached almost within touch, and then Edmund stood forth, fearless and splendid as Caesar, and conducted his "parley." When it was over, there was a flashing of aerial colors between Ala's ship and the others, and then all, including ours, set out to return to the capital. After a while Edmund, who had been very thoughtful, turned to us and said:

"You can make your minds easy. Of course you'll understand there is a certain amount of guesswork in what I tell you, but you can depend upon the correctness of my general conclusions. I believe that I have made it perfectly clear that we intended no harm, and that we are not dangerous characters. At least Ala understands it perfectly. As for Ingra, perhaps he doesn't want to understand it. I can't make out the cause of his enmity, but it is certain that he doesn't like us, and if it all depended upon him, it would go hard with us. I believe that we shall have to stand a trial of some kind, but remember that we've got a powerful advocate. I don't regret our running off, for, as I anticipated, it afforded us the opportunity to establish some sort of terms. The mere fact that we return willingly when they know that we might have fled beyond their reach should count in our favor, for, as I have always insisted, these are highly intelligent people, with civilized ideas. If I had not been sure of that I should have continued the flight and depended upon some other means of recovering the car—or constructing a new one."

We had become so much accustomed to accept Edmund's decisions as final that none of us thought of objecting to what he had done; unless it might have been Henry, but he kept his thoughts to himself.

CHAPTER XI
BEFORE THE THRONE OF VENUS

While we were dropping down toward the city, with a great fleet of air ships attending, Edmund opened his mind upon another curious difficulty besetting us.

"You, of course, noted," he said, "how close we approached at one time to the cloud dome. The existence of that sky screen is a circumstance which may possibly be decisive in the determination of our fate."

"Favorable or unfavorable?" I asked.

"Unfavorable, for this reason. If these people could be made to understand that we are visitors from another world, and not inhabitants of the other side of their own planet, they might treat us with greater consideration, and even with a certain superstitious deference. The imagination is doubtless as active with them as with terrestrial beings, and if you can once touch the imagination, even of the most intelligent and instructed persons, you can do almost anything you choose with them. But how am I to convey to them any idea of this kind? Seeing neither sun, nor moon, nor stars, they can have no conception of such a thing as another world than their own."

"Couldn't you persuade them," said Jack, "that we come from the upper side of the cloud dome? You could pretend that it's very fine living up there—plenty of sunshine and good air."

Edmund laughed.

"I'm afraid, Jack, that they are too intelligent to believe that a person of your avoirdupois could walk on the clouds. You're not quite angelic enough for that. I'm sure that they know perfectly well what the dome consists of."

"The presence of Juba with us is another difficulty," I suggested. "If, as you suppose, they recognize certain racial characteristics in him, which convince them that he belongs to the other side of Venus, then they are sure to believe that we belong there, too."

"Certainly. But I must find some way round the difficulty. I depend upon the intelligence of Ala. If she had been killed, nothing could have saved us. We have had an unpleasant escape from something too closely resembling the misfortune of Oedipus."

In the meanwhile, we reached the capital and disembarked on the great tower. To our intense surprise and delight, instead of being reconducted to prison, we were led into a magnificent apartment, with open arches facing toward the distant mountains, and a repast was spread before us. Juba, to our great contentment, was allowed to accompany us. I think that Jack was the most pleased member of the party at the sight of the food. We sat at a round table, and I observed that the eatables consisted, as with Juba's people, exclusively of vegetables, except that there were birds, of species unknown to us, but of most exquisite flavor, and a light, white wine, the most delicious that I ever tasted.

When we had finished eating, we fell to admiring the view, and Jack pulled out his pipe, and, aided by Edmund's pocket lamp, which possessed an attachment for cigar lighting, began to smoke, leaning back luxuriously in his seat, with as much nonchalance as if he had been in the smoking room at the Olympus. I think I may say that we all exhibited a *sang froid* amidst our novel surroundings that would have astonished us if we had stopped to analyze our feelings, but in that respect

Jack was often the coolest member of the party, although he had not the iron nerves of Edmund. On this occasion, he was not long in producing a sensation. No sooner had the smoke begun to curl from his lips than the attendants in the room were thrown into a state of laughable consternation. Evidently they thought, like the servant of Walter Raleigh, that the smoke must come from an internal fire. Their looks showed alarm as well as astonishment.

"Keep your pipe concealed," whispered Edmund. "Take a few strong whiffs, and hide it in your pocket before they observe whence the smoke really comes. This may do us some good; it will, at least, serve to awake their imagination, and that is what we need."

Jack did as requested, first filling his mouth with smoke, and then slowly letting it out in puffs that more and more astonished the onlookers, who kept at a respectful distance, and excitedly discussed the phenomenon. Suddenly, Jack, with characteristic mobility of thought, turned to Edmund and demanded:

"Edmund, why didn't those fellows shoot us when we were running away? There were enough of them to bring us down with the wildest sort of shooting."

"They didn't shoot," was the reply, "because they had nothing to shoot with. I have made up my mind that they are an unwarlike people. I don't believe that they have the slightest idea what a gun is. Yet they are no cowards, and they'll fight if there is need of fighting, and no doubt they have weapons of some kind; only they are not natural slaughterers like ourselves, and I shouldn't be surprised if war is unknown on Venus.

"All the same," said Jack, "I wish I had my pistol back. I tried to hide it, but those fellows had their eyes on it, and it's confiscated. I'm glad you think they don't know how to use it."

"And I'm glad," returned Edmund, "that you haven't got your pistol. You've been altogether too handy with it. Now," he continued, "let us consider our situation. You see at a glance that we have gained a great deal as a result of the parley; the way we have just been treated here shows plainly enough that we shall, at least, have a fair trial, and we couldn't have counted on that before. You can never make people listen to reason against their inclination unless you hold certain advantages, and our advantage was that we clearly had it in our power to continue our flight. My only anxiety now is in regard to the means of holding them to the agreement—for agreement it certainly was—and of impressing them not only with a conviction of our innocence but with a sense of our reserve power, and the more mysterious I can make that power seem to them, the better. That is why I welcomed even the incident of Jack's smoking. We shall surely be arraigned before a court of some kind, and I imagine that we shall not have long to wait. What I wish particularly is that all of you shall desist from every thought of resistance, and follow strictly such instructions as I may have occasion to give you."

He had hardly ceased speaking when a number of official-looking persons entered the room where we were.

"Here come the cops," said Jack. "Now for the police court."

He was not very far wrong. We were gravely conducted to one of the little craft which served for elevators, and after a rapid descent, were led through a maze of passages terminating in a vast and splendid apartment, apparently perfectly square in plan, and at least three hundred feet on a side. It was half filled with a brilliant throng, in which our entry caused a sensation. Light entered through lofty windows on all four sides. The floor seemed to be of a rose-colored marble, with inlaid diapering of lapis lazuli, and the walls and ceiling were equally rich. But that which absolutely fascinated the eye in this great apartment was a huge circle high on the wall opposite the entrance door, like a great clock face, or the rose window of a cathedral, from which poured trembling streams of colored light.

• GARRETT P. SERVISS

"Chromatic music, once more," said Edmund, in a subdued voice. "Do you know, that has a strange effect upon my spirits, situated as we are. It is a prelude that may announce our fate; it might reveal to us the complexion of our judges, if I could but read its meaning."

"It is too beautiful to spell tragedy," I said.

"Ah, who knows? What is so fascinating as tragedy for those who are only lookers-on?"

"But, Edmund," I protested, "why do you, who are always the most hopeful, now fall into despondency?"

"I am not desponding," he replied, straightening up. "But this soundless music thrills me with its mysterious power, and sometimes it throws me into dejection, though I cannot tell why. To me, when what I firmly believe was the great anthem of this wonderful race, was played in the sky with spectral harmonies, there was, underlying all its mystic beauty, an infinite sadness, an impending sense of something tragic and terrible."

I was deeply surprised and touched by Edmund's manner, and would have questioned him further, but we were interrupted by the officials, who now led us across the vast apartment and to the foot of a kind of throne which stood directly under the great clock face. Then, for the first time, we recognized Ala, seated on the throne. Beside her was a person of majestic stature, with features like those of a statue of Zeus, and long curling hair of snowy whiteness. The severity of his aspect struck cold to my heart, but Ala's countenance was smiling and full of encouragement. As we were led to our places a hush fell upon the throng of attendants, and the colors ceased to play from the circle.

"Orchestra stopped," whispered the irrepressible Jack. "Curtain rises."

The pause that followed brought a fearful strain upon my nerves, but in a moment it was broken by Ala, who fixed her eyes upon Edmund's face as he stood a little in advance of the rest of us. He returned her regard unflinchingly. Every trace of the feeling which he had expressed to me was gone. He stood erect, confident, masterful, and as I looked, I felt a thrill of pride in him, pride in his genius which had brought us hither, pride in our mother earth—for were we not her far-wandering children?

I summoned all my powers in the effort to understand the tongueless speech which I knew was issuing from Ala's eyes. And I did understand it! Although there was not a sound, I would almost have sworn that my ears heard the words:

"Who and what are you, and whence do you come?"

Breathlessly I awaited Edmund's answer. He slowly lifted his hand and pointed upward. He was, then, going at once to proclaim our origin from another world; to throw over us the aegis of the earth!

The critical experiment had begun, and I shivered at the thought that here they knew no earth; here no flag could protect us. I saw perplexity and surprise in Ala's eyes and in those of the stern Zeus beside her. Suddenly a derisive smile appeared on the latter's lips, while Ala's confusion continued. God! Were we to fail at the very beginning?

Edmund calmly repeated his gesture, but it met with no response; no indication appeared to show that it awakened any feeling other than uncomprehending astonishment in one of his judges and derision in the other. And then, with a start, I caught sight of Ingra, standing close beside the throne, his face made more ugly by the grin which overspread it.

I was almost wild; I opened my mouth to cry I know not what, when there was a movement behind, and Juba stepped to Edmund's side, dropped on his knees, rose again, and fixed his great eyes upon the judges!

My heart bounded at the thoughts which now raced through my brain. Juba belonged to their world, however remote the ancestral connection might be; he possessed at least the elements of their unspoken language; and *it might be a tradition among his people, who we knew worshipped the earth-star, that it was a brighter world than theirs.* Had Edmund's gesture suddenly suggested to his mind the truth concerning us—a truth which the others had not his means of comprehending—and could he now bear effective testimony in our favor?

With what trembling anxiety I watched his movements! Edmund, too, looked at him with mingled surprise and interest in his face. Presently he raised his long arm, as Edmund had done, and pointed upward. A momentary chill of disappointment ran through me—could he do no more than that? But he *did* more. Half unconsciously I had stepped forward where I could see his face. *His eyes were speaking.* I knew it. And, thank God! there was a gleam of intelligence answering him from the eyes of our judges.

He had made his point; he had suggested to them a thought of which they had never dreamed!

They did not thoroughly comprehend him; I could see that, for he must have been for them like one speaking a different dialect, to say nothing of the fundamental difficulty of the idea that he was trying to convey, but yet the meaning did not escape, and as he continued his strange communication, the wonder spread from face to face, for it was not only the judges who had grasped the general sense of what he was telling them. Even at that critical moment there came over me a feeling of admiration for a language like this; a truly universal language, not limited by rules of speech or hampered by grammatical structure. At length it became evident that Juba had finished, but he continued standing at Edmund's side.

Ala and her white-headed companion looked at one another, and I tried to read their thoughts. In her face, I believed that I could detect every sign of hope for us. Occasionally she glanced with a smile at Edmund. But the old judge was more implacable, or more incredulous. There was no kindness in his looks, and slowly it became clear that Ala and he were opposed in their opinion.

Suddenly she placed her hand upon her breast, where the bullet must have grazed her, and made an energetic gesture, including us in its sweep, which I interpreted to mean that she had no umbrage against those who had unintentionally injured her. It was plain that she insisted upon this point, making it a matter personal to herself, and my hopes rose when I thought that I detected signs of yielding on the part of the other. At this moment, when the decision seemed to hang in the balance, a new element was introduced into the case with dramatic suddenness and overwhelming force.

For several minutes I had seen nothing of Ingra, but my thoughts had been too much occupied with more important things to take heed of his movements. Now he appeared at the left of the throne, leading a file of fellows bearing a burden. They went direct to the foot of the throne, and deposited their burden within a yard of the place where Edmund was standing. They drew off a covering, and I could not repress a cry of consternation.

It was the body of one of their compatriots, and a glance at it sufficed to show the manner in which death had been inflicted. It had been crushed in a way which could probably mean nothing else than a fearful fall. The truth flashed upon me like a gleaming sword. The victim must have been precipitated from the air ship which we had struck at the beginning of our flight!

And there stood our enemy, Ingra, with exultation written on his features. He had made a master stroke, like a skillful prosecutor.

"Hang him!" I heard Jack mutter between his teeth. "Oh, if I only had my pistol!"

"Then you would make matters a hundred times worse," I whispered. "Keep your head, and remember Edmund's injunction."

The behavior of the latter again awoke my utmost admiration. Contemptuously turning his back upon Ingra, he faced Ala and old Zeus, and as their regards mingled, I knew well what he was trying to express. This time, since his meaning involved no conception lying utterly beyond their experience, he was more successful. He told them that the death of this person was a fact hitherto unknown to us, and that, like the injury to Ala, it had been inflicted without our volition. I believed that this plea, too, was accepted as valid by Ala; but not so with the other. He understood it perfectly, and he rejected it on the instant. My reason told me that nothing else could have been expected of him, for, truly, this was drawing it rather strong— to claim twice in succession immunity for evils which had undeniably originated from us.

Our case looked blacker and blacker, as it became evident that the opposition between our two judges had broken out again, and was now more decided than before. The features of the old man grew fearfully stern, and he rejected all the apparent overtures of Ala. He had been willing to pardon the injury and insult to her person, since she herself insisted upon pardon, but now the affair was entirely different. Whether purposely or not, we had caused the death of a subject of the realm, and he was not to be swerved aside from what he regarded as his duty. My nerves shook at the thought that we knew absolutely nothing about the social laws of this people, and that, among them, the rule of an eye for an eye, and blood for blood, might be more inviolable than it had ever been on the earth.

As the discussion proceeded, with an intensity which spoken words could not have imparted to it, Ala's cheeks began to glow, and her eyes to glitter with strange light. One could see the resistance in them rising to passion, and, at last, as the aged judge again shook his head, with greater emphasis than ever, she rose, as if suddenly transformed. The majestic splendor of her countenance was thrilling. Lifting her jeweled arm with an imperious gesture, she commanded the attendants to remove the bier, and was instantly obeyed. Then she beckoned to Edmund, and without an instant's hesitation, he stepped upon the lower stage of the throne. With the stride of a queen, she descended to his side, and, resting her hand on his shoulder, looked about her with a manner which said, as no words could have done:

"It is the power of my protection which encircles him!"

CHAPTER XII
MORE MARVELS

It was not until long afterwards that we fully comprehended all that Ala had done in that simple act; but I will tell you now what it meant. By the unwritten law of this realm of Venus, she, as queen, had the right to interpose between justice and its victim, and such interposition was always expressed in the way which we had witnessed. It was a right rarely exercised, and probably few then present had ever before seen it put into action. The sensation which it caused was, in consequence, exceedingly great, and a murmur of astonishment arose from the throng in the great apartment, and hundreds pressed around the throne, staring at us and at the queen. The majestic look which had accompanied her act gradually faded, and her features resumed their customary expression of kindness. The old judge had risen as she stepped from her place beside him, and he seemed as much astonished as any onlooker. His hands trembled, he shook his head, and a single word came from his mouth, pronounced with a curious emphasis. Ala turned to him, with a new defiance in her eyes, before which his opposition seemed to wither, and he sank back into his seat.

But there was at least one person present who accepted the decision with a bad grace—Ingra. He had been sure of victory in his incomprehensible persecution of us, he had played a master card, and now his disappointment was written upon his face.

With surprise, I saw Ala approach him, smiling, and I was convinced that she was trying to persuade him to cease his opposition. There was a gentleness in her manner—almost a deference—which grated upon my feelings, while Jack's disgust could find no words sufficient to express itself:

"Beauty and the beast!" he growled. "By Jo, if he's got any influence over her, I'm sorry for her."

"Well, well, don't worry about him," I said. "He's played his hand and lost, and if you were in his place, you wouldn't feel any better about it."

"No, I'd go and hang myself, and that's what he ought to do. But isn't *she* a queen, though!"

Ala now resumed her place upon the throne, and issued orders which resulted in our being conducted to apartments that were set aside for us in the palace. There were four connecting rooms, and Juba had one of them. But we immediately assembled in the chief apartment, which had been assigned to Edmund. There was much more deference in the manner of our attendants than we had observed before, and as soon as they left us we fell to discussing the recent events. Jack's first characteristic act was joyously to slap Juba on the back:

"Bully old boy!" he exclaimed. "Edmund, where'd we have been without Juba?"

"I ought to have foreseen that," said Edmund. "If I had been as wise as I sometimes think myself, I'd have arranged the thing differently. Of course it should have been obvious all the while that Juba would be our trump card. I dimly saw that, but I ought to have instructed him in advance. As it was, his own intelligence did the business. He understood my claim to an origin outside this planet, when they could not. It must have come over him all at a flash."

"But do you think that they understand it now?" I asked.

"To a certain extent, yes. But it is an utterly new idea to them, and all the better for us that it is so. It is so much the more mysterious; so much the more effective with the imagination. But this is not the end of it; they will want to know more—especially Ala—and now that Juba has broken the ice, it will be comparatively easy to fortify the new opinion which they have conceived of us."

"But Ingra nearly wrecked it all," I remarked.

"Yes, that was a stunning surprise. How devilish cunning the fellow is; and how inexplicable his antipathy to us."

"I believe that it is a kind of jealousy," I said.

"A kind of natural cussedness, *I* guess," put in Jack.

"Why should he be jealous?" asked Edmund.

"I don't know, exactly; but you know we are not simple barbarians in their eyes, and Ingra may have conceived a prejudice against us, somehow, on that very account."

"Very unlikely," Edmund returned, "but we shall find out all about it in time; in the meanwhile, do nothing to prejudice him further, for he is a power that we have got to reckon with."

The conversation then turned upon the mysterious language that had been employed at what we called the trial. I expressed the admiration which I had felt for such a means of communication when I had observed the effect that Juba had been able to produce.

"Yes," said Edmund, "it seems as wonderful as it is beautiful, but there is no reason why it should not have been acquired by the inhabitants of the earth. We have the elements, not merely in what we call telepathy, or mind reading, but in our everyday converse. Try it yourself, and you will be astonished at what the eyes, the looks, are able to convey. Even abstract ideas are not beyond their reach. Often we abandon speech for this better method of conveying our meaning. How many a turn in the history of mankind has depended upon the unspoken diplomacy of the eyes; how many a crisis in our personal lives is determined, not by words, but by looks."

"That's right," said Jack, "more matches are made with eyes than with lips."

Edmund smiled and continued: "There's nothing really

mysterious about it. It has a purely physical basis, and only needs attention and development to become the most perfect mode of mental communication that intellectual beings could possibly possess."

"And the music and language of color?" I asked. "How has that been developed?"

"As naturally as the silent speech. We have it, and we feel it, in pictures, in flower gardens, and in landscapes; only with us it is a frozen music. Living music exists on the earth only in the form of sonorous vibrations because we have not developed our sense of the harmony of colors except when they lie dead and motionless before us. A great painting by Raphael or Turner is to one of these color hymns of Venus like a printed score, which merely suggests its harmonies, compared with the same composition when poured forth from a perfect instrument under the fingers of a master player."

"Well, Edmund," interposed Jack, "I've no doubt it's all as you say, and I'd like to know just enough of their speechless speech to tell Ingra what he ought to hear; and if I understood their music, I'd play him a dead march, sure."

"But," continued Edmund, disregarding Jack's interruption, "mark me, there's something else behind all this. I have a dim foreglimpse of it, and if we have luck, we'll know more before long."

I find that the enthusiasm which these wonderful memories arouse, as they flood back into my mind, is leading me to dwell upon too many details, and I must sum up in fewer words the story of the events which immediately followed our acquittal, although it involves some of the most astonishing discoveries that we made in the world of Venus.

As Edmund had surmised, Ala lost no time in seeking more light upon the mystery surrounding us. Within twenty-four hours after the dramatic scene in the hall of judgment, we were summoned before her, in a splendid apartment, which was apparently an audience chamber, where we found her surrounded by several of her female attendants, as well as by what seemed to be high officers of the court; and among them, to our displeasure, was Ingra. He, in fact, appeared to be the most respected and important personage there, next to the queen herself, and he kept close by her side. Edmund glanced at him, and half turning to us, shook his head. I took his meaning to be that we were not to manifest any annoyance over Ingra's presence.

The queen was very gracious, and seats were offered to us. Immediately she began to question Edmund, as I could see; but with all my efforts I could make out nothing of what was "said." But Juba evidently was able to follow much of the conversation, in which he manifested the liveliest interest. The conference lasted about an hour, and at its conclusion, we retired to our apartments. There we eagerly questioned Edmund concerning what had occurred.

He seemed to be greatly impressed and pleased. He told us that he had learned more than he had communicated, but that he had succeeded, as he believed, in making clearer to Ala our celestial origin. Still, he doubted if she fully comprehended it, while as for Ingra, he was sure that the fellow rejected our claim entirely, and persisted in regarding us as inhabitants of the dark hemisphere.

"Bosh!" cried Jack. "He's too stupid to understand anything above the level of his nose, and I'd like to flatten that for him!"

"No," said Edmund, "he's not stupid, but I'm afraid he's malicious. If he were a little more stupid, it would be the better for us."

"But does Ala comprehend the difference between us and Juba—I mean in regard to origin?" I asked.

"I think so. In fact Juba bears unmistakable signs that he is of their world, although so different in physical appearance. His remarkable comprehension of their method of mental communication is alone sufficient to stamp him as ancestrally one of them. And yet," Edmund continued, musing, "think of the vast stretch of ages that separates the inhabitants of the two sides of this planet, the countless eons of evolution that have brought about the differences now existing! I am delighted to find that Ala has some understanding of all this. She has had good teachers—do not smile—for what you have seen of their mechanical achievements proves that science exists and is cultivated here; and from her savants she has learned—what our astronomers have deduced—that formerly Venus turned rapidly on her axis, and had days and nights swiftly succeeding one another. But they do not know the scientific reasons as completely as we do. With them this is knowledge based largely upon tradition, 'ancestral voices' echoing down through periods of time so vast that our most ancient legends seem but tales of yesterday. Whatever may be the measure of man's antiquity on the earth, I am certain that here intellectual life has existed for millions upon millions of years, and its history stretches back beyond the time when the brake of tidal friction had so far destroyed the rotation of the planet that its surface became permanently divided between the reigns of day and night."

I listened with amazement and could not help exclaiming:

"But, Edmund, how could you learn all this in so short a time?"

"Because," he replied, smiling, "the language of the mind, unhampered by dragging words and blundering sentences, plays back and forth with the quickness of thought. There is another thing, too, which I have learned, a thing so amazing that it daunts me. I have found, I believe, the explanation of that minor note of infinite sadness which, as I told you, I always feel, even in the most joyous-seeming paeans of their color music. I think it is due to their forereaching science, which assures them that this world has entered upon the last stage of its existence which began with the arrest of its axial rotation, and which will end with the total extinction of life through the evaporation of all the waters under the never-setting sun, and the consequent complete desiccation of this now so beautiful land."

"But," I objected, "you have said that they never see the sun."

"That was, I believe, a mistake, I am sure that they never see the stars or the planets, but I think that sometimes they see the sun, or, at least that there is a tradition of its having been seen. The whole thing is yet obscure to me, but I have received an inkling of something very, very strange in that regard."

"Then, Ala may think that it is from the sun that we claim to come," I said, disregarding his last remark, which had a significance which even he could not then have appreciated.

"I am not sure; we must wait for further light. But I have still another communication not so instinct with mystery. We are to be shown the sources of their mechanical power—the means by which they run all their motors."

"Hurrah," cried Jack. "Now, that's something I like! I can understand a machine—if you don't ask me to run it—but as for this talking through the eyes, and playing Jim Crow with rainbows, it's too much for me."

It was not many hours later when we were conducted by Ala, accompanied as usual by the inevitable Ingra, and a brilliant cortege of attendants, upon our first excursion through the capital. We embarked in a gorgeous air ship, and flying low at first, skirted the roofs of the innumerable houses which constituted the bulk of the city resting on the ground. The oriental magnificence of the views which we caught in the winding streets and frequent squares crowded with people, excited our interest to the utmost. But we kept on without descending or stopping until, at length, we passed the limits of the immense metropolis, and, flying more rapidly, and at a greater elevation, soon approached what, at a distance, appeared to be a waterfall, greater than Niagara, pouring out of the air!

"What marvel can this be?" I asked.

"A fountain," responded Edmund.

"A cataract turned upside down," exclaimed Jack. "Well, I've ceased to be surprised at anything I see here. I wouldn't be astonished now to find that their whole old planet was hollow, and full of gnomes, or whatever you call 'em."

When we got nearer we saw that Edmund's description was substantially correct. The vast mass of water gushed from the top of a broad plateau, in the form of a gigantic vertical fountain, with a roar so stupendous that Ala and her attendants immediately covered their ears with protectors, and we should not have been sorry to follow their example, for our eardrums were almost burst by the billowing force of the sound waves. The water shot upward four or five hundred feet with geyser-like plumes reaching a thousand feet, and then descended in floods on all sides. But the slope of the ground was such that eventually it was all collected in a river, which flowed away with great swiftness, past the distant city, and disappeared in the direction of the sea from which we had come. The solid column of rising water must have been, at its base, three hundred feet in diameter!

But our amazement was redoubled when we recognized, at various points of vantage, squat, metallic towers of enormous strength, which caught the descending water, allowing it to issue in roaring torrents from their bases.

"Those," shouted Edmund in our ears, "are power houses. I knew already that these people had learned the mechanical uses of electricity; and if we have seen no electric lights as yet, it is because, in a world of perpetual daylight, they have little or no use for them. They employ the power for other purposes."

"But how do you account for this incredible fountain?" I asked.

"It must be due to geological causes, if I may use a terrestrial term. You observe that the land all has a slope hitherward from the distant range of mountains, and that between us and the sea there is a chain of hills. The metropolis lies at the lower edge of a vast basin, and it must be that the relatively porous surface, over many thousands of square miles, is underlain by an almost unbroken shell of rock, impermeable to water. The result is that the drainage of this whole immense region, after being collected under ground, flows together to this point, where the existence of a huge vent in the upper layer offers it a way of escape, and it comes spouting out of the great crater with the consequences which you behold."

Many objections to Edmund's theory occurred to my mind; but he spoke so confidently, the course of things on this strange planet had so often followed his indications, and I felt myself so incapable of suggesting a more satisfactory hypothesis, that I made no reply, as a geologist, perhaps, would have done. At any rate the wonderful phenomenon existed before our eyes, explanation or no explanation. We learned afterwards that the river formed by the giant fountain passed through a gap in the hills to the seaward, and the more I reflected upon Edmund's idea the more acceptable I found it.

A great deal of the water was led away from the foot of the plateau out of which the fountain issued by ditches constructed to irrigate the rich gardens surrounding the metropolis and the open agricultural country for many miles around. At the queen's invitation, although she did not accompany us, we inspected one of the power houses, and Edmund found the greatest delight in studying the details of the enormous dynamos and the system of cables by which, quite in our own manner, the electric power was conveyed to the city. We noticed that everywhere the most ingenious devices were employed for killing noise.

"I knew we should find all this," said Edmund—"although I did not precisely anticipate the form that the natural supply of energy would take—as soon as I saw the aerial screws that give buoyancy to the great towers. In fact, I foresaw it as soon as I found, in inspecting the machinery of the air ship which brought us from the sea, that their motors were driven by storage batteries. It was obvious, then, that they had some extraordinary source of energy."

"Oh, of course, you knew it all!" muttered Henry under his breath. "But if you were as omniscient as you think yourself, you'd not be in this fool's paradise."

"What's that you're saying?" demanded Jack, partly catching the import of Henry's remark, and beginning to ruffle his feathers.

"Oh, nothing," mumbled Henry, and I shook my head at Jack to keep quiet. We all felt at times Edmund's assumption of superiority, but Jack and I were willing to put up with it as one of the privileges of genius. If Edmund had not believed in himself, he would never have brought us through. And besides, we always found that he was right, and if he sometimes spoke rather boastingly of his knowledge and foresight, at least it was real knowledge and genuine foresight.

CHAPTER XIII
WE FALL INTO TROUBLE AGAIN

It was not long after our visit to the marvelous fountain when Jack proposed to me that he and I should make a little excursion on our own account in the city. Edmund was absent at the moment, engaged in some inquiries which interested him, under the guidance of Ala and her customary attendants. I forget why Jack and I had stayed behind, since both Juba and Henry had accompanied Edmund, but it was probably because we wished to make some necessary repairs to our garments for I confess that I shared a little of the coquettishness of Jack in that matter. At any rate, we grew weary of being alone, and decided to venture just a little way in search of adventure. We calculated that the tower of the palace, which was so conspicuous, would serve us as a landmark, and that there was no danger of getting lost.

Nobody interfered with us at our departure, as we had feared they might, and in a short time we had become so absorbed in the strange spectacles of the narrow streets, lined with shops and filled with people on foot, while small air ships continually passed just above the roofs, that we forgot the necessity of keeping our landmark constantly in view, and were lost without knowing it.

One thing which immediately struck us was the entire absence of beasts of burden—nothing like horses or mules did we see. There were not even dogs, although, as I have told you, some canine-like animals dwelt with the people of the caverns. Everybody went either on foot or in air ships. There were no carriages, except a kind of palanquin, some running on wheels and others borne by hand.

"I should think they would have autos," said Jack, "with all their science and ingenuity which Edmund admires so much."

But there was not a sign of anything resembling an auto; the silence of the crowded streets was startling, and made the scene more dreamlike. Everybody appeared to be shod with some noise-absorbing material. We strolled along, turning corners with blissful carelessness, staring and being stared at (for, of course, everybody knew who we were), peering into open doors and the gaping fronts of bazaars, chattering like a couple of boys making their first visit to a city, and becoming every moment more hopelessly, though unconsciously, lost, and more interested by what we saw. The astonishing display of pleasing colors and the brilliancy of everything fascinated us. I had never seen anything comparable to this in beauty, variety, and richness. We passed a market where we saw some of the bright-plumaged birds that we had eaten at our first repast hung up for sale. They had a way of serving these birds at table with the brilliant feathers of the head and neck still attached, as if they found a gratification even at their meals in seeing beautiful colors before them.

Other shops were filled with birds in gilded cages, which we should have taken for songsters but for the fact that, although crowds gathered about and regarded them with mute admiration, not a sound issued from their throats—at least we heard none. A palanquin stopped at one of these shops, and a lady alighted and bought three beautiful birds which she carried away in their cages, watching them with every indication of the utmost pleasure, which we ascribed to the splendor of their plumage and the gracefulness of their forms. As a crowd watched the transaction without interference on the part of the shopkeeper, or evidence of annoyance on that of the lady, we took the liberty of a close look ourselves. Then we saw their money.

"Good, yellow gold," whispered Jack.

Such, indeed, it seemed to be. The lady took the money, which consisted of slender rings, chased with strange characters, from a golden purse, and the whole transaction seemed so familiar that we might well have believed ourselves to be witnessing a purchase in a bazaar of Cairo or Damascus. This scene led to a desire on Jack's part to buy something himself.

"If I only had some of their money," he said, "I'd like to get some curiosities to carry home. I wonder if they'd accept these?" and he drew from his pocket some gold and silver coins.

"No doubt they'd be glad to have a few as keepsakes," I said.

"By Jo! I think I'll try it," said Jack, "but not here. I'm not a bird fancier myself. Let's look a little farther."

We wandered on, getting more and more interested, and followed by a throng of curious natives, who treated us, I must say, much more respectfully than we should have been treated in similar circumstances at home. Many of the things we saw, I cannot describe, because there is nothing to liken them to, but all were as beautiful as they were strange. At last we found a shop whose contents struck Jack's fancy. The place differed from any that we had yet seen; it was much larger, and more richly fitted up than the others, and there were no counters, the things that it contained being displayed on the inner walls, while a single keeper, of a grave aspect, and peculiarly attired, all in black, occupied a seat at the back. The objects on view were apparently ornaments to be hung up, as we hang plaques on the wall. They were of both gold and silver, and in some the two metals were intermixed, with pleasing effects. What seemed singular was the fact that the *motif* of the ornaments was always the same, although greatly varied in details of execution. As near as I could make it out, the intention appeared to be to represent a sunburst. There was invariably a brilliant polished boss in the center, sometimes set with a jewel, and surrounding rays of crinkled form, which plunged into a kind of halo that encircled the entire work. The idea was commonplace, and it did not occur to me amidst my admiration of the extreme beauty of the workmanship that there was any cause for surprise in the finding of a sunburst represented here. Jack was enthusiastic.

"That's the ticket for me," he said. "How would one of those things look hanging over the fireplace of old Olympus? You bet I'm going to persuade the old chap to exchange one for a handful of good solid American money."

I happened to glance behind us while Jack was scooping his pocket, and was surprised to see that the crowd of idlers, which had been following us, had dispersed. Looking out of the doorway, I saw some of them furtively regarding us from a respectful distance. I twitched Jack by the sleeve:

"See here," I said, "there's some mistake about this. I don't believe that this is a shop. You'd better be careful, or we may make a bad break."

"Oh, pshaw!" he replied; "it's a shop all right, or if it isn't exactly a shop that old duffer will be glad to get a little good money for one of his gimcracks."

My suspicion that all was not right was not allayed when I noticed that the old man, whose complexion differed from the prevailing tone here, and who was specially remarkable by the possession of an eagle-beaked nose, a peculiarity that I had not before observed among these people, began to frown as Jack brusquely approached him. But I could not interfere before Jack had thrown a handful of coin in his lap, and, reaching up, had put his hand upon one of the curious sunbursts, saying:

"I guess this will suit; what do you say, Peter?"

Instantly the old fellow sprang to his feet, sending the coins rolling over the polished floor, and with eyes ablaze with anger, seized Jack by the throat. I sprang to his aid, but in a second four stout fellows, darting out of invisible corners, grappled us, and before we could make any effective resistance, they had our arms firmly bound behind our backs! Jack exerted all his exceptional strength to break loose, but in vain.

"I tried to stop you, Jack—" I began, in a tone of annoyance, but immediately he cut me off:

"This is on *me*, Peter; don't you worry. *You* haven't done anything."

"I'm afraid it's on all of us," I replied. "The whole party, Edmund and all, may have to suffer for our heedlessness."

"Fiddlesticks," he returned. "I haven't got his old ornament, but he's got my coin. This looks like a skin game to me. What in thunder did he hang the things up for if he didn't want to sell 'em?"

"But I told you this wasn't a shop."

"No, I see it isn't; it's a trap for suckers, I guess."

Jack's indignation grew hotter as we were dragged out into the street, and followed by a crush of people drawn to the scene, were hurried along, we knew not whither. In fact, his indignation swallowed up the alarm which he ought to have experienced, and which I felt in full force. I beat my brains in vain to find some explanation for the merciless severity with which we were treated so out of all proportion to the venial fault that had unconsciously been committed, and my perplexity grew when I saw in the faces of the crowd surrounding us, and running to keep up, a look of horror, as if we had been guilty of an unspeakable crime. We were too much hurried and jolted by our captors to address one another, and in a short time we were widely separated, Jack being led, or rather dragged, ahead, as if to prevent any communication between us. Once in a while, to my regret, I observed him exerting all his force to break his bonds and slinging his custodians about; but he could not get away, and at last, to my infinite comfort, he ceased to struggle, and went along as quietly as the rapid pace would permit.

Presently an air ship swooped down from above, and alighted in a little square which we had just entered. Immediately we were taken aboard, with small regard to our comfort, and the air ship rose rapidly, and bore off in the direction of the great tower of the palace which we could now see. Upon our arrival we were taken through the inevitable labyrinth of corridors, and finally found ourselves in a place that was entirely new to us.

It was a round chamber, perhaps two hundred feet in diameter, lighted, like the Roman Pantheon, by a huge circular opening in the vaulted roof, through which I caught a glimpse of the pearl-tinted cloud dome, which seemed infinitely remote. No opposition was made when I pushed ahead in order to be at Jack's side, and as a throng quickly hedged us round, our conductors released their hold, although our arms remained bound. When at last we stood fast we were in front of a rich dais, containing a thronelike seat occupied by a personage attired in black, the first glimpse of whose face gave me such a shock as I had not experienced since the priest of the earth-worshipers seized me for his prey. I have never seen anything remotely resembling that face. It was without beard, and of a ghastly paleness. It was seen only in profile, except when, with a lightning-like movement, it turned, for the fraction of a second, toward us, and was instantly averted again. It made my nerves creep to look at it. The nose was immense, resembling a huge curved beak, and the eyes, as black and glittering as jet, were roofed with shaggy brows, and seemed capable of seeing crosswise.

Sometimes one side of the face and sometimes the other was presented, the transition being effected by two instantaneous jerks, with a slight pause between, during which the terrible eyes transfixed us. At such moments the creature—though he bore the form of a man—seemed to project his dreadful countenance toward the object of his inspection like a monstrous bird stretching forth its neck toward its prey. The effect was indescribable, terrifying, paralyzing! The eyes glowed like fanned embers.

"In God's name," gasped Jack, leaning his trembling shoulder upon me, "what is it?"

I was, perhaps, more unmanned than he, and could make no reply.

Then there was a movement in the throng surrounding us, and the old man of the sunbursts appeared before the throne, and, after dropping on his knees and rising again, indicated us with his long finger, and, as was plain, made some serious accusation. The face turned upon us again with a longer gaze than usual, and we literally shrank from it. Then its owner rose from his seat, towering up, it seemed, to a height of full seven feet, shot his hand out with a gesture of condemnation, and instantly sat down again and averted his countenance. There seemed to have been a world of meaning in this brief act to those who could comprehend it. We were seized, even more roughly than before, and dragged from the chamber, and at the end of a few minutes found ourselves thrown into a dungeon, where there was not the slightest glimmer of light, and the door was locked upon us.

It was a long time before either of us summoned up the courage to speak. At length I said faintly:

"Jack, I'm afraid it's all over with us. We must have done something terrible, though I cannot imagine what it was."

But Jack, after his manner, was already recovering his spirits, and he replied stoutly:

"Nonsense, Peter, we're all right, as Edmund says. Wait till he comes and he'll fix it."

"But how can he know what has happened? And what could he do if he did? More likely they will all be condemned along with us."

Jack felt around in the dark and got me by the hand, giving it a hearty pressure.

"Remember Ala," he said. "She's our friend, or Edmund's, and they'll bring us out of this. You want to brace up."

"Remember Ingra!" I responded with a shiver, and I could feel Jack start at the words.

"Hang him!" he muttered. "If I'd only finished him when I had the drop!"

After that neither spoke. If Jack's thoughts were blacker than mine he must have wished for his pistol to blow out his own brains. At no time since our arrival on the planet had I felt so depressed. I had no courage left; could see no lightening of the gloom anywhere. In the horror of the darkness which enveloped us, the *horror of space* came over my spirit. One feels a little of that sometimes when the breadth of an ocean separates him from home, and from all who really care for him—but what is the Atlantic or the Pacific to millions upon millions of leagues of interplanetary space! To be cast away among the inhabitants of another world than one's own! To have lost, as we had done (for in that moment of despair I was sure Edmund could never repair the car), the only possible means of return! To have offended, just because we were strangers, and could not know better, some incomprehensible social law of this strange people, who owned not a drop of the blood of our race, or of any race whatsoever dwelling on the earth! To lie under the condemnation of that goblin face, without the possibility of pleading even the mercy that our hearts instinctively grant to the smallest mite of fellow life on our own planet! To be alone! friendless! forsaken! condemned!—in a far-off, kinless world! I could have fallen down in idolatry before a grain of sand from the shore of the Atlantic!

In the murkiest depth of my despair a sound roused me with a shock that made my heart ache. In a moment the door opened, light streamed in, and Edmund stood there.

CHAPTER XIV
THE SUN GOD

Strangely enough, I, who have an exceptional memory for spoken words, cannot, by any effort, recall what Edmund said, as his face beamed in upon us. I have only a confused recollection that he spoke, and that his words had a marvelous effect upon my broken spirit. But I can see, as if it were yet before me, the smile that illumined his features. My heart bounded with joy, as if a messenger had come straight from the earth itself, bearing a reprieve whose authority could not be called in question.

Jack's joy was no less than mine, although he had not suffered mentally as I had done. And the sight of Ala was hardly less reassuring to us, but to find Ingra, too, present was somewhat of a shock to our confidence in speedy delivery from trouble. And, in fact, we were not at once delivered. We had to spend many weary hours yet in our dark prison, but they were rendered less gloomy by Edmund's assurance that he would save us. The confidence that he always inspired seems to me to have been another mark of his genius. We had an instinct that he could do in any circumstances what was impossible to ordinary men.

At last the welcome moment came, and we were led forth, free, and rejoined Edmund, Henry, and Juba in our apartments. Then, for the first, we learned what we had done, and how narrow had been our escape from a terrible doom. It was a new chapter of wonder that Edmund opened before us. I shall tell it in his own words.

"When I returned to the palace and found you missing I was greatly wrought up. Immediately I applied to Ala for aid in finding you. She was quickly informed of all the circumstances of your arrest, and I saw at once, by the expression of her features, that it was a matter of the utmost gravity. I was not reassured by Ingra's evident joy. I could read in his face the pleasure that the news gave him, and I perceived that there was again opposition between him and Ala, and that she was trying, with less success than I hoped for, to bring him round to her view.

"With no little trouble I finally discovered the nature of your offense. I understood it the more readily because I had already begun to suspect the existence among these people of a strange form of idolatry, in some respects akin to the earth-worship of the cavern dwellers. I have told you that certain things had led me to think that they occasionally see the sun here. It is a phenomenon of excessive rarity, and whole generations sometimes pass without its recurrence. It is due to an opening which at irregular periods forms for a brief space of time in the cloud dome. I imagine that it may be in some way connected with sunspots, but here they have no notion of its cause, and look upon it as entirely miraculous.

"Whenever this rare event occurs it gives rise to extraordinary religious excitement, and ceremonies concerning which there is some occult mystery that I have not yet penetrated. I suspect that the ceremonies are not altogether unlike the Bacchanalian festivals of ancient Greece. At any rate the momentary appearance of the sun at these times is regarded as the avatar of a supreme god, and their whole religious system is based upon it. So universal and profound is the superstition to which it gives rise that the most instructed persons among them are completely under its dominion. The eagle-beaked individual who condemned you, and whom I have since seen, is the chief priest of this superstition, and within his sphere his power is unlimited. It is solely to the belief—which, through Ala, I have succeeded in impressing upon him—that we are *children of the sun* that I owe the success of my efforts in your behalf. Without that you would surely have been sacrificed, and we with you.

"One of the forms which this superstition takes is a belief that the anger of the sun god can be mollified by offerings of images, made in his likeness, which are first consecrated by the chief priest, and then hung up on the walls of certain small temples, which are scattered through the city, and are always kept open to the air under the guard of a minor priest and his attendants. A whole family, as I understand it, deems itself protected by one of these images, which are made by artists who never touch any other work, and which are only granted to those who have undergone a painful series of purifications in the great temple. The preliminary ceremonies finished, the images are suspended, and at certain times those to whom they belong go and kneel and pray before them, as before their guardian saints."

"What a fool I was not to understand it," I murmured.

"You will understand now," Edmund continued, "how serious was Jack's offense in insulting a priest, and laying impious hands upon a sacred image, belonging, no doubt, to a family whose antiquity of descent would make our oldest pedigrees on the earth seem as ephemeral as the existence of a May fly; for I am convinced that here life has gone on, uninterrupted by wars and changes of dynasty, for untold ages.

"It is a marvel that you escaped, for already they were preparing the awful sacrifice. The chief priest was amazed when an interposition was made on your behalf. Such a thing had never been known, and, as I have said, it was only by acting upon his superstition that I succeeded, with Ala's assistance, in obtaining a reprieve. As the case stands, we find ourselves occupying a dangerous eminence, which it may be difficult for

A Columbus of Space •

us to maintain. I must beseech you to be on your guard, and to act only under my direction. It is all the more serious for us because I am convinced that Ingra has no faith whatever in the legend which protects us. He persists in believing that we are simply interlopers from the dark hemisphere, and the opposition between him and Ala has now become so sharp that he would gladly witness our destruction. I am sure that he will do his utmost to unmask us, and thus send us to our death."

"But—" I began.

"Wait a moment," said Edmund, "I have not yet finished. I must now tell you who Ingra is. *He is the destined consort of Ala.* That explains his influence over her. From what I can make out, it appears that he is of the royal blood, and that the marriage of the queen is arranged, not by her preference, but by an unwritten law, administered by the chief priest. She has no choice in the matter."

"I should say not," broke in Jack. "She never would have chosen that jackanapes! If you hadn't spoiled my aim I'd have relieved her of the burden."

"Not another word of that!" said Edmund severely. "In no manner, not even by a look, are you ever to express your dislike of him. And remember, you must govern your very thoughts, for here they lie open, as legible as print."

"Hang me," growled Jack, "if I like a world where a man can't even think his own thoughts because his mind goes bare! Take me back where you have to speak before you are understood."

"When you have wicked thoughts don't look them in the eyes," said Edmund, half smiling, "and then you will run no danger. It is through the eyes that they read. Now, to resume what I was saying, I am more than ever anxious to recover the car, and to find the materials that will enable me to repair its machinery. With it in our possession, and in good shape, we shall be in a position to run away whenever it may seem

GARRETT P. SERVISS

"It curled itself over the edge of the hovering air ship and drew it down."
Page 172.

necessary to do so, and in the meantime to impose our legend upon them by the possession of so apparently miraculous a means of conveying ourselves through space. It will be overwhelming proof of the truth of our assertion of an origin outside their world, and perhaps, upon the whole, it is just as well that they should think that we belong to the sun, of whose existence they have some knowledge, rather than to the earth, of which they know nothing, in spite of the inkling that Juba succeeded in conveying to them."

"The car is here, isn't it?" I asked.

"Yes, it is in the great tower, but it is useless in its present condition."

"And what materials do you want to find?"

"Primarily nothing but uranium. They understand chemistry here. They have the apparatus that I need, but they do not know how to use it as I do. The uranium certainly exists somewhere. They mine gold and silver, and other things, and when I can find their mines, without exciting their suspicion, and can get the use of a laboratory in secret, I shall soon have what I need. But I must be very circumspect, for it would not do to let them perceive that chemistry really lies at the basis of our miracle. It is this necessity for secrecy which troubles me most. But I shall find a way."

"For God's sake, find it quick," Henry burst out. "And then get away from this accursed planet."

Edmund looked at him a moment before replying:

"We shall go when the necessity for going arises, and not before. We have not yet seen all the interesting things of this world."

I believe that even Jack and I shared to some extent Henry's disappointment on hearing this announcement. We should have been glad to know that we were to start on the return journey as soon as the car was in shape to transport us. But the event proved that Edmund's instinct was, as usual, right, and that the things which were yet to be seen and experienced were well worth the fearful risk we ran in remaining.

While Edmund undertook the delicate inquiries which were necessary in order to determine the direction that his search for uranium should take, and to enable him to conduct his chemical processes without awaking suspicion as to his real purpose, we were left much of the time in charge of a party of attendants who, by his intercession, had been selected to act as our guides when we wished to examine the wonders of the palace and the capital. Sometimes he accompanied us; but more often he was with Ala and her suite, including her uneludable satellite, Ingra.

"I bless my stars that he doesn't favor *us* with his delightful company," was Jack's comment, when he saw Ingra tagging along after Ala and Edmund.

I privately believed that Ingra had his spies among our attendants, but I was careful not to mention my suspicions to Jack.

But, oh, the delight of those excursions! Those streets; and those aerial towers, which rose like forests of coral in a gulf of liquid ether! They shine often in my dreams. A thousand times I have tried to put into words, simply for my own satisfaction, a description of the things that we saw, and the impressions that they made on my mind—but it is impossible. I understand now why the tales of travelers into strange lands never convey a tithe of what is in the writers' minds; they simply cannot; the necessary words and analogies do not exist. I can only use general terms, ransacking the vocabulary of adjectives—"beautiful," "wonderful," "fascinating," "marvelous," "indescribable," "magical," "enchanting," "amazing," "inexplicable," "*sans pareil*"—what you will—but all that says nothing except to my own mind. Only the language of Venus could describe the charms and the wonders of Venus!

There was one thing, however, which was sufficiently comprehensible—*the great library*. Edmund was not with us when we paid our first visit to it; but he had predicted its existence during one of our conversations, when we were talking of the silent language.

"This people," he had said, "has a great history behind it, extending over periods which would amaze our disinterrers of human antiquity, but an intelligent race cannot make history without also keeping records of it. Tradition alone, handed on from mind to mind, would not answer their requirements. The possession of the power to communicate thought without spoken language does not presuppose a power of memory any more perfect than we have. The brain forgets, the imagination misleads, with them as with us, and consequently they must have books of some kind—which implies a written or printed language. It is probable that this language does not correspond with the very meager one of which we occasionally hear them pronounce a few words. The latter is, I am convinced, used only for names and interjections, and sometimes to call the attention of the person addressed, while the former must be a rich and carefully elaborated system of literary expression, which may not be phonetic at all. We shall find that this is so; and there are unquestionably libraries—probably a great imperial library—devoted to history and science. There must be schools also."

Thus Edmund had spoken, and thus we found it to be. The great library was in a building separate from the palace. It was admirably lighted from without, and its nature was apparent the moment we were led into it. The "books" were long scrolls, which might have been taken for parchment or papyrus, and the characters written on them resembled those of the Chinese language, but worked out in exquisite colors, which might themselves have had a meaning. The rolls were kept in proper receptacles under the charge of librarians, and we saw many grave persons at desks poring over them. Absolute silence reigned, and as I gazed at the scene I found admiration for this extraordinary people taking the place of the prejudice which I had recently been led to feel against them.

Jack, unusually impressed, whispered to me that Edmund

must have been playing us some Hindoo bedevilment trick, for he could not believe that we were actually in a foreign world. The same impression came over me. This was too earthlike; too much as if, instead of being on the planet Venus, we had been transported to some land of antique civilization in our own world. But, after all, we *knew where we were*, and as the realization of that fact came to us we could only stare with increasing astonishment at the scene before us. I may say here that Edmund subsequently visited this great library, and also some of the schools, and I know that he made notes of what he discovered and learned in them, with the purpose, as I supposed, of writing upon the subject after his return. But the expected book, which would have supplemented and clarified much of what I have undertaken to tell, with but a half understanding of what we saw, never appeared.

Our wonderful excursions came to an end when Edmund at length announced that he had obtained the information he needed, and that we were about to make a trip to some of the mines of Venus.

"I have discovered," he said, "that Venus is exceedingly rich in the precious metals, as well as in iron and lead. They mine them all, and we shall visit the mines under Ala's escort. My real purpose, of course, is to find uranium, of whose properties, strangely—and for us luckily—enough, they seem to have no knowledge. Nevertheless, they are capital chemists as far as they go, and possess laboratories provided with all that I shall need. They refine the metals at the mines themselves, so that I am sure of finding everything necessary to do my work right on the ground. The substance which I obtain from uranium is so concentrated that I can carry in my pocket all that will be required to repair the damage done to the transformers in the car. A careful examination, which I have made of the car, proves that the terrific shocks the machinery suffered in the crystal mountains caused an atomic readjustment which destroyed the usefulness of the material in the transformers, and while I might, by laboratory treatment, possibly restore its properties, I think it safer to obtain an entirely fresh supply. We shall start with the queen's ship within a few hours; so you had better make your preparations at once."

CHAPTER XIV
AT THE MERCY OF FEARFUL ENEMIES

I f we could have foreseen what was to happen during this trip, even Edmund, I believe, would have shrunk from undertaking it. But we all embarked upon it gladly, because we had conceived the highest expectations of the delight that it would afford us; and at the news that we were to visit mines of gold richer than any on the earth, Henry exhibited the first enthusiasm that he had shown since our departure from home.

Embarked on Ala's splendid "yacht," as Jack called it, and attended by her usual companions, we rapidly left the city behind, and sped away toward the purple mountains, so often seen in the distance. The voyage was a long one, but at length we drew near the foothills, and beheld the mountains towering into peaks behind. Lofty as they looked, there was no snow on their summits. We now descended where plumes of smoke had for some time attracted our attention, and found ourselves at one of the mines. It was a gold mine. The processes of extracting the ore, separating the metal, etc., were conducted with remarkable silence, but they showed a knowledge of metallurgy that would have amazed us if we had not already seen so much of the capacity of this people. Yet similarly to the scene in the library, its earth-likeness was startling.

"This sort of thing is uncanny," said Jack, as we were led through the works. "It makes me creep to see them doing things just as we do them at home, except that they are so quiet about it. If everything was different from our ways it would seem more natural."

"Anyhow," I replied, "we may take it as a great compliment to ourselves, for it shows that we have found out ways of doing things which cannot be improved even in Venus."

I should like to describe in detail the wonders of this mine, but I have space for only a few words about it. It was, Edmund learned, the richest on the planet, and was the exclusive property of the government, furnishing the larger part of its revenues, which were not comparable with those of a great terrestrial nation because of the absence of all the expenditures required by war. No fleets and no armies existed here, and no tariffs were needed where commerce was free. This great mine was the Laurium of Venus. The display of gold in the vaults connected with it exceeded a hundredfold all that the most imaginative historian has ever written of the treasures of Montezuma and Atahualpa. Henry's eyes fairly shone as he gazed upon it, and he could not help saying to Edmund:

"You might have had riches equal to this if you had stayed at home and developed your discovery."

Edmund contemptuously shrugged his shoulders, and turned away without a word.

We were afterwards conducted to a silver mine, which we also inspected, and finally to a lead mine in another part of the hills. This was in reality the goal at which Edmund had been aiming, for he had told us that uranium was sometimes found in association with lead. Our joy was very great when, after a long inspection, he informed us that he had discovered uranium, and that it now remained only to submit it to certain operations in a laboratory in order to prepare the substance that was to give renewed life to those lilliputian monsters in the car, which fed upon men's breath and begot power illimitable.

"I must now contrive," said Edmund, "to get admission

to the laboratory connected with the mine, and to do my work without letting them suspect what I am about."

He managed it somehow, as he managed all things that he undertook, and within forty-eight hours after our arrival he was hard at work, evidently exciting the admiration of the native chemists by the knowledge and skill which he displayed. At first they crowded around him so that he was hampered in his efforts to conceal the real object of his labors; but at last they left him comparatively alone, and I could see by his expression whenever I visited the laboratory that things were going to his liking. But the work was long and delicate. Edmund had to fabricate secretly some of the chemical apparatus he needed, destroying it as fast as it served its purpose, so that weeks of time rolled by before he had what he called the "thimbleful of omnipotence" that was to make us masters of our fate. As fast as he produced it he put it in a metal box, shaped like a snuffbox, and covertly he showed it to us. It consisted of brilliant black grains, finer than millet seeds.

"Every one of those minute grains," he told us, "is packed with as much potential energy as that of a ton's weight suspended a mile above the earth."

But while the little box was being gradually filled with crystallized powder, we, who could lend no aid in the fabrication of Edmund's miracle, improved the opportunity to make acquaintance with the beauties of the surrounding country. Ala had returned to the capital, leaving an air ship at our disposal, and, of all persons in the world, *Ingra in command*! We refused all invitations to accompany him in the air ship, preferring to make our excursions on foot, accompanied at first by some of the attendants that Ala had left. Edmund did not share our fears that Ingra meditated mischief.

"He doesn't dare," was his reply to all our representations. But nothing could induce Jack and me to trust to Ingra's tender mercies.

Among the favorite spots which we had found to visit in

the neighborhood of the mine was a little knoll crowned with a group of the most beautiful trees that I ever saw, and washed at its base by a brook of exquisitely transparent water which tinkled over a bed of white and clear-yellow pebbles, sparkling like jewels. More than once at the beginning I fished some of them out in the belief that they were nuggets of pure gold polished by the water. In a pool under the translucent shadow of the overhanging trees played small fish so splendid in their varied hues that they looked like miniature rainbows darting about beneath the water. Birds of vivid color sometimes flitted among the branches overhead. There was but one "rainy day" while we were at the mine; all the rest of the time not a cloud appeared under the great dome, and a scented zephyr continually drew down from the mountains and fanned us. Here, then, we passed many hours and many days, chatting of our adventures and our chances, drowsily happy in the pure physical enjoyment which this charming spot afforded.

When at last Edmund informed us that his box was full, and he was ready to return to the capital, we would not let him go without first conducting him to our little paradise. All together, then, with the exception of Juba, who, by some interference of an overlooking providence, was left at the mine, we set out in the highest spirits to be for once our leader's leaders in the exploration of some of the charms of Venus. Edmund was no less delighted than we had been with the place, and yielding to its somnolent influences we were soon stretched side by side on the spreading roots of a giant tree, and sleeping the sleep of sensuous languor.

Our waking was as terrible as it was sudden. I heard a cry, and at the same instant felt an irresistible hand grasping me by the throat. As I opened my eyes I saw that the whole party were prisoners. Nearby an air ship was quivering, as, held in leash, it lightly touched the ground; and a dozen gigantic fellows, whipping our hands behind our backs, hurried us aboard, the great mechanical bird, which instantly rose, describing a circle that carried us above the treetops. I did not try to struggle, for I felt how vain would be any effort that I could make.

Glancing about me, the very first features I recognized were those of Ingra. At last he had us in his power!

I looked at Edmund, but his face was set in thought, and he did not return my glance. Henry, as usual, had plunged into silent hopelessness, and Jack was a picture of mingled rage and despair. Although we were loosely fastened side by side to a rail on the deck, neither of us spoke for perhaps half an hour. In the meantime the air ship rose to a height greater than that of the nearby mountains, and then more slowly approached them. At last it began to circle, as if an uncertainty concerning the route to be chosen had arisen, and I observed, for we could look all about in spite of our bonds, that Ingra and one who appeared to be his lieutenant were engaged in an animated discussion. They pointed this way and that, and the debate grew every moment more earnest. This continued for a long time, while the ship hovered, running slowly in the wide circles. We could not then know how much this hesitation meant for us. If Ingra had been as rapid in his decision now as he was in the act of taking us prisoners, this history would never have been written. I watched Edmund, and saw that his attention was absorbed by what our captors were about, and even in that emergency I felt a touch of comfort through my unfailing confidence in our leader.

Finally a decision seemed to have been reached, and we set off over the crest of the range. As its huge peaks towered behind us and we descended nearer the ground, my heart sank again, for now we were cut off from the world beyond, and in the improbable event of any pursuit, how could the pursuers know what course we had taken, or where to look for us? And, then, who would pursue? Juba could do nothing, Ala was far away at the capital, even supposing that she should be disposed to set out in search of us, and hours, perhaps days, must elapse before she could be informed of what had happened. Not even when

Jack and I were in the dungeon had our case seemed so desperate.

But how the gods repent when they have sunk men in the blackest pit of despair, sending them a messenger of hope to steady their hearts!

Good fortune had willed that we should be so placed upon the deck that we faced most easily sternward. Suddenly, as I gazed despondently at the serrated horizon receding in the distance, a thrill ran through my nerves at the sight of a dark speck in the sky, which seemed to float over one of the highest peaks. A second look assured me that it was moving; a third gave birth to the wild thought that it was in chase. Then I turned to Edmund and whispered:

"There is something coming behind us."

"Very well, do nothing to attract attention," he returned. "I have seen it. They are following us."

I said nothing to Jack or Henry, who had not yet caught sight of the object; but I could not withdraw my eyes from it. Sometimes I persuaded myself that it was growing larger, and then, with the intensity of my gaze, it blurred and seemed to fade. At last Jack spied it, and instantly, in his impetuous way, he exclaimed:

"Edmund! Look there!"

His voice drew Ingra's attention, and immediately the latter observed the direction of our glances, and himself saw the growing speck. He turned with flushed face to his lieutenant and in a trice the vessel began fairly to leap through the air.

"Ah, Jack," said Edmund reproachfully, but yet kindly, "if only you could always think before you speak! It is certain from Ingra's alarm that we are pursued by somebody whom he does not wish to meet. Most likely it is the queen, although it seems impossible that she could so quickly have learned of our mishap. Peter and I have been watching that object, which is unquestionably an air ship, in silence for the last twenty minutes, during which it has perceptibly gained upon us. But for your lack of caution it might have come within winning distance before it was discovered by Ingra, but now—"

The rebuke was deserved, perhaps, but yet I wished that Edmund had not given it, so painful was the impression that it made upon Jack's generous heart. His countenance was convulsed, and a tear rolled down his cheek—all the more pitiful to see because his arms were pinioned, and he could do nothing to conceal his agitation. Edmund was stricken with remorse when he saw the effect of his words.

"Jack," he said, "forgive me; I am sorry from the bottom of my heart. I should not have blamed you for a little oversight, when I alone am to blame for the misfortunes of us all."

"All right, Edmund, all right," returned Jack in his usual cheerful tones. "But, see here, I don't admit that you are to blame for anything. We're all in this boat together and hanged if we won't get out of it together, too, and you'll be the man to fetch us out."

Edmund smiled sadly, and shook his head.

Meanwhile Ingra, with the evident intention of concealing the movements of the vessel, dropped her so low that we hardly skipped the tops of the trees that we were passing over, for now we had entered a wide region of unbroken forest. Still that black dot followed straight in our wake, and I easily persuaded myself that it was yet growing larger. Edmund declared that I was right, and expressed his surprise, for we were now flying at the greatest speed that could be coaxed out of the motors. Suddenly a shocking thought crossed my mind. I tried to banish it, fearing that Ingra might read it in my eyes, and act upon it. Suppose that he should hurl us overboard! It was in his power to do so, and it seemed a quick and final solution. But he showed no intention to do anything of the kind. He may have had good reasons for refraining, but, at the time I could only ascribe his failure to take a summary way out of his difficulty to a protecting hand which guarded us even in this extremity.

On we rushed through the humming air, and still the pursuing speck chased us. And minute by minute it became more distinct against the background of the great cloud dome. Presently Edmund called our attention to something ahead.

"There," he said, "is Ingra's hope and our despair."

I turned my head and saw that in front the sky was very dark. Vast clouds seemed to be rolling up and obscuring the dome. Already there was a twilight gloom gathering about us.

"This," said Edmund, "is apparently the edge of what we may call the temperate zone, which must be very narrow, surrounding in a circle the great central region that lies under the almost vertical sun. The clouds ahead indicate the location of a belt of contending air currents, resembling that which we crossed after floating out of the crystal mountains. Having entered them, we shall be behind a curtain where our enemy can work his will with us."

Was it knowledge of this fact which had restrained Ingra from throwing us overboard? Was he meditating for us a more dreadful fate?

It was, indeed, a land of shadow which we now began to enter, and we could see that ahead of us the general inclination of the ground was downward. I eagerly glanced back to see if the pursuers were yet in sight. Yes! There was the speck, grown so large now that there could be no doubt that it was an air ship, driven at its highest speed. But we had entered so far under the curtain that the greater part of the dome was concealed, the inky clouds hanging like a penthouse roof far behind. We could plainly perceive the chasers; but could they see us? I tried to hope that they could, but reason was against it. Still they were evidently holding the course.

But even this hope faded when Ingra cunningly changed our course, turning abruptly to the left in the gloom. He knew, then, that we were invisible to the pursuers. But not content with one change, he doubled like a hunted fox. We watched for the effect of these maneuvers upon those behind us, and to our intense disappointment, though not to our surprise, we saw that they were continuing straight ahead. They surely could not have seen us, and even if they anticipated Ingra's ruse, how could they baffle it, and find our track again? At last the spreading darkness swallowed up the arc of illuminated sky behind, and then we were alone in the gloom.

This, you will understand, was not the deep night of the other side of the planet; it was rather a dusky twilight, and as our eyes became accustomed to it, we could begin to discern something of the character of our surroundings. We flew within a hundred yards of the ground, which appeared to be perfectly flat, and soon we were convinced by the pitchy-black patches which frequently interrupted the continuity of the umbrageous surface beneath, that it was sprinkled with small bodies of water—in short, a gigantic Dismal Swamp, or Everglade. I need hardly say that it was Edmund who first drew this inference, and when its full meaning burst upon my mind I shuddered at the hellish design which Ingra evidently entertained. Plainly, he meant to throw us into the morass, either to drown in the foul water, whose miasma now assailed our nostrils, or to starve amidst the fens! But his real intention, as you will perceive in a little while, was yet more diabolical.

The bird ship stooped lower, just skimming the tops of strange trees, the most horrible vegetable forms that I have ever beheld. And then, without warning, we were seized and pushed overboard, while the vessel, making a broad swoop, quickly disappeared. Henry alone uttered a loud cry as we fell.

We crashed through the clammy branches and landed close together in a swamp. Fortunately the water was not deep, and we were able to struggle upon our feet and make our way to a comparatively dry open place, perhaps half an acre in extent. No sooner were we all safe on the land than I noticed Edmund struggling violently and then he exclaimed:

"Here, quick! Hold a hand here!"

As he spoke he backed up to me.

A Columbus of Space

"Take a match from this box which I have twisted out of my pocket, and while I hold the box, scratch it, and hold the flame against the bonds around my wrists."

I managed to get out a match, and scratched it. But the match broke. Edmund, with the skill of a prestidigitator, got out another match, and pushed it into my fingers. It failed again.

"It's got to be done!" he said. "Here, Jack, you try."

Again he extracted a match, as Jack backed up in my place. Whether his hands happened to be less tightly bound, or whether luck favored him, Jack, on a second attempt, succeeded in illuminating a match.

"Don't lose it," urged Edmund, as the light flashed out; "burn the cord."

Jack tried. The smell of burning flesh arose, but Edmund did not wince. In a few seconds the match went out.

"Another!" said Edmund, and the operation was repeated. A dozen separate attempts of this kind had been made, and I believe that I felt the pain inflicted by them more than Edmund did, when, making a tremendous effort, he burst the charred cord. His hands and wrists must have been fearfully burned, but he paid no attention to that. In a flash he had out his knife and cut us all loose. It was a mercy that they had not noticed the flame of the matches from the air ship, for if they had, unquestionably Ingra would have returned and made an end of us.

After our release we stood a few moments in silence, awaiting our leader's next move. Presently a sonorous sign startled us, followed by a sticky, tramping sound.

"In God's name, what's that?" exclaimed Jack.

"We'll see," said Edmund quietly, and threw open his pocket lantern.

As the light streamed out there was a rustle in the branches above us, and the form of an air ship pushed into view.

Ingra!

No, it was not Ingra! Thank God, there was the bushy head of Juba visible on the deck as the ship drifted over us! And near him stood Ala and a half dozen attendants.

As one man we shouted, but the sound had not ceased to echo when, out of the horrible tangle about us, rose, with a swift, sinuous motion, a monstrous anacondalike arm, flesh pink in the electric beam, but covered with spike-edged spiracles! It curled itself over the edge of the hovering air ship and drew it down.

CHAPTER XVI
DREADFUL CREATURES

The deck of the air ship was tipped up at an angle of forty-five degrees by the pressure, and with inarticulate cries most of those on board tumbled off, some falling into the water and some disappearing amidst the tangled vegetation. Ala was visible, as the machine sank lower, and crashed through the branches, clinging to an upright on the sloping deck, while Juba, who hung on like a huge baboon, was helping her to maintain her place.

Almost at the same moment I caught sight of the head of the monstrous animal which had caused the disaster. It was as massive as that of an elephant or mammoth; and the awful arm resembled a trunk, but was of incredible size. Moreover, it was covered with sucking mouths or disks. The creature apparently had four eyes ranged round the conical front of the head where it tapered into the trunk, and two of these were visible, huge, green, and deadly bright in the gleam of the lantern.

For a moment we all stood as if petrified; then the great arm was thrown with a movement quick as lightning round both Ala and Juba as they clung to the upright! My heart shot into my mouth, but before the animal could haul in its prey, a series of terrific reports rattled like the discharge of a machine gun at my ear. The monstrous arm released the victims, and waved in agony, breaking the thick, clammy branches of the vegetation, and the vast head disappeared. Edmund had fired all the ten shots in his automatic pistol with a single pressure of the double trigger and an unvarying aim, directed, no doubt, at one of the creature's eyes.

"Quick!" he shouted, as the air ship, relieved from the stress, righted itself; "climb aboard."

The vessel had sunk so low, and the vegetation was so crowded about it, that we had no great difficulty in obeying his commands. He was the last aboard, and instantly he grasped the controlling apparatus, and we rose out of the tangle. We could hear the wounded monster thrashing in the swamp, but saw only the reflection of its movements in the commotion of the branches.

I had expected that Edmund would immediately fly at top speed away from the dreadful place, but, instead, as soon as we were at a safe elevation, he brought the air ship to a hover, circling slowly above the comparatively open spot of dry ground at the edge of the swamp.

"We cannot leave the poor fellows who have fallen overboard," he said, as quietly as if he had been safely aboard his own car. "We must stay here and find them."

Soon their cries came to our ears, and turning down the light of the lantern we saw five of them collected together on the solid ground, and gesticulating to us in an agony of terror. Edmund swept the ship around until we were directly over the poor fellows, and then allowed it to settle until it rested on the ground beside them. I trembled with apprehension at this bold maneuver, but Edmund was as steady as a rock. Ala instantly comprehended his intention, and encouraged her followers, who were all but paralyzed with fright, to clamber aboard. A momentary communication of the eyes took place between Edmund and Ala, and I understood that he was demanding if all had been found.

There was another—and not a trace of him could be seen.

"We must wait a moment," said Edmund, reloading the chamber of his pistol while he spoke. "I'll look about for him."

"In God's name, Edmund! You don't think of going down there!"

"But I do," he said firmly, and before I could put my hand on his arm he had dropped from the deck. The gigantic creature that he had wounded was still thrashing about a little distance off, occasionally making horrible sounds, but Edmund seemed to have no fear. We saw him, with amazement, walk collectedly round the ground encircled by the swamp, peering into the tangle, and frequently uttering a call. But his search was vain, and after five minutes of the most intense nervous strain that I ever endured, I thanked Heaven for seeing him return in safety, and come slowly aboard. There was another consultation with Ala, which evidently related to the ability of the engineer of the ship to resume his functions. This had a satisfactory result, for the fellow took his place, and the vessel finally quitted the ground. But, at Edmund's request, it rose only to a moderate height, and then began again to circle about. He would not yet give up the search.

We flew in widening circles, Edmund keeping his lantern directed toward the ground, and the full horror of these interminable morasses now became plain. I was in a continual shudder at the evidence of Ingra's pitiless scheme for our destruction. He had meant that we should be the prey of the unspeakable inhabitants of the fens, and had believed that there was no possibility of escape from them. We became aware that there was a great variety of them in the swamps and thickets beneath through the noises that they made—heart-quaking cries, squealing sounds, gruntings, and, most trying of all, a loud, piercing whistle whose sibilant pulsations penetrated the ear like thrusts of a needle. I pictured to myself a colossal serpent as the most probable author of this terrifying sound, but the error of my fancy was demonstrated by a tragedy which shook even Edmund's iron nerves.

Always circling, and always watching what was below by the light of the lantern, which was of extraordinary power for so small an instrument, we saw occasionally a curling trunk uplifted above the vegetation, as if its owner imagined that the strange light playing on the branches was some delicate prey that could be grasped, and sometimes a gliding form whose details escaped detection, when, upon passing over a relatively open place, like that where our adventure had occurred, a blood-curdling sight met our eyes.

Directly ahead, in the focus of the reflector of the lantern, and not more than a hundred feet distant, stood a prodigious black creature, on eight legs, rolling something in its mandibles, which were held close to what seemed to be its mouth.

"Good Lord!" cried Jack. "It's a tarantula as big as a buffalo!"

"It has caught the missing man!" said Edmund. "Look!"

He pointed to a shred of garment dangling on a thorny branch. I felt sick at heart, and I heard a groan from Jack. After all, these people were like us, and our feelings would not have been more keenly agitated if the victim had been a descendant of Adam.

"He is beyond all help," I faltered.

"But he can be avenged," said Edmund, in a tone that I had never heard him use before.

As he spoke he whipped out his pistol, and crash! crash! crash! sounded the hurrying shots. As their echo ceased, the giant arachnid dropped his prey, and then there came from him—clear, piercing, quivering through our nerves—that arrowy whistle that had caused us to shudder as we unwillingly listened to it darting out of the gloom of the impenetrable thickets.

Then, to our horror, the creature, which, if touched at all by the shots, had not been seriously injured, picked up its prey and bounded away in the darkness. Edmund instantly turned to Ala, and I knew as well as if he had spoken, what his demand was. He wished to follow, and his wish was obeyed. We swooped ahead, and in a minute we saw the creature again. It had stopped on another oasis of dry land, and it still carried its dreadful burden. Its head was toward us, and it appeared to be watching our movements. Its battery of eyes glittered wickedly, and I noticed the bristle of stiff hairs, like wires, that covered its body and legs.

Again Edmund fired upon it, and again it uttered its stridulous pipe of defiance, or fear, and leaped away in the tangle. We sped in pursuit, and when we came upon it for the third time it had stopped in an opening so narrow that the bow of the air ship almost touched it before we were aware of its presence. This time its prey was no longer visible. There was no question now that its attitude meant defiance. Cold shivers ran all over me as, with fascinated eyes, I gazed at its dreadful form. It seemed to be gathering itself for a spring, and I shrank away in terror.

Crash! bang! bang! bang! sounded the shots once more, and in the midst of them there came a blinding tangle of bristled, jointed legs that thrashed the deck, a thud that shook the air ship to its center, and a cry from Jack, who fell on his back with a crimson line across his face.

"Give me your pistol!" shouted Edmund, snatching my arm.

I hardly know how I got it out of my pocket, I was so unnerved, but it was no sooner in Edmund's hand than he was leaning over the side of the deck and pouring out the shots. When the pistol was emptied he straightened up, and said simply:

"*That* devil is ended."

Then he turned to where Jack lay on the deck. We all bent over him with anxious hearts, even Ala sharing our solicitude. He had lost his senses, but a drop from Edmund's flask immediately brought him round, and he rose to his feet.

"I'm all right," he said, with a rather sickly smile; "but," drawing his hand across his brow and cheek, "he got me here, and I thought it was a hot iron. Where is he now?"

"Dead," said Edmund.

"Jo, I'd have liked to finish him myself!"

We were worried by the appearance of the wound, like a long, deep scratch, on Jack's face, but, of course, we said nothing about our worriment to him. Edmund bound it up, as best he could, and it afterwards healed, but it took a long time about it, and left a mark that never disappeared. There was probably a little poison in it.

Edmund himself needed the attention of a surgeon, for his wrists had been cruelly burned by the matches, but he would not allow us to speak of his sufferings, and putting on some slight bandages, he declared that it was time now to get out of this wilderness of horrors. He communicated with Ala, and in a few minutes we were speeding, at a high elevation, toward the land of the opaline dome. So far above the morasses we no longer heard the brute voices of its terrible inhabitants, nor saw the swaying of the branches as they looked about in search of prey.

"This," said Edmund, "exceeds everything that I could have imagined. I do not know in what classification to put any of the strange beasts that we have seen. They can only be likened to the monsters of the early dawn on the earth, in the age of the dinosaurs. But they are *sui generis*, and would make our anatomists and paleontologists stare. I am only surprised that we have encountered no flying dragons here."

"But was it really a—a giant spider that captured Ala's man?" I asked with a shudder.

"God knows what it was! It had the form of a spider, and it leaped like one. If it had been armored I could never have killed it. I think the shock of its impact against the air ship helped to finish it."

It was only after we had issued from under the curtain of twilight that we learned the story of the chase which had brought our salvation. Edmund first obtained it from Ala and Juba, filling out the outlines of their wordless narrative with his ready power of interpretation, and then he told it to us."

"We owe our lives to Juba," he said. "Ala had just returned to the mine from the capital when our abduction took place. Juba, who had wandered out on our track, saw from a distance the seizure, and a few minutes afterwards Ala's air ship arrived. He instantly communicated the facts to her, and without losing an instant the chase was begun. Ingra's delay in choosing his course was the thing that saved us. They knew that they must not lose sight of us for an instant, and their motors were driven to their highest capacity. Fortunately, Ala's vessel is one of the speediest, and they were able to gain on us from the start. Slowly they drew up until the border of the twilight zone was reached. Then as we entered under the clouds we were swallowed from the sight of all except Juba. But for his wonderful eyes, there would have been no hope of continuing the chase. He had lived all his life in a land of darkness and now he began to feel himself at home. Throwing off the shades which he has worn since our arrival, he had no difficulty in following the movements of Ingra, even after our vessel had completely faded from the view of all the others. So, without abating their fearful speed, they plunged into the gloom straight upon our track. The nose of the bloodhound is not more certain in the chase than were Juba's eyes in that terrible flight through the darkness. When Ingra changed his course and doubled, Juba saw the maneuver and turned the dodge against its inventor, for now Ingra could not see them, and did not know that they were still on his track. They cut off the corners, and gained so rapidly that they were close at hand when Ingra rose from the swamp after pitching us overboard. They had heard Henry's cry, which served to tell them what had happened, and to direct them to the spot. But even Juba could not discern us in the midst of the vegetation, and it was the sudden flashing out of our lamp which revealed our location when they were about to pass directly over us."

I need not say with what breathless attention we listened

to this remarkable story, which Edmund's scientific imagination had constructed out of the bones of fact that he had been able to gather.

"Jo," said Jack, "our luck is simply outlandish!"

Then he broke out in one of his fits of enthusiasm. Slapping Juba on the shoulder, he danced around him, laughing joyously, and exclaiming:

"Bully old boy! Oh, you're a trump! Wait till I get you in New York, and I'll give you the time of your life! Eh, Edmund, won't we make him a member of Olympus? Golly, won't he make a sensation!"

And Jack hugged himself again with delight. His reference to home threw us into a musing. At length I asked:

"Shall we ever see the earth again, Edmund?"

"Why, of course we shall," he replied heartily. "I have the material I need, and it only remains to repair the car. I shall set about it the moment we reach the capital. Do you know," he continued, "this adventure has undoubtedly been a benefit to us."

"How so?"

"By increasing our prestige. They have seen the terrible power of the pistols. They have seen us conquer monsters that they must have regarded as invincible. When they see what the car can do, even Ingra will begin to fear us, and to think that we are more than mortal."

"But what will Ala think of Ingra now?"

"Ah, I cannot tell; but, at any rate, he cannot have strengthened himself in her regard, for it is plain that she, at least, has no desire to see us come to harm. But he is a terrible enemy still, and we must continue to be on our guard against him."

"I should think that he would hardly dare to show himself now," I remarked.

"Don't be too sure of that. After all, we are interlopers here, and he has all the advantages of his race and his high rank.

Ala is interested in us because she has, I believe I may say, a philosophical mind, with a great liking for scientific knowledge. It was she who planned and personally conducted the expedition toward the dark hemisphere. From me she has learned a little. She appreciates our knowledge and our powers, and would ask nothing better than to learn more about us and from us. Her prompt pursuit and interference to save us when she must have understood, perfectly, Ingra's design, shows that she will go far to protect us; but we must not presume too much on her ability to continue her protection, nor even on her unvarying disposition to do so. For the present, however, I think that we are safe, and I repeat that our position has been strengthened. Ingra made a great mistake. He should have finished us out of hand."

"His leaving us to be devoured by those fearful creatures showed an inexplicable cruelty on his part; he chose the most horrible death he could think of for us," I said.

"Oh, I don't know," replied Edmund. "Did you ever see a laughing boy throw flies into a spider's den? It is my idea that he simply wished to have us disappear mysteriously, and then *he* would never have offered an explanation, unless it might have been the malicious suggestion that we had suddenly decamped to return to the world we pretended to have come from. And but for Ala's unexpected return to the mine he would have succeeded. No doubt his crew were pledged to secrecy."

CHAPTER XVII
EARTH MAGIC ON

We were no sooner installed again at the capital than Edmund began his "readjustment of the atomic energies."

"Blessed if I know what he means," said Jack; "but he gets the goods, and that's enough for me."

In reality I did not understand it any better than Jack did, only I had more knowledge than he of the nature of the forces that Edmund employed. We went with him to the place in the great tower where the car had been stored, and where it seemed to be regarded with a good deal of superstitious awe. But they had not yet the least idea of its marvelous powers. We were preparing for them the greatest surprise of their lives, and our impatience to see the effect that would be produced when we made our first flight grew by day, while Edmund, shut up alone in the car, labored away at his task.

"I wonder what they think he is doing in there," I said, the third day after our return, as we sat on a balcony of the floating tower, with our feet nonchalantly elevated on a railing, and our eyes drinking in the magnificent prospect of the vast city, as brilliant in variegated colors as a flower garden, while a soft breeze, that gently swayed the gigantic gossamer, soothed us like a perfumed fan.

"Worshipping the sun god, I reckon," laughed Jack. "But,

see here, Peter, what do you make of this religion of theirs, anyway?"

"I don't know what to make of it," I replied. "But if the sun really does appear to them once in a lifetime, or so, as Edmund thinks, it seems to me natural enough that they should worship it. We have done more surprising things of the kind on the earth."

"Not civilized people like these."

"Oh, yes. The Egyptians were civilized, and the Romans, and they worshipped all sorts of strange things that struck their fancy. And what can you say to the Greeks—they were civilized enough, and look what a collection of gods they had."

"But the wise heads among them didn't really believe in their gods."

"I'm not sure of that; at any rate they had to pretend that they believed. No doubt there were some who secretly scoffed at the popular belief, and it may be the same here. I shouldn't wonder if Ingra were one of the scoffers. Edmund has a great opinion of his intelligence, and if he really doesn't believe in the thing, he is all the more dangerous for us, because you know that now we are depending a good deal on their superstition for our safety."

"But Ala is very intelligent, a regular wonder, I should think, from what Edmund says; and yet she accepts their superstition as gospel."

"Lucky for us that she does believe," I said. "But there's some great mystery behind all this; Edmund has convinced me of that. We don't begin to understand it yet, and there are moments when I think that Edmund is afraid of the whole thing. He seems dimly to foresee some catastrophe connected with it, though what it may be I cannot imagine, and I think he doesn't know himself."

Henry listened to our conversation without proffering a remark—quite the regular thing with him—and at this point Jack, yielding to the overpowering sense of well-being, and the soothing influence of the delicious air and delightful view, closed his eyes for a nap.

Presently Edmund came and roused us all up with the remark that he had finished his work. Jack was instantly on his feet:

"Hurrah!" he exclaimed. "Now for another trip that will open the eyes of these Venusians. Where shall we go, Edmund?"

"We shall go nowhere just at present. I want first to make sure by a trial trip that everything is in perfect shape. For that purpose I shall wait for the hours of repose when there will be nobody to watch us."

I must here explain more fully what I have already said—that in this land of unceasing daylight, everybody took repose as regularly as on the earth. That is a necessity for all physical organisms. When they slept, they retired into darkened chambers, and passed several hours in peaceful slumber. We had learned the time when this periodical need for sleep seized upon the entire population, and although, naturally, there were a few wide-awakes who kept "late hours," yet within a certain time after the habitual hour for repose had arrived it was a rare thing to see anybody stirring. We had, then, only to wait until "the solemn dead of night" came on in order that Edmund might try his experiment with almost a certainty of not being observed. This was the easier, since latterly there had been no guard kept over our movements. We were not confined in any way, and could go and come as we pleased. Evidently, if anybody thought of such a thing as an attempt to escape on our part, they trusted to the fact that we had no means of getting away, for after our first exploit of that kind, all the air ships were carefully guarded, and placed beyond our reach. As to the car, there was nothing about it to suggest that it could fly, and probably they took it simply for some kind of boat, since they had seen us employ it only in navigating the sea. I have often thought, with wonder, of their unsuspiciousness in permitting

Edmund to spend so much time alone and undisturbed in the car. Possibly, there was something in Jack's suggestion, that they supposed it to be connected with our religious observances. Anyhow, so it was; and I can only ascribe the fact to the kindness of that overlooking Power which so often interfered in our behalf, making it no disparagement of our claim upon its protection that we had abandoned our mother earth and ventured so far away into space!

One thing decidedly in our favor was that, since our return from the mine (the adventure in the land of bogs and monsters was, as far as Edmund could ascertain, unknown at the capital, except by those who had taken part in it), we had been accustomed to pass the hours of repose in the tower. We should thus be close to the car when we got ready to start. Another equally favorable circumstance—and perhaps it was even more important—was the absence of Ingra, who, either because he did not care just now to face Ala, or because he had gone off somewhere after throwing us to the animals and was not yet aware of our escape, had not shown himself. If he had been present it might not have been so easy for Edmund to make his preparations.

Never had the great city seemed to me so long in quieting down for its periodical rest as on this occasion. After all was deserted in the streets below, people were still moving about on the tower, and it did seem as if they had taken a fit of wakefulness expressly to annoy us and interfere with our plans. We kept stealing out of our sleeping room, and looking cautiously about, for at least two hours, but always there was some one stirring in the immediate neighborhood. At last a tall fellow, who had been standing an interminable time at the rail directly in front of the storage place of the car, and whom Jack had half seriously threatened to throttle if he stood there any longer, turned and went yawning away. No sooner was he out of sight than Edmund led the way, and with the slightest possible noise, aided by Juba, who was as strong as three men, we got the car out on the platform. I was in a fever lest there should be a squeak from the little wheels that carried it. But they ran as still as rubber.

"Get in," whispered Edmund; and we obeyed him with alacrity.

Would it go?

Even Edmund could not answer that question. He pulled a knob, and I held my breath. There was the slightest perceptible tremor. Was it going to balk? No, thank Heaven! It was under way. In a few seconds we were off the tower in the free air. Edmund pressed a button, and the speed instantly increased. The gorgeous tower seemed to be flying away from us like a soap bubble. Jack, in ecstasy, could hardly repress a cheer.

"Hurrah, if you want to,'" said Edmund.

"They won't hear you, and now I don't care if they do. The apparatus is all right, and we'll give them something to wake up for. My only anxiety was lest they should witness a failure, which might have led to disagreeable consequences. There must be no dropping of knives in our juggling."

"Good!" cried Jack. "Then let's give 'em a salute."

Edmund smiled and nodded his head:

"The guns are in the locker," he said.

Jack had one of the automatic rifles out in a hurry.

"Shoot high," said Edmund, "and off toward the open country. The projectiles fly far, and I guess we can take the risk."

He threw both windows open, and Jack aimed skyward and began to pull the trigger.

Bang! bang! bang! Heavens, what a noise it was! The car must have seemed a flying volcano. And it woke them up! The sleeping city poured forth its millions to gaze and wonder. Surely they had never heard such a thundering. Within five minutes we saw them on the roofs and in the towers. Many were staring at us through a kind of opera glasses which they had. Then from a dozen aerial pavilions the colors broke forth and quivered through the air.

"Saluting us!" exclaimed Jack, delighted.

"Asking one another questions, rather," said Edmund.

They certainly asked enough of them, and I wondered what answers they returned.

"Probably they think we're off for good," said I.

"And aren't we?" asked Henry anxiously.

"Not yet," Edmund replied, and Henry's countenance fell.

The car turned and approached the great tower again. We swept round it within a hundred yards, and could see the amazement in the faces that watched us. But if they were astonished they were not terror-stricken. Within ten minutes twenty air ships were swiftly approaching us. Edmund allowed them to come within a few yards, and then darted away, rushed round the whole city like a flying cloud, and finally rose straight up with dizzying velocity, which made the vast metropolis shrink to a colored patch, as if we had been viewing it through the wrong end of a telescope.

"I'll go right up through the cloud dome now," he said. "Nothing could more impress them with a sense of our power than that; and when we come back again they will know that we have no fear, and the very act will be a proof of origin from the sky."

When we were in the midst of the mighty curtain of vapor, I was interested in noticing the peculiar quality of the light that surrounded us. We seemed to be immersed in a rose-pink mist.

"I do not understand," I said to Edmund, "how this dome is maintained at so great an elevation, and in apparent independence of the rain clouds which sometimes form beneath. No rain ever falls from the dome itself, and yet it consists of true clouds."

"I think," he replied, "that the dome is due to vapors which assemble at a general level of condensation, and do not form raindrops, partly because of the absence of dust to serve as nuclei at this great height, and partly because of some peculiar electrical condition of the air, arising from the relative nearness of Venus to the sun, which prevents the particles of vapor from gathering into drops heavy enough to fall. You will observe that there is a peculiar inner circulation in the vapor surrounding us, marked by ascending and descending currents which are doubtless limited by the upper and lower surfaces of the dome. The true rain clouds form in the space beneath the dome, where there seems to be an independent circulation of the winds."

On entering the cloud vault Edmund had closed the windows, explaining that it was not merely the humidity which led him to do so, but the diminishing density of the air which, when we had risen considerably above the dome, would become too rare for comfortable breathing. In a little while his conjecture about a peculiar electrical condition was justified by a pale-blue mist which seemed to fill the air in the car; but we felt no effects and the mechanism was not disturbed. Owing to our location on Venus, still at a long distance from the center of the sunward hemisphere, the sun was not directly overhead, but inclined at a large angle to the vertical, so that when we began to approach the upper surface of the vault, and the vapor thinned out, we saw through one of the windows a pulsating patch of light, growing every moment brighter and more distinct, until as we shot out of the clouds it instantly sharpened into a huge round disk of blinding brilliance.

"The sun! The sun!" we cried.

We had not seen it for months. When it had gleamed out for a short time during our drift across the water from the land of ice into the belt of tempests, we had been too much occupied with our safety to pay attention to it; but now the wonder of it awed us. Four times as large and four times as bright and hot as it appears from the earth, its rays seemed to smite with terrific energy. Juba, wearing his eye shades, shrank into a corner and hid his face.

"It is well that we are protected by the walls of the car and

A Columbus of Space

the thick glass windows," said Edmund, "for I do not doubt that there are solar radiations in abundance here which scarcely affect us on the earth, but which might prove dangerous or even mortal if we were exposed to their full force."

Even at the vast elevation which we had now attained there was still sufficient air to diffuse the sunlight, so that only a few of the brightest stars could be glimpsed. Below us the spectacle was magnificent and utterly unparalleled. There lay the immense convex shield of Venus, more dazzling than snow, and as soft in appearance as the finest wool. We gazed and gazed in silent admiration, until suddenly Henry, who had shown less enthusiasm over the view than the rest of us, said, in a doleful voice:

"And now that we are here—free, free, where we can do as we like—with all means at our command—oh! why will you return to that accursed planet? Edmund, in the name of God, I beseech you, go back to the earth! Go now! For the love of Heaven do not drag us into danger again! Go home! Oh, go home!"

The appeal was pitiful in its intensity of feeling, and a shade of hesitation appeared on Edmund's face. If it had been Jack or I, I believe that he would have yielded. But he slowly shook his head, saying in a sympathetic tone:

"I am sorry, Henry, that you feel that way. But I *cannot* leave this planet yet. Have patience for a little while and then we will go home."

I doubt whether afterwards, Edmund himself did not regret that he had refused to grant Henry's prayer. If we had gone now when it was in our power to go without interference, we should have been spared the most tragic and heart-rending event of all that occurred during the course of our wandering. But Edmund seemed to feel the fascination of Venus as a moth feels that of the candle flame.

When we emerged again on the lower side of the dome we were directly over the capital. We had been out of view for at least three hours, but many were still gazing skyward, toward the point where the car had disappeared, and when we came into sight once more there were signs of the utmost agitation. The prismatic signals began to flash from tower to tower, conveying the news of the reappearance of the car, and as we drew near we saw the crowds reassembling on every point of vantage. We went out on the window ledges to watch the display.

"Perhaps they think that we have been paying a visit to the sun," I suggested.

"Well, if they do I shall not undeceive them," said Edmund, "although it goes against the grain to make any pretense of the kind. Ala, particularly, is so intelligent, and has so genuine a desire for knowledge, that if I could only cause her to comprehend the real truth it would afford me one of the greatest pleasures of my life."

"I hope old Beak Nose is getting his fill of this show," put in Jack. "He'll be likely to treat us with more respect after this. By the way, I wonder what's become of my money. I think I'll sue out a writ of replevin in the name of the sun to recover it."

Nobody replied to Jack's sally, and the car rapidly approached the great tower.

"Are you going to land there?" I asked.

"I certainly shall," Edmund responded with decision.

"But they'll seize the car!" exclaimed Henry in affright.

"No, they won't. They are too much afraid of it."

Any further discussion was prevented by a sight which arrested the eyes of all of us. On the principal landing of the tower, whence we had departed with the car, stood Ala with her suite, and by her side was Ingra!

His sudden apparition was a great surprise, as well as a great disappointment, for we had felt sure that he was not in the city, and I, at least, had persuaded myself that he might be in disgrace for his attempt on our lives. Yet here he was, apparently on terms of confidence with her whom we had regarded as our only sure friend.

"Hang him!" exclaimed Jack. "There he is! By Jo, if Edmund had only invented a noiseless gun of forty million atom power, I'd rid Venus of *him*, in the two-billionth part of a second!"

"Keep quiet," said Edmund, sternly, "and remember what I now tell you; in no way, by look or act, is any one of us to indicate to him the slightest resentment for what he did. Ignore him, as if you had never seen him."

By this time the car had nearly touched the landing. Edmund stepped inside a moment and brought it completely to rest, anchoring it, as he whispered to me, by "atomic attraction." When the throng on the tower saw the car stop dead still, just in contact with the landing, but manifestly supported by nothing but the air—no wings, no aeroplanes, no screws, no mechanism of any kind visible—there arose the first *voice of a crowd* that we had heard on the planet. It fairly made me jump, so unexpected, and so contrary to all that we had hitherto observed, was the sound. And this multitudinous voice itself had a quality, or timbre, that was unlike any sound that had ever entered my ears. Thin, infantine, low, yet multiplied by so many mouths to a mighty volume, it was fearful to listen to. But it lasted only a moment; it was simply a universal ejaculation, extorted from this virtually speechless people by such a marvel as they had never dreamed of looking upon. But even this burst of astonishment, as Edmund afterwards pointed out, was really a tribute to their intelligence, since it showed that they had instantly appreciated both the absence of all mechanical means of supporting the car and the fact that here was something that implied a power infinitely exceeding any that they possessed. And to have produced in a world where aerial navigation was the common, everyday means of conveyance, such a sensation by a performance in the *air* was an enormous triumph for us!

No sooner had we gathered at the door of the car to step

out upon the platform than an extraordinary thing occurred. The front of the crowd receded into the form of a semicircle, of which the point where we stood marked the center, and in the middle of the curve, slightly in advance of the others, stood forth the tall form of the eagle-beaked high priest with the terrible face, flanked on one side by Ala and on the other by the Jovelike front of the aged judge before whom our first arraignment had taken place. Directly behind Ala stood Ingra. The contrast between the three principal personages struck my eye even in that moment of bewilderment—Ala stately, blonde, and beautiful as a statue of her own Venus; the high priest ominous and terrifying in aspect, even now when we felt that he was honoring us; and the great judge, with his snow-white hair and piercing eyes, looking like a god from Olympus.

"Do you note the significance of that arrangement?" Edmund asked, nudging me. "Ala, the queen, yields the place of honor to the high priest. That indicates that our reception is essentially a religious one, and proves that our flight sunward has had the expected effect. Now we have the head of the religious order on our side. Human nature, if I may use such a term, is the same in whatever world you find it. Touch the imagination with some marvel and you awaken superstition; arouse superstition and you can do what you like."

It would be idle for me to attempt to describe our reception because Edmund himself could only make shrewd guesses as to the meaning of what went on, and you would probably not be particularly interested in his conjectures. Suffice it to say that when it was over, we felt that, for a time at least, we were virtually masters of the situation.

Only one thing troubled my mind—what did Ingra think and what would he do? At any rate, he, too, for the time being, seemed to have been carried away with the general feeling of wonder, and narrowly as I watched him I could detect in his features no sign of a wish to renew his persecution.

CHAPTER XVIII
WILD EDEN

The next day after our return from the trip above the cloud dome, and our astonishing reception (you will, of course, understand the sense in which I use the term "day"), Edmund sprang another surprise upon us.

"I have persuaded Ala," he said, "to make a trip in the car."

"You don't mean it!"

"Oh, yes, and I am sure she will be delighted."

"But she is not going alone?"

"Surely no; she will be accompanied by one of her women—and by Ingra."

"*Ingra!*"

"Of course. Did you suppose that he would consent to be left behind? Ala herself would refuse to go without him."

"Then," I said, with deep disappointment, "he has resumed all his influence over her."

"I'm not sure he ever lost it," returned Edmund. "You forget his rank, and his position as her destined consort. Whatever we do we have got to count him in."

Jack raged inwardly, but said nothing. For my part, I almost wished Jack's bullet had not gone astray at that first memorable shooting.

"Now," Edmund continued, "the car, as you know, has but a limited amount of room. I do not wish to crowd it uncomfortably, but I can take six persons. Ala's party comprises three, so there is room for just two besides myself. You will have to draw lots."

"Is Juba included in the drawing?"

"Yes, and I'm half inclined to take him anyway, and let you three draw for the one place remaining."

"You can count me out," said Henry. "If there is another to stay with me I prefer to remain."

"Very well," said Edmund, "then Peter and Jack can draw lots."

"Since we can't all go," said Jack, "and since that fellow is to be of the party, I'll stay with Henry."

So it was settled without an appeal to chance, and I went with Edmund and Juba. As usual Edmund immediately put his project into execution. It showed an astonishing confidence in us that Ala should consent to make such a trip, and that her people, and especially Ingra, should assent to it, and I could not sufficiently wonder at the fact. But we were now at the summit of favor and influence, and it is impossible to guess what thoughts may have been in their minds. At any rate, it showed how completely Edmund had established himself in Ala's esteem, and I suspect that her woman's curiosity had played a large part in the decision. There was another thing which astonished me yet more, and, in fact, awakened a good deal of apprehension in my mind. I could not but wonder that Edmund, after all the precautions that he had previously taken, should now think of admitting these people into the car, where they could witness his manipulations of the mechanism. I spoke to him about it. "Rest your mind easy about that," he said. "Now that everything goes like a charm, they will suspect nothing. It will be all a complete mystery to them. Even the gods used natural agencies when they visited the earth without shaking the belief of mankind in them. I employ no force of which they have the least idea, and if they see me touch a button, or pull a knob, what can that convey to their minds except an impression of mysterious power?"

I said no more, but I was not convinced, and the sequel proved that, for once, Edmund had made a serious mistake, the more amazing because he had been the first to detect the exceptional intelligence and shrewdness of Ingra. But, no doubt, in the exultation of his recent triumph, he counted upon the strength of the superstitious regard in which we were held.

Our departure from the tower was the signal for the assembling of great crowds of spectators again, and we sailed away with the utmost *eclat*. Ala at once showed all the eager excitement of a child over so novel and enjoyable an experience. The motion of the car was entirely unlike that of the air ships. Perfectly steady, it skimmed along at a speed which filled her with amazement and delight. The city, with its towers, seemed to fly away from us by magic, and the trees and fields beneath ran into streaming lines. The windows were thrown wide open, and all stood by them, watching the scene. Finally Ala wished to go out on the window ledges, where one was perfectly secure if he kept a firm hold on the supports. Edmund was most of the time with us outside, only stepping within when he wished to change the course. I thought that he showed a disposition to conceal his manipulations as much as possible, as if what I had said had made an impression. But all were so much occupied with their novel sensations that, for the time at least, there was no danger of their taking note of anything else.

I believe that it must have been some intimation from Ala which finally led Edmund to hold his course toward the mountains, but in a direction different from that which led to the mines. When he had once chosen this direction he worked up the speed to fully a hundred miles an hour, and all were compelled to go inside on account of the wind created by our rush through the air. We held on thus for five hours. During this time Edmund spread a repast made up of dishes chosen from the supplies in the car, and, of course, utterly strange to our guests. They found them to their taste, however, and were delighted with Edmund's entertainment. We spent a long time at our little table, and I was surprised at the variety of delicious things which Edmund managed to extract from his stores. There was even some champagne, and I noticed that Edmund urged it upon Ingra, who, nothing loth, drank enough to make him decidedly tipsy, a fact which was not surprising since we had found that the wines of Venus were very light, and but slightly alcoholized.

At length we began to approach what proved to be the goal of our journey. Before us spread a vast extent of forest composed of trees of the most beautiful forms and foliage. Some towered up to a great height, spreading their pendulous branches over the less aspiring forms, like New England elms; others were low and bushy, and afire with scarlet blossoms, whose perfume filled the air; a few resembled gigantic grasses or great timothy stems, surmounted with nodding plumes of golden leaves, streaming out like gilt gonfalons in the breeze; but there was one species, as tall and massive as oaks, and scattered everywhere through the forest, that I could liken to nothing but enormous rose bushes in the full bloom of June. When we began to pass above this strange woodland, Ala made some communication to Edmund which caused him to slow down the movement of the car. By almost imperceptible touches he controlled the motive power, and presently we came to rest above a delightful glade, where a small stream ran at the foot of a gravelly slope, crowned with grass and overhung by trees.

Here the car was allowed to settle gently upon the ground, and all alighted. Ingra, over whom the influence of the champagne had been growing, tottered on his legs in a way that would have filled Jack with uncontrollable delight, but Edmund gravely helped him out of the car and steadied him to a seat on the soft turf under the tree. I saw Ala regarding Ingra with a puzzled look, and no wonder, for Edmund had been careful that no one else should take enough of the wine to produce more than the slightest exhilaration of spirits. It is possible that Edmund had plied Ingra with the idea of rendering him less observant, and it probably had that effect; but it resulted, as you will see presently, in a revelation which finally put Edmund on guard against the very danger to which he had seemed so insensible when I mentioned it to him before our start.

The place where we now were was, beyond comparison, the most charming that we had yet seen. A very Eden it seemed, wild, splendid, and remote from all cultivation. The air was loaded with indescribable fragrance shed from the thousands of strange blossoms that depended from trees and shrubs, and starred the rich grass. I learned afterwards from Edmund, who had it from Ala, that the spot was famous for its beauty and other attractions, and was sometimes visited in air ships from the capital. But for them, what took us but a few hours was a trip extending over several days of time. One would have said that the forest was imbedded in a garden of the most extraordinary orchids. The shapes of some of the flowers were so fantastic that it seemed impossible that Nature could have produced them. And their colors were no less unparalleled, inimitable, and incredible.

The flowery bank on which we had chosen our resting place was removed a few yards from the spot where the car rested, and the latter was hidden from view by intervening branches and huge racemes of gorgeous flowers, hanging like embroidered curtains about us. A peculiarity of the place was that little zephyr-like breezes seemed to haunt it, coming one could not tell whence, and they stirred the hanging blossoms, keeping them in almost continual rhythmic motion. The effect was wonderfully charming, but I observed that Ala was especially influenced by it. She sat with her maid beside her, and fixed her eyes, with an expression of ecstasy, upon the swinging flowers. I whispered to Edmund to regard her singular absorption. But he had already noticed it, and seemed to be puzzling his brain with thoughts that it suggested to him.

Thus as we sat, the leaves of a tree over our heads were lightly stirred, and a bird, adorned with long plumes more beautiful than those of a bird of paradise, alighted on a branch, and began to ruffle its iridescent feathers in a peculiar way. With every movement waves of color seemed to flow over it, merging and dissolving in the most marvelous manner. As soon as this bird appeared, Ala gave it all her attention, and the pleasure which she experienced in watching it was reflected upon her countenance. She seemed positively enraptured. After a few moments the conviction came to me that she was *listening!* Her whole attitude expressed it. And yet not an audible sound came from the bird. At last I whispered to Edmund:

"Edmund, I believe that Ala hears something which we do not."

"Of course she does," was his reply. "There is music here, such music as was never heard on earth. That bird is *singing*, but our ears are not attuned to its strain. You know the peculiarity of this atmosphere with regard to sound, and that all of these people have a horror of loud noises. But their ears detect sounds which are beyond the range of the vibrations that affect ours. If you will observe the bird closely you will perceive that there is a slight movement of its throat. But that is not the greatest wonder, by any means. I am satisfied that there is *a direct relation here between sounds and colors.* The swaying of the flowers in the breeze and the rhythmic motion of the bird's plumage produce harmonious combinations and recombinations of colors which are transformed into sounds as exquisite as those of the world of insects. A cluster of blossoms, when the wind stirs them, shake out a kind of aeolian melody, and it was that which so entranced Ala a few moments ago. She hears it still, but now it is mastered by the more perfect harmonies that come from the bird, partly from its throat but more from

A Columbus of Space •

the agitation of its delicate feathers."

You may imagine the wonder with which I listened to this. It immediately recalled what Jack and I had observed at the shop of the bird fancier, and when the lady carried off her seemingly mute pets in the palanquin.

"But," I said, after a moment of reflection, "how can such a thing be? To me it seems surely impossible."

"I can only try to explain it by an analogy," said Edmund. "You know how, by a telephone, sounds are first transmuted into electric vibrations and afterwards reshaped into sonorous waves. You know, also, that we have used a ray of light to send telephonic messages, through the sensitiveness of a certain metal which changes its electric resistance in accord with the intensity of the light that strikes it. Thus with a beam of light we can reproduce the human voice. Well, what we have done awkwardly and tentatively by the aid of imperfect mechanical contrivances, Nature has here accomplished perfectly through the peculiar composition of the air and some special adjustment of the auditory apparatus of this people.

"Light and sound, color and music, are linked for them in a manner entirely beyond our comprehension. It is plain to me now that the music of color which we witnessed at the capital, was something far more complete and wonderful than I then imagined. Together with the pleasure which they derive from the harmonic combinations of shifting hues, they drink in, at the same time, the delight arising from sounds which are associated with, and, in many cases, awakened by, those very colors. It is probable that all their senses are far more fully, though more delicately, developed than ours. The perfume of these wonderful flowers is probably more delightful to Ala than to us. As there are sounds which they hear though inaudible to us, and colors visible to them which lie beyond the range of our vision, so there may be vibrations affecting the olfactory nerves which make no impression upon our sense of smell."

"Well, well," I exclaimed, "this seems appropriate to Venus."

"Yes," said Edmund with a smile, "it is appropriate; and yet I am not sure that some day we may not arrive at something of the kind on the earth."

I was about to ask him what he meant when there came an exciting interruption. Ingra, who had fallen more and more under the influence of the champagne, had stumbled to the other side of the little glade, virtually unnoticed, and Juba had wandered out of sight. Suddenly there came from the direction of the car the sound of a struggle mingled with inarticulate cries. We sprang to our feet, and, running to the car, found both Ingra and Juba inside it. The former had his hands on one of the knobs controlling the mechanism, and Juba had grasped him round the waist and was trying to drag him away. Ingra was resisting with all his strength, and uttering strange noises, whose sense, if they had any, we, of course, did not comprehend. Just as we reached the door, Juba succeeded in wrenching his opponent from his hold, and immediately gave him a fling which sent him clear out of the car, tumbling in a heap at our feet. Juba's eyes were ablaze with a dangerous light, but the moment he encountered Edmund's gaze he quietly walked away and sat down on the bank. Ala was immediately by our side, and I thought that I could read embarrassment as well as surprise in her looks. Fortunately the knob that Ingra had grasped had been thrown out of connection; else he and Juba might have made an involuntary voyage through space.

We picked up Ingra, found a seat for him, and Edmund, going down to the brook, filled a pocket flask with water and flung it in the fellow's face. This was repeated several times with the effect of finally straightening out his muddled senses sufficiently to warrant us in embarking for the return trip. All the way home Ingra was in a sulky mood, like any terrestrial drunkard after a debauch, but he kept his eyes on all Edmund's movements with an expression of cunning, which he had not sufficient self-command to conceal, and which could leave no doubt in our minds as to the nature of the quest which had led him into the car. As to Juba—although his interference had been of no practical benefit, since Ingra, especially in his present state, could surely have made no discovery of any importance—the devotion which he had again shown to our interests endeared him the more to us. Ala's manner showed that she was deeply chagrined, and thus our trip, which had opened so joyously, ended in gloom, and we were glad when the car again touched the platform, and our guests departed.

CHAPTER XIX
THE SECRET OF THE CAR

Jack and Henry were overjoyed to see us again, for after our departure they had fallen into a despondent mood, and began to imagine all sorts of evil.

"Jo!" was Jack's greeting; "I never was so glad to see anybody in my life. Edmund, don't you ever go off and leave any of us alone again."

"I'll never leave you again," responded Edmund. "You can count on that."

Then we told them the story of what we had seen, and of what had happened in the wild Eden that we had visited. They were not so much interested in the most wonderful thing of all—the combination of sound and color—as they were in the conduct of Ingra. Jack laughed until he was tired over Ingra's drunkenness, but he drew a long face when he heard of the adventure in the car.

"Edmund," he said earnestly, "I am beginning to be of Henry's opinion; you had better get away from here without losing a moment."

"No," said Edmund, "we'll not go yet. The time hasn't come to run away. What difference does it make even if Ingra does suspect that the car is moved by some mechanism instead of by pure magic? He could not understand it if I should explain it to him."

"But you have said that he is extraordinarily intelligent."

"So he is, but his intelligence is limited by the world he lives in, and while there are many marvelous things here, nobody has the slightest conception of inter-atomic force. They have never heard even of radioactivity. At the same time I don't mean that they shall go nosing about the car. I'll take care of that."

"But," said Jack, "it grinds me to see that brute Ingra get off scot-free after trying to murder us. And what has he got against us, anyway? But for him we should never have had any trouble. He was against us from the beginning."

"I don't think he was particularly *against* us at the start," said Edmund. "Only he was for treating us with less consideration than Ala was disposed to show. But after the first accidental shooting, and the drubbing that Juba gave him, naturally his prejudices were aroused, and he could hardly be blamed for thinking us dangerous. Then, when he found himself defeated, and his wishes disregarded, on all sides, he began to hate us. It is easy enough to account for his feelings. Now, since our recent astonishing triumph, being himself incredulous about our celestial origin, he will try to undermine us by showing that our seeming miracle is no miracle at all."

"And you gave him the chance by taking him in the car!" I could not help exclaiming.

"Yes," said Edmund, with a smile. "I admit that I made a mistake. I counted too much upon the influence of the sense of mystery. But it will come out all right."

"I doubt it," I persisted. "He will never rest now until he has found out the secret."

Nothing more was said on the subject, but Edmund was careful not to leave the car unguarded. It was always kept afloat, though in contact with the landing. The expenditure of energy needed to keep it thus anchored without support was, Edmund assured us, insignificant in comparison with the quantity stored in his mysterious batteries.

We were not long in finding, on all sides, evidence that our trip up through the cloud dome had been a master stroke, and that the presumable incredulity of Ingra with regard to our claims was not shared by others. He might have his intimates, who entertained prejudices against us resembling his own, but if so we saw nothing of them. In fact, Ingra was much less in evidence than before, but I did not feel reassured by that; on the contrary, it made me all the more fearful of some plot on his part, and Jack was decidedly of my opinion.

"Hang him!" he said, "he's up to some mischief, and I know it. Much as I detest him, I'd rather have him *in* sight than *out*, just now. He makes me feel like a snake in a bush; if he'd only show his ugly head, or spring his rattle, I'd be more comfortable."

But the kindness and deference with which we were treated, and the new wonders that were shown to us in the capital, gradually drove Ingra from our minds. Now we were permitted to enter the temples without opposition, our presence there according with our new character of "children of the sun." We saw the worship that was offered before the solar images by family parties, and attended, as favored guests, the periodical ceremonies in the great temple. Edmund confessed that the high priest greatly embarrassed him by staring into his eyes, and plainly assuming that he knew things of which he was profoundly ignorant.

"The hardest thing I ever undertook," he said, "is to hold my mind in suspense during these trying interviews, when he endeavors to read the depths of my soul, and I to throw a veil over them which he cannot penetrate."

In some way, Edmund discovered that the high priest and all the priests connected with the sun worship (and they certainly bore a family likeness) belonged to a special race, whose roots ran back into the most remote antiquity, and about whose persons clung a sacredness that placed them, in some respects, above the royal family itself. We frequently visited the great library, where Edmund undertook a study of the language of the printed rolls, though what he made of it I never clearly understood. I do not think that he succeeded in deciphering any of it. He also spent much time studying their mechanics and engineering, for which he professed great admiration.

But most interesting of all to us was what Edmund himself accomplished. I have told you of his remark about the color-sound music, viz., that he thought it not impossible that even human senses might be enabled to appreciate it. Well, he actually realized that wildly improbable dream! He fitted up a laboratory of his own in which he labored sometimes for twenty hours at a stretch, and at last he brought to us the astonishing invention he had made.

I can make no pretense of understanding it; although Edmund declared that, in substance, it was no more wonderful than a telephone. The machine consisted of a little metal box. (He made three of them, and I have mine yet, but it will not work on the earth, and it lies on my table as I write, serving for the most wonderful paper weight that a man ever possessed.) When this box was pressed against the ear in front of one of the revolving disks that threw out blending colors, or in the presence of a "singing" bird, the most divine harmonies seemed to awake *in the brain*. I cannot make the slightest approach to a description of the marvelous phenomenon. One felt his whole being infused with ecstatic joy. It was the very soul of music itself, celestial, ineffable! The wonder-box also enabled us to catch many sounds peculiar to the atmosphere of Venus, formed of vibrations, as Edmund had explained, that lie outside our gamut. But to these, apart from the music, I could never listen. They were *too* abnormal, filling one with inexplicable terror, as if he had been snatched out of nature and compelled to listen to the sounds of a preternatural world. The only sound that I ever heard with my natural ear which bore the slightest resemblance to these was the awful piercing whistle of the monster that killed Ala's man.

Yet we derived immense pleasure from the possession of those little boxes. With their aid, we could appreciate the exquisite melodies that were played everywhere—in great halls where thousands were assembled, in the temples great and small, and in the homes of the people, to which we were often admitted. In every house there was on one of the walls a "musical rose," whose harmonies entranced the visitor. And the variety of musical *motifs* seemed to be absolutely without limit. One was never tired of the entertainment because there was so little repetition.

On one ever-memorable occasion we heard the great national, or, as Edmund preferred to call it, "racial" hymn, played in the air from the principal tower. When we had only beheld the play of colors characterizing this composition we had found it altogether delightful, although, as I have said, Edmund detected, even then, some underlying tone of sadness or despair; but when its *sounds* broke into the brain the effect was overwhelming. The entire thing seemed to have been "written in a minor key," of infinite world-embracing pathos. The listener was plunged into depths of feeling that seemed unfathomable, eternal—and unendurable.

"Heavens!" whispered Jack to me in an awed voice, dropping the box from his ear, "I can't *stand* it!"

I saw tears running down his face, and felt them on my own. Edmund and Henry were equally affected, and could not continue to listen. Edmund said nothing, but I recalled his words about the traditional belief of this people that their world had entered upon the last stage of its existence. Then I watched the countenances about us; they wore an expression of solemnity, and yet there was something which spoke of an uplifting pride, awakened by the great paean, and swelling the heart with memories of interminable ages of past glory.

"Come," said Edmund at last, turning away, "this is not for us. The measureless sadness we feel, but the triumphant reflection of ancestral greatness is for them alone. Heavens!

A Columbus of Space

what an artist he must have been who composed this!—if it be not like the Iliad, the work of an age rather than of a man."

We almost forgot the passage of time in the enjoyment of our now delightful and untroubled existence, but there came at last a rude awakening from this life, which had become for us like a dream.

As I have said, we had ceased to worry about Ingra, whom we seldom saw, and who, when we did see him, gave no indication of continued enmity. At first we had kept the car under continual surveillance, but as time went on we became careless in this respect, and at last we did not guard it at all.

One day, during the time of repose, I happened to be, with Juba, in our room on that stage of the great tower where the car was anchored, while Edmund and the others were below in the palace. Juba was already asleep, and I was lying down and courting drowsiness, when a slight noise outside attracted my attention. I stepped softly to the door and looked out. The door of the car was open! Supposing that Edmund was there I approached to speak to him. By good fortune I was wearing the soft slippers worn by everybody here, and which we had adopted, so that my footsteps made no sound.

As I reached the car door and looked in, I nearly dropped in the intensity of my surprise and consternation. There, at the farther end, was Ingra, on his knees before the mechanical mouths which swallowed the invisible elements of power from the air; and beside him was another, also on his knees, and busy with tools, apparently trying to detach the things. The explanation flashed over my mind; Ingra had brought a skilled engineer to aid him in discovering the secret of the car, and, no doubt, to rob it of its mysterious mechanism. They seemed to fear no interruption, because Ingra had undoubtedly informed himself of the fact that for a day or two past we had abandoned the use of our room in the tower, and taken our repose in our apartments in the palace. It was by mere chance that Juba and I had, on this occasion, remained so long aloft that I had decided to take our sleep in the tower room.

Anticipating no surveillance, Ingra was not on his guard, and had no idea that I was behind him. Instinctively I grasped for my pistol but instantly remembered that it was with my coat in the room. I tiptoed back, awoke Juba, making him a sign to be noiseless, got the pistol, and returned, without a sound, to the open door of the car with Juba at my heels. They were yet on their knees, with their heads under the shelf, and I heard the slight grating made by the tool that Ingra's assistant was using. The pistol was in my hand. What should I do? Shoot him down without warning, or trust to the strength of Juba to enable us to overcome them both and make them prisoners?

While I hesitated, and it was but a moment, Ingra suddenly rose to his feet and confronted us. An exclamation burst from his lips, and the other sprang up. I covered Ingra with the pistol and pulled the trigger. There was not a sound! The sickening remembrance then burst over me that I had not reloaded the pistol since Edmund had emptied its whole chamber in the closing fight with the tarantula of the swamps. Ingra, followed by his man, sprang upon me like a tiger. In a twinkling I lay on my back, and before I could recover my feet, I saw Juba and Ingra in a deadly struggle, while the other ran away and disappeared. Jumping up I ran to Juba's assistance, but the fight was so furious, and the combatants whirled so rapidly, that I could get no hold. I saw, however, that Juba was more than a match for his opponent, and I darted into the car to get one of the automatic rifles, thinking that I could use it as a club to put an end to the struggle if the opportunity should offer. But the locker was firmly closed and I could not open it. After a minute of vain efforts I returned to the combatants and found that Juba had nearly completed his mastery. He had Ingra doubled over his knee and was endeavoring to pinion his hands.

At this instant, when the victory seemed complete, and our enemy in our power, Juba uttered a faint cry and fell in a heap. Blood instantly stained the floor around him, and Ingra, with a bound, dropping a long knife, attained the door of a nearby chamber, and was out of sight before I could even start to pursue him. Nevertheless, I ran after him, but quickly became involved in a labyrinth where it was useless to continue the search, and where I nearly lost my way.

I then returned to see how seriously Juba had been wounded. He had crawled into the car. I bent over him—he was dead! The knife had inflicted a fearful wound, and it seemed wonderful that he could have made his way unassisted even over the short distance from where he was struck down to the door of the car.

Juba dead! I felt faint and sick! But the critical nature of the emergency helped to steady my nerves by giving me something else to think of and to do. Edmund must be called at once. There were no "elevators" running regularly during the general hours of repose, and I did not know the way up and down the tower by the ladder-like stairways which connected the stages. But there were signals by which the little craft that served as elevators could be summoned in case of necessity, and I pulled one of the signal cords. It seemed an age before the air ship came, and another before I could reach Edmund.

His great self-control enabled him to conceal his grief at my news, but Jack was overcome. He had really loved Juba almost as if he had been human and a brother. The big-hearted fellow actually sobbed as if his heart would break. Then came the reaction, and I should never have believed that Jack Ashton could exhibit such malevolent ferocity. His lips all but foamed, as he fairly shouted, striking his big fists together:

"This'll be *my* job! Edmund! Peter! You hear me! Don't either of you dare to lay a hand on *that devil!* He's *mine!* Oh! I'll—" But he could not finish his sentence for gnashing his teeth.

We calmed him as best we could and then summoned an air ship. While we waited, Edmund suddenly put his hand in his pocket, and withdrawing it quickly, said, with a bitter smile:

"What a fool I have been in my carelessness. Ingra has had the key abstracted from my pocket by some thief. That explains how he got the car open."

The moment the ship came we hurriedly ascended to the platform. When Edmund saw poor Juba's body lying in the car and learned how he had made his way there to die, he was more affected than when he first heard of his death.

"He has died for us," he said solemnly; "he has crawled here as to a refuge, and here he shall remain until I can bury him among his people in his old home. Would to God I had never taken him from it!"

"Then you will start at once for the dark hemisphere?" I asked.

"At the earliest possible moment; and it shall be on the way to our own home."

But we were not to depart before even a more terrible tragedy had darkened over us, for now the tide of fate was suddenly running at flood.

CHAPTER XX
THE CORYBANTIA OF THE SUN

I have several times mentioned Edmund's half-formed impression that there was some very remarkable ceremony connected with the cyclical apparition of the sun before the eyes of its worshipers. He had said, you may recall, that it seemed probable that the religious rites on these rare occasions bore some resemblance to the *bacchanalia*, or *dionysia*, of ancient Greece. How he had derived that idea I do not know, but it proved to have been but too well founded—only he had not guessed the full truth. The followers of Dionysus made themselves drunken with the wine of their god and then indulged in the wildest excesses. Here, as we were now to learn, the worshipers of the sun were seized with another kind of madness, leading to scenes that I believe, and hope, have never had their parallel upon the earth.

With our hearts sore for Juba, we had completed our preparations for departure within six hours after his tragic death. Ala had been informed of the tragedy, and had visited the car and looked upon the dead form, which I thought greatly affected her. Edmund held little communication with her, but it was evidently with her cooperation that he was able to procure a kind of coffin, in which we placed Juba's body. I do not know whether Edmund informed her of his purpose to quit the planet, but she must have known that we were going to convey our friend somewhere for interment.

We were actually on the point of casting loose the car, Ala and a crowd of attendants watching our movements, when there came the second great sound of united voices which we had heard in this speechless world. It rose like a sudden wail from the whole city. There was a rushing to and fro, Ala's face grew as pale as death, and her attendants fell upon their knees and began to lift their hands heavenward, with an expression of terror and wild appeal.

At the same time we noticed a sudden brightening about us, and Edmund stepping out on the platform, immediately beckoned, with the first signs of uncontrollable excitement that I had ever seen him display. I was instantly at his side, and a single glance told the story.

High in the heavens, the sun had burst forth in all its marvelous splendor!

A vast rift was open in the cloud dome, through which the gigantic god of day poured down his rays with a fierceness that was inconceivable. The heat was like the blast of a furnace, and I felt my head beginning to swim.

"Quick!" cried Edmund, grasping my sleeve and pulling me into the car. "These rays are fatal! My God, what a sight!"

As by magic the atmosphere had become crowded with air ships, and throngs of thousands were pouring from them upon the great platform and the other stages, as well as upon the surrounding towers. Every available space was filling up with people hastening from below. As fast as they arrived they threw themselves into the most extraordinary postures of adoration, lifting hands and eyes to the sun. I remember thinking, in a flash, that the intense glare of light must burn to the very sockets of their eyes—but they did not flinch. It was evident, however, that those who looked directly in the sun's face were blinded.

I looked round for Ala, and noticed with a thrill that her beautiful eyes were wide open and glancing with an expression that I cannot describe, over her kneeling people. Beside her was the towering form of the great priest, who was staring straight at the sun—and yet, although his eyes were open, it was evident that they were not rendered altogether sightless even by that awful light. They burned like coals. He was making strange gestures with his long arms, and in unison with his every movement a low, heart-thrilling sound came from the throats of the multitude.

Edmund, at my shoulder, muttered under his breath:

"Shall I try to save her from this?—But to what good?"

For a moment he seemed to hesitate, and I thought that he was about to rush out upon the platform and seize Ala in order to rescue her from some danger that he foresaw; when, all at once, the multitude rose to its feet, staggering, and began to rush to and fro, colliding with one another, falling, rising again, grappling, struggling, uttering terrible cries—and then I saw the flash of knives.

"Good heavens!" shouted Edmund. "It is the ultraviolet rays! They have gone mad!"

In the meantime the gigantic high priest whirled upon his heel, swinging his arms abroad and uttering a kind of chant which was audible above the dreadful clamor of the rabid multitude. Though he had no weapon, he seemed the inspirer of this Aceldama, and around him its fury raged. Presently he drew close to Ala, who still stood motionless, as if petrified by the awful scene. I felt Edmund give a violent start, and before I comprehended his intention, he had dashed from the car, and was forcing his way through the struggling throng toward the queen.

"Edmund!" I shouted. "For God's sake, come back!"

Jack started to follow him, but I held him back with all my strength.

"Let me go!" he yelled. "Edmund will be killed!"

"And you, too!" I answered. "Break open the locker and get the guns!"

Jack threw himself upon the door of the locker, and strove

to wrench it open. Meanwhile, half paralyzed with excitement, I remained standing at the door. I saw Edmund hurl aside those who attacked him, and push on toward his goal. But a minute later a knife reached him, and he fell.

"Quick, Jack, quick!" I shouted; "Edmund is down!"

He had not got the locker open, but he darted to my side, and together we rushed out into the press. Shall I ever forget that moment! We were pushed, hustled, struck, hurled to and fro; but we had only a few steps to go, and we reached our leader where he lay. Seizing him, we succeeded somehow in carrying him into the car. Our clothes were torn, our hands and faces were bleeding, and there was blood on Jack's shoulder. Edmund was alive. We placed him on a bench, and then the fascination of the spectacle without again enchained us.

Suddenly my eyes fell upon Ingra, who had not previously made his appearance. He was as insane as the others, and like many of them had a knife in his hand. In a moment he pushed his way toward Ala, and my heart rose in my throat, for I did not know what mad thought might be in his mind. If I had had a weapon, I believe I should have shot him, but before he had arrived within three yards of the queen there came an explosion of flame—I do not know how else to describe it, for it was so sudden—and the great platform was instantly wrapped in licking tongues of fire.

The wickerwork caught like tinder, and the gauzy screws threw off streams of sparks like so many Fourth of July pinwheels. The gush of heat from the conflagration was terrible, and I turned my eyes in horror from the stricken multitude which seemed to have been shocked back into sanity by the sudden universal danger only to find itself a helpless prey to the flames.

"It's all over with them!" cried Jack.

His words awoke me to our own danger. We must get away instantly. Knowing the proper button to touch to throw the mechanism into action, I pushed it forcibly and pulled out a knob which I had often seen Edmund manipulate in starting the car. It responded immediately, and in a second we were afloat, and clear of the tower. Seeing that the direction which the car was taking would remove us from the reach of the flames, and that there was nothing ahead to obstruct its progress, and knowing that Edmund often left it to run of itself when the speed was slow, and there was no occasion to change its course, I now hurried with Jack to Edmund's side. Henry all this time had been lying on a bench like one in a trance.

Jack and I stripped off Edmund's coat, and at once saw the nature of his wound. A knife had penetrated his side, and there was considerable effusion of blood, but I was surgeon enough to feel sure that the wound was not mortal. He roused up as he felt us working over him, and opening his eyes, said faintly:

"You will find bandages under the locker. What has happened? We are moving."

"The tower is all in flames!" exclaimed Jack, before I could interrupt him, for I should have preferred not to tell Edmund the real situation just at that moment.

Jack's words roused him like an electric shock. He pushed us aside, and struggled to his feet. Then he sprang to a knob, and brought the car to rest.

We had been moving slowly, and had not gone more than a quarter of a mile from the tower. The car had swung round so that the fire was not visible from the open door, but now, as Edmund arrested its progress, it swayed back again and the spectacle burst into view. The heat smote us in the face even at this distance. In the few minutes since I had last seen the tower the flames had made incredible progress. The whole of the immense structure was blazing. Spires of flame leaped and swayed from its summit, partitions were falling, platforms giving way, and hundreds of air ships caught by the sheets of fire were crumpling and falling in swooping curves like birds whose wings had been seared. I was thankful that we could not see the unfortunates who were perishing in that furnace. It was but too evident that not a soul on the tower could have escaped.

I glanced at Edmund's face. It was pale and set—the face of a man gazing upon an awful tragedy with which he is absolutely powerless to interfere. His breath came quick, but he did not utter a word. Then came the reaction, and, staggering, he leaned on my shoulder, and I led him to the bench from which he had risen. For a moment I thought he had fainted, but when I put a flask to his lips he swallowed a mouthful and immediately recovered sufficient strength to sit up, resting his head on his hand.

"Had we not better go on?" I asked.

"Ye-es," he replied, after a moment's hesitation. "We can do nothing. They are all gone; the queen has perished with the rest! Pull out that knob on the right, but gently, and then push this button. We must circle round the outskirts until we see whether the fire will seize upon the other towers and extend to the city below."

I followed his directions, and, as we started our circuit, the vast tower suddenly swayed aside, and then, tumbling in upon itself, it went down in a whirl of smoke and eddying sparks.

As far as we could see none of the other aerial structures had caught fire. The entire absence of wind was no doubt the favorable circumstance that saved them. But all the towers were swaying under the impulse imparted to them by the excited multitudes that crowded their platforms. Although the light of the conflagration faded as soon as the principal tower fell, the others continued to shine brilliantly in the solar rays, but suddenly, as we watched, the splendor failed, and the subdued illumination characteristic of the endless daylight under the great dome took its place. The rift in the clouds above had closed as unexpectedly as it had recently opened, and the sun was no longer visible. It had been in view less than an hour, but in that brief space what scenes had been enacted!

Presently Edmund, shaking his head sadly, said:

A Columbus of Space •

"It is useless to stay longer. Even if the conflagration should spread we could do nothing to help the unfortunates. They must depend upon themselves."

He then gave me directions for changing our course to a direct line away from the city, at the same time increasing the speed. In the meantime he himself aided in binding up his wound.

"If there were the slightest chance that Ala could have escaped," he said, after a few minutes, "I would remain here, and search for her, but it is only too clear what her fate has been. She was really our only friend, and now that she is gone, we must get away from the sight and memory of these things as quickly as possible."

Seeing that his strength was gradually coming back to him, and secretly rejoicing that he bore this terrible blow so stoically, I felt that we might now converse about the catastrophe which we had witnessed.

"What do you think was the cause of the sudden outburst of fire?" I asked.

"It could hardly have been the direct action of the sunlight," he replied. "It must have resulted from some accidental concentration of the solar rays upon an inflammable substance by a mirror."

"I recall seeing a large concave glass on the principal platform in which they were fond of looking at their magnified images," I said.

"Yes, and no doubt that was the instrument chosen by fate to bring about this terrible end. The power of the sunbeams is twice as great here as upon the earth, and the heat in the focus of a mirror a couple of feet in diameter would suffice to set fire to the flimsy materials which abounded on the tower. Once started in such a place it ran like sparks in a train of gunpowder."

"But the madness that seized the multitude before the catastrophe—what did you mean by saying that it was the ultraviolet rays?"

"I used the term," Edmund replied slowly, "without attaching a very clear meaning to it. It simply expressed the general thought that was in my mind. It may be some other form of solar radiation to which we are not accustomed on the earth, but which is specially effective here when the sun is uncovered because of the greater nearness of Venus. This atmosphere, notwithstanding its density, may well be diaphanous to the ultraviolet rays, owing to some peculiarity in its composition which I have not had time to study. At any rate, it is evident, from what we have seen, that the rays of the unclouded sun almost instantly affect the brain. I, myself, felt them as if a thousand needles had been thrust through my skull; and I believe that they are responsible, rather than the shock of the wound in my side, for my present weakness."

"And did you foresee the consequences of the uncovering of the sun?"

"Not altogether. I had been led to think that something extraordinary must accompany the periodical appearances of the great orb, and if I could have known that an apparition was at hand I might have made preparations for it and we might have been able to save Ala. When I saw what was going on, I tried to reach her, and you know the result."

"But is it not incredible that a people of so peaceable a disposition should be seized with such murderous instincts when driven out of their senses by the effect of the rays?"

"No, it does not seem so to me. You know the general tendency of sudden madness, which usually produces a complete reversal of the ordinary instincts of the demented persons, making them dangerous to their dearest friends. But why talk longer of this? It is too painful—too overwhelming. What can man do against the great forces of Nature? At this moment I solemnly declare to you that I regret that I ever entered upon this expedition."

While we had been talking, the car had receded to a great

distance from the city, and now all but the tops of a few of the airy pinnacles were lost to our sight forever. But as we gazed, straining our sight for a last look, we perceived a familiar flickering of prismatic lightning on the horizon. We glanced at each other meaningly. It was the color speech again. But, oh, what must be the burden of their communications now! Suddenly, Edmund, whose eyes were fixed with intensity upon the scene, remarked, half shuddering:

"It is the great Paean."

Seized with curiosity, I pressed the magic box to my ear, and faintly there echoed in my brain a few disconnected strains of that solemn music. But now, more than ever, it was insufferable to me, and I dropped the box with a crash.

As Edmund recovered his strength he once more took charge of the car, and in a little while he had risen to a great height in order to take advantage of the easier going in the lighter atmosphere above. Thus we ran on for several hours until we began to catch sight of the sea, which was soon beneath us, while far ahead we saw the tumbling clouds marking the location of the belt of tempests behind which we knew lay the range of the crystal mountains. At length we issued from beneath the cloud dome, and then we saw the sun again, and the storms whipping the waters, whose waves occasionally flashed up at us through rifts in the streaming clouds beneath. And at last the icy peaks began to glitter on the horizon, and we knew that we were nearing the world of eternal night and frost. It was with strange feelings that we once more beheld the crystal mountains, for our minds were filled with the recollection of the scenes that had occurred among them when we were helpless in the grasp of their tempests. But now there was a certain exhilaration in the thought that this time we could safely sail over their summits. As we passed over them we looked eagerly for landmarks that might show where our former passage had occurred, and as Edmund purposely dropped as close to their summits as it was safe to go, I at last believed that

I recognized the mighty peak of rainbows that had so nearly wrecked us.

When we had left the mountains behind and entered into the region of night, I asked Edmund how he would proceed in order to find the location of the caverns.

"I shall go by the stars," he said. "I noted the bearing of the place, and I have no doubt that I can find it again."

CHAPTER XXI
THE EARTH

Edmund's reference to the stars instantly drew my attention to the heavens. They were ablaze with amazing gems, but at first I could not see the earth among them.

"I know what you are looking for," said Edmund. "Here, look through the peephole in the bow. From our present position the earth appears but little elevated above the horizon, but when we reach the caverns, which are in the center of the dark hemisphere, we shall see her overhead."

I knelt at the peephole, and my heart was in my throat. There was our glorious planet, oh, so bright! and close beside her the moon. At the sight, an irrepressible longing arose in me to be once more at home. Jack and Henry took their turns at looking, and they were no less affected than I had been. But Edmund retained a perfect self-command:

"Do you know," he asked with an odd smile (for now the lamps were glowing, and we had plenty of light in the car), "how long we have been absent from home?"

Not one of us had kept a record.

"It is just six hundred and four days," he continued, "since we left New York. We were sixteen days on our way to Venus; six days after our arrival at the caverns occurred the conjunction of the earth, and the ceremonies that Peter will not forget as long as he refrains from hair dye; two days later we departed for the sun lands; and since then five hundred and eighty days have passed. Now, between one conjunction of the earth and Venus to the next, five hundred and eighty-four days elapse. Already five hundred and eighty-two of those days have passed, so that within two days another conjunction will occur, and if we are then at the caverns we shall doubtless witness another sacrifice to the earth and the moon."

"God forbid!" I exclaimed.

"I feel as you do," said Edmund. "We have seen enough of such things. In order, then, to hasten our arrival at the caverns, where we must bury Juba, for on that I insist, I am going to rise up out of the atmosphere, in order that we may fly with planetary speed. We can thus reach the caverns, traversing the five thousand miles of distance that yet remain, in something like an hour, for some time must be lost in rising out of and returning into the atmosphere, and in the meantime I must make observations to determine our location. Having found the caverns we will complete our rites at Juba's grave, and get away for good before the sacrificial ceremonies begin."

It was a programme that suited us all, and it was quickly carried out. I had not thought that my admiration of Edmund's ability could be increased, but it was carried a notch higher when I saw how easily, guiding himself by the ever-visible stars, he located the caverns. When he knew that he was directly over them he dropped the car swiftly, and we could not repress a cry as we saw directly beneath us the familiar shafts of light issuing from the ground.

"We may have to do a little searching," said Edmund, as we approached the lights, "for, of course, my observations are not accurate enough to enable me to locate the exact spot where we landed before."

But fortune favored us marvelously, and the very first opening that we approached was at once recognized, for there stood the sacrificial altar.

We anchored the car near the shaft, and carried out Juba's coffin.

A Columbus of Space

"Wait here," said Edmund, "while I descend."

"No, you're not going alone," exclaimed Jack. "I'll go with you."

Edmund made no objection and he and Jack descended the steps. Half an hour elapsed before they returned, accompanied by a dozen of the natives, stolid, and not exhibiting the signs of surprise over our return which I had expected to see. Edmund had now made so much progress in their strange means of communication that he had little difficulty in causing them to comprehend what was wanted. They easily carried the coffin, and all of us followed down into the depths. It was the strangest funeral procession that ever a man saw!

While the grave was being prepared in the underground cemetery where we had witnessed the interment of the first victim of our pistols, Henry and I remained as a sort of guard of honor for Juba in the lower of the two great chambers which have been described in the earlier chapters of this history, and there a most singular thing occurred. We were startled by a low whining, and looking about saw one of the doglike creatures which appeared to be the only inhabitants of the caverns except the natives seated on its haunches close to the coffin, and exhibiting exactly the signs of distress that a dog sometimes displays over its dead master. That we were taken aback by this scene I need not assure you. We had never observed, during our former visit, that either Juba or any of his people was followed by these creatures; in fact, they had always fled at our approach, and we had paid little attention to them.

But now, if the poor animal could have spoken, he could not more plainly have told us that, by means of the mysterious instinct which beings of his kind possess, he had recognized the presence of his old master, and was mourning for him. It was truly a touching spectacle, and Henry was hardly less moved by it than I. When Edmund and Jack came back, having superintended the preparations, Jack was cut to the heart by the sight. Immediately he declared that the "dog" must accompany us in the car, and Edmund assented by a grave inclination of the head. The animal followed us to the grave, and remained there watching us intently. He seemed to have dismissed his fear, as if he comprehended that we were friends of his master.

There were not more than twenty of the natives present at the interment, and none of them showed signs of sorrow. And when the grave was closed and we turned away, the little creature followed at our heels. Edmund had carved on a flat stone the word "JUBA," and left it lying on the grave, and Jack, having nothing else, threw a silver dollar on top of it. The natives probably regarded these things as talismans, or religious symbols, for they treated them with the greatest deference, and no doubt they lie there yet, and will continue to lie there through all the eons, for in those dry caverns the progress of decay can hardly be perceptible even after the passage of ages. It was a singular fact, noted by Edmund, that the natives exhibited not the slightest curiosity concerning their comrades who had been lost in the crystal mountains, and I really doubt whether they knew what the coffin contained.

When we had paid the last honors to Juba, we began to think of our final departure. This place had become disagreeable to us. After the brilliant scenes that we had witnessed on the other side of the planet, the gloom here, and the absence of all that had made the land of perpetual daylight seem a paradise of beauty, were intensely oppressive to our spirits. But Edmund still wished to make some investigations, and we were compelled to await his movements. What the nature of his investigations was I do not know, for I was devoured by the desire to get away, and did not inquire. But fully twenty-four hours had elapsed before our leader was ready to depart. In the meanwhile "Juba's dog" had become firmly attached to Jack, who petted it as probably no creature of its race had ever been petted before. It was a strange-looking animal; about as large as a terrier, with a big square head, covered with long black hair, while, in startling imitation of the hirsute adornment of the natives themselves, its body was clothed with a golden-white pelt of silky texture. It would eat anything we offered it, and seemed immensely pleased with its new master, as it had every reason for being.

During the last hours of our stay we noticed unmistakable indications of preparation for the dreaded ceremonies of the conjunction, and our departure was hastened on that account. The priests, whom Edmund had been compelled to put out of the way of further mischief on the former occasion, had been replaced by others, and we thought that, perhaps, this being the first opportunity for the display of their functions, they would try to make it memorable—which presented a still stronger reason why we should not delay. But, with one thing and another, we were held back until the very eve of the ceremonies.

When we finally stood ready to enter the car, with Juba's dog at Jack's heels, the procession up the steps had already begun. Edmund decided to wait until the multitude had all assembled. They came trooping up into the starlight, and I am sure that they had no idea of what we intended to do. Undoubtedly they must have recalled what had happened on the other occasion, but they showed no sign of either regret or anxiety on that account. They arranged themselves in a dense circle, as before, and the priests took their place in the center. At this moment Edmund gave the word to enter the car. We sprang into it, and immediately Jack and I went out on a window ledge in order to get a better view of the scene. Edmund started the car, and we rose straight toward the earth which glowed in the zenith. Our movement was unexpected, and we at once arrested the attention even of the priests. The beginning of the ceremony was stopped short. All eyes were evidently drawn to us, and when they saw the direction that we were taking a low murmur arose.

"Let me give them a parting salute," said Jack.

Edmund thought a moment, and then said:

• GARRETT P. SERVISS

"Very well, take a gun, but don't fire at them. If it terrifies them into abandoning their sacrifice we shall have done one good thing in this world."

Jack instantly had the gun roaring, and although we were now high above their heads, we could see that they were seized with consternation, rising from their knees, and running wildly about. Whether the noise and the sight of us flying toward the earth, had the effect which Edmund had hoped for, will never be known; but the last sight we had of living beings on Venus was the spectacle of those white forms darting about in the starry gloom.

Our long journey home was interrupted by one more almost tragic episode. When we had been ten days in flight, and the earth had become like a round moon of dazzling brilliance, Juba's dog, which had grown feeble and refused to eat, died. Jack was broken-hearted, and protested when Edmund said that the body of the animal must be thrown out. He would have liked to try to stuff the skin, but Edmund was firm.

"But if you open a window," I said, "the air will escape."

"Some of it will undoubtedly escape," Edmund replied. "But, luckily, this is the air of Venus which we are carrying, and being very dense, we can spare a little of it without serious results. I shall be quick, and there will be no danger."

It was as he had said. When the window was partially opened, for only a second or two, we distinctly felt a lowering of the atmospheric pressure that made us gasp for a moment, but instantly Edmund had the window closed again, and we were all right. As we shot away we saw the little white body gleaming in the sunlight like a thistledown, and then it disappeared forever.

"It is a new planet born," said Edmund, "and the law of gravitation will pay it as much attention as if it were a Jupiter. It may wander in space for untold ages, and sometime it may even fall within the sphere of the earth's attraction, and then Jack's wish will have been fulfilled; but it will be but a flying spark, flashing momentarily in the heavens as it shoots through the air."

* * * *

Our home-coming was a strange one. For some reason of his own Edmund did not wish to take the car to New York. He landed in the midst of the Adirondack woods, far from any habitation, and there, concealed in a swamp, he insisted upon leaving the car. We made our way out of the wilderness to the nearest railway station, and our first care was to visit a barber and a clothing merchant. Probably, as we carried some of the guns, they took us for a party of hunters who wished to furbish up before revisiting civilization.

On reaching New York, we went, in the evening, straight to the Olympus Club, where our arrival caused a sensation. We found Church in the old corner, staring dejectedly at a newspaper. He did not see who was approaching him. Jack slapped him on the shoulder, and as he looked up and recognized us he fell back nearly fainting, and with mouth open, unable to utter a word.

"Come, old man," said Jack, "so we've found you! What did you run away for? Let me introduce you to the Columbus of Space, and don't you forget that I'm one of his lieutenants."

I don't think that Church has ever fully believed our story. He thinks, to this day, that we lost our "balloon," as he calls it, and invented the rest. We purposely allowed the newspaper reporters to take the same view of the case, but when we four were alone we unburdened our hearts, and relived the marvelous life of Venus. I use the past tense, because I have yet to tell you most disquieting news.

Edmund has disappeared.

Within three months after our return he bade us good night at an unusually early hour and we have never seen him since, although more than a year has now elapsed since he went out of the room at the Olympus. Jack and I have made every effort to find a trace of him, without avail. Led by a natural suspicion, we have ransacked the Adirondack woods, but we could never satisfy ourselves that we had found the place where the car was left. Henry persists in the belief that Edmund is trying in secret to develop his invention, with the intention of "revolutionizing industry and making himself a multibillionaire." But Jack and I know better! Wherever he may be, whatever may occupy his wonderful powers, we feel that the ordinary concerns of the earth have no interest for him. Yet we are sure that if he is alive he often thinks of us.

Last night as Jack and I were walking to the club with my completed manuscript under my arm, a falling star shot across the sky.

"Do you know what that recalls to me?" asked Jack, with a far-off expression in his eyes.

"What?"

"Juba's dog."

Neither of us spoke again before we reached the clubhouse steps, but I am certain that through both our minds there streamed a glittering procession of such memories as life on this planet could never give birth to. And they ended with a sigh.

AFTERWORD
BY ROB GODWIN

The very same month that Robert Goddard chose to do his first serious calculations on rockets one of his earlier ideas appeared in a story of space fiction published in one of Frank Munsey's magazines. Starting in January 1909 and running monthly until June, Garrett Serviss' story *A Columbus of Space* appeared in the pages of *All-Story* magazine. Munsey had launched the magazine four years earlier and from a very early point his editors had recognized the appeal of scientific fiction. Serviss was already a well-respected scientist and a brilliant writer. The latest subject at the forefront of the debate among astronomers was regarding the nature of Venus. It was supposed that Venus (still considered to be much older than the Earth) had been subjected to eons of tidal drag. It was suggested that it was now spinning on its axis only once for each Venusian year. Like the Earth's moon, Venus was supposed to only show one side to the sun, while the other half was in a perpetual state of frozen night. Serviss decided to send a group of gentlemen explorers on a trip to Venus using a nuclear-powered space ship. It was exactly the sort of thing which Goddard had proposed in an article he had submitted to *Popular Science* three years earlier, but while Goddard was young, with little influence and his article was rejected, Serviss was already a 58-year-old elder statesman of astronomy. Unlike Serviss' previous interplanetary adventure, *Edison's Conquest of Mars*, this time he wasted little time cluttering up his story with technology. *A Columbus of*

• GARRETT P. SERVISS

Space is a straight ahead adventure story which derives its drama from the two completely polarized hemispheres of the Venusian ecology.

The half that permanently faces the sun is enshrouded in cloud for years at a time, protecting an advanced, intellectually adept society, led by an enigmatic and beautiful queen. They communicate using light, and they travel about their planet using air ships. Meanwhile, the night side is inaccessible to the light-side inhabitants due to a mountainous wall of ice that is engulfed by fierce weather systems. The night side people are primitive ape-like creatures who are superstitious and unpredictable. Serviss flies his hardy team of explorers to Venus on his nuclear-powered ship which derives its main source of power from uranium. The ship also converts pollutants in the ship's atmosphere to fuel, a sort of primitive fusion device. During the voyage to Venus they encounter a large dumb-bell shaped asteroid which they deflect by, "setting up atomic reaction against it, as a boatman pushes with his pole." The description is uncannily like that science fiction staple, the force-field. Serviss also makes a short reference to the Martians proposed by Richard Proctor in the nineteenth century when one of his characters says, "I'm glad you made it Venus instead of Mars, from all I've heard of Mars with its fourteen foot giants, I don't think I should like to try…that direction." Then Serviss takes a sarcastic shot at Venusian "angels" which suggests he might have read Griffith's *Honeymoon in Space* from eight years earlier. The overall tone of the book is much less serious than anything from Wells. It's a brilliant and entertaining story for its time and extremely well written. It is possible that Robert Goddard may have read it, due to his proclaimed fondness for Serviss, but there are no references to the story in Goddard's memoirs and it seems likely that he would have made some mention of the idea of nuclear propulsion being used in such a way by one of his favorite authors had he been aware of the story. Serviss may have introduced many of the staples of space fiction in his earlier work, but in *A Columbus of Space* he seemed to be more interested in spinning a good adventure story, propelled for the first time in history by nuclear energy.

  Present:
The most comprehensive series of vintage space fiction ever published!
Look for these & other titles!

For details contact: Apogee Science Fiction
www.apogeespacebooks.com
email: marketing@cgpublishing.com
Tel: 905 637 5737—Fax: 905 637 2631